Black Crucifix

Louis Park

Chapter 1

Nothing quite dampens your day like a four-year-old kid pissing on your leg.

A big part of me—fortunately, not the part that controls my leg—wanted to kick him in the chest. It would have probably been pleasurable for the briefest of seconds, but then insurmountable guilt and the inevitable assault from his very round grandparent would have come. Also, as a social worker, I had to protect kids, not kick them.

"OI! Mary, please, can you stop him!" I cried as I leapt to the side.

"Stop what?" she tilted her head and feigned ignorance.

Unfortunately, Peter trapped me in the living room's corner, so he only had to change his aim to hit me with his stream of urine as I hopped on one foot to the other to avoid the onslaught. I growled at the obese grandmother who sat planted into the sofa next to us.

Rather than continue to dance and try to avoid the yellow fountain, I went on the offence. I quickly reached down, grabbed the four-year-old by the shoulders and spun him around so his piss went up and all onto his grandmother's lap. She yelped and screamed, but still lay implanted into the grooves of the tattered tan leather couch. Fortunately for her, it was only a few seconds later that he finished.

When he finished, the grime-covered gremlin giggled and ran across the room to play with a dirt-stained Barbie doll that had half its hair pulled out. Just before this assault of bodily liquids, I tried my hardest not to stare at the grandmother's oddly hypnotising and disfigured legs. Her blotchy, saggy, rotund, and varicose vein-covered limbs rooted out of a stained and tattered pale-yellow summer dress. The fat from the appendages sunk down and drooped so much so it appeared as if the skin flowed into the ground. Only the semblance of toes sticking out showed that what was below was feet.

"THAT'S ASSAULT! THAT IS ASSAULT! I'm going to have you struck off from the social worker register, you goddamn black bas—" she screamed but was just about able to stop herself before she completed the final expletive.

"I'm what? Go on, please, tell me. It'll just be more to feed into the assessment about you and your parenting!" I snapped.

I glared down at her until she turned away.

"I'm not the parent, though. It should be my poor Sue…my poor, poor Sue," she moaned.

Again, the feelings of rage crept up because of the attempted emotional manipulation. The want, a damn near need, to slap the selfishness out of this old woman filled me from head to toe. If only it was so easy. Slap em' until you've cured em! If it was actually like that, then every damn person in England would want to sign up to be a social worker, and then finally councils wouldn't be so short-staffed with them.

One deep and ammonia-filled breath later, I squashed all such feelings deep down into me, and I put my work mask of polite professionalism back on. Even though I knew what she was doing, I played along.

"It isn't good, Mary, I know. I wish I had the power to have stopped her from overdosing. Peter needed her," I sighed.

The old woman lifted her chubby and blotchy red face. Her bloodshot, pale-blue eyes looked into mine. For the briefest second, her eyes moistened, and I saw all the sufferings I had read up about in assessments and court reports. Her late husband was a sadistic paedophile. He, fortunately, ended up locked away and beaten to death in prison, but he did enough damage on Peter's mother, Sue, to leave her a hollowed out and fractured husk.

What followed in Sue's life was so predictable it seemed like she didn't have a choice, and whenever there seemed to be a glimmer of hope for her, the poverty and the predators made damn sure she stayed down. As broken as Mary was, to her credit, she did eventually try in her own twisted way to save her daughter. Of course, the local authority eventually stepped in but, by then, it was like trying to remould a cooked clay sculpture.

"I raised her good and proper. I made sure she was fed, loved, and she had clothes on her back. She had everything a daughter could have wanted. Why did she...why?" Mary quavered.

Because your late husband repeatedly raped her whilst you sat downstairs watching telly night after night. You must have known, and worse is that you let it happen! You're as guilty as him. How in the hell did the court assess you as a viable carer for your grandson?! I thought whilst I nodded with a look of concern on my face.

I took a deep gulp, turned away, so I could force the anger back down, and then looked back at her again with a placid look on my face. Just before I spoke, I wrinkled my nose as the smell of urine wafted back up my nose again. I grimaced as I remembered what had just happened.

"I hear what you're saying, and I am sorry you had to go through all that, but we've got to think about what we can do at present. Peter needs you, and he also needs a lot more because of what has happened to him. Come on, let's go over the plan again, and you can tell me how we can make it better for you and him."

I put a hand on a shoulder to reassure her. She flinched, and for a split-second, I saw a flash of disgust on her face before it became crinkled with anxiety. The grandmother looked up at me and looked at Peter, who smacked his frayed

Barbie against the corner of the couch. She then crinkled her nose as she smelt the piss as well.

"Sorry, love, let's do that next time. I'm covered in the little bastard's piss, and so are you. I need to wash me sen and get clean. Do what you got to do and bugger off...please."

I raised an eyebrow.

"Please, don't call him that...or, at the very least, not in front of him," I sighed.

"What!? He is a bastard. He is the very definition of one!"

I growled in frustration and shook my head before I turned around and headed out of the living room. I opened the grime-covered and once white baby gate, then stomped up the high steps that were without carpet, made up only of bare wood boards. With each step, I felt my wet jeans slide lecherously against my knees and shins, and wafts of urine fill my nostrils.

I had to be careful on the stairs as there was only a minimal amount of light because there was no bulb in the light socket at the top of the landing. However, I could still make out that the walls were garish pink, mottled with dirt and mould that gave it a cowhide pattern. Each step creaked, saying they wanted to give up and cave in, adding to my fear that I'd slip and fall back.

When I reached the top, I saw that the upstairs landing window remained broken and jagged. There was a case note I read before the visit that the previous social worker had a long conversation about housing standards with the landlord a month ago. Clearly, the owner ignored the complaints.

I went and looked in Peter's room, which was tidier and more homely than the rest of the house. There were still touches of dirt and grime on the walls, but they were at least decorated with wallpaper that had cartoon planets and stars. Even the ceiling had a matching dark navy-blue colour and had stuck on glow-in-the-dark stars on it. There were a lot of toys of various kinds inside bright boxes, and his tiny race car bed even had bedding. My mouth fell open as there was also carpet and a cupboard in the room.

I wondered why if he had so many toys, then why did he opt to play with such a shabby Barbie doll. It wasn't the bomb site I had expected but I knew the state of his bedroom could be a one-off or she simply tidied the room up when she knew when a social worker was coming around. Still, at least it meant I could leave without having to lecture the cantankerous troll again.

I quickly turned around and had a nosey peak in the other rooms. The bathroom's toilet seat and cupboard mirror were hanging onto dear life by the hinges, but aside from that, it was clean. A second after I poked my head in Mary's room, the smell of it hit me and almost made me retch. It was a combination of body odour, damp, and a faint something that was quite reminiscent of a cheese called Stinking Bishop. That being said, it was tidy, and there were no signs of drug use. By that point, I felt I had enough for the visit, and I wanted out, so I quickly headed back downstairs.

I peeked my head into the living room to see that Mary had somehow pushed herself out of the sofa. I saw where the indentation of her bottom was on the chair that there were a couple of flattened cupcakes. Suddenly, the image of me falling to my knees and eating the food up flashed into my head, and a feeling of revulsion quickly followed. I realised my face had lost its mask, so I quickly forced it back on so I still had the look of a non-judgemental professional on.

Mary was much taller than I expected. My eyes went down to her rippling legs, and I had to bring my gaze back up to hers, so she did not notice my curiosity.

"Well, I'm off. We'll talk soon and arrange another visit. See you, Peter!" I exclaimed and waved at the feral child who seemed oblivious to me as he swung the Barbie doll at his grandmother's backside.

Mary grunted at me and rolled her eyes. I didn't fancy another argument, so I turned heel, and I was soon out of the front door. As the cold winter morning air hit me, it reminded me of the wet patches on my jeans as they quickly turned ice cold. I softly shut the door behind me and avoided the dog excrement on the pavement just outside. Even though the sky was a beautiful crisp blue, it could not make the street look any better.

Sentries of red-brick terraced houses, each with grime stained doors that were once pristine white, surrounded the road. Even though it was cold, there was a group of elderly women and frowning young men who stood outside a nearby house, completely blocking the entire pavement, and speaking a language I thought was possibly Roma. I huffed and puffed as I'd have to walk by the loud group to get to my car.

Whilst I walked, I looked down to avoid the rubbish and dog excrement that littered the road, and also so I didn't make eye contact with the people. I imagined they were the types who would have found it a bloody magnificent show if a social worker was set on fire, an entertainment that the whole neighbourhood could enjoy and watch.

I walked in the middle of the road so I didn't have to walk through them, and I quickly reached my beat-up, 2002 silver Ford Ka. The sorry vehicle's left rear corner stuck out onto the road. Even with such a compact car, I still couldn't park properly. As much as I loved its quirks, I knew it was a machine that should be turned into scrap.

The hubcaps had long since fallen off, and they showed the blackened and rusty wheels underneath. Rust crept up from the cracked and flaking body paint around the front doors. Bird shit covered the silver bonnet, and splashes of dried mud covered the plastic wheel guards on both sides.

I opened the passenger side with my key, and a damp musk invaded my nostrils. A sigh of disappointment escaped my lips as there was no smell of used cigarettes. I put my rucksack in the car's foot-well and then reached across to unlock the driver's side door—this being the only way to open it. I pushed myself back out, shut the door, and went around to get in.

As soon as I was inside, I shut the door, locked it, and I breathed a deep sigh of relief as I was finally safe in my cocoon. I moved my left foot, and it landed on something that caused a plastic crinkle noise. I reached down and picked up the empty bottle of cola and chucked it onto the back seat so it could mingle with the other assortments of rubbish.

I quickly vowed to myself that I needed to tidy it up as soon as possible as there were possibly novel forms of life growing from the mess back there. Just as I pulled my phone out to zombify myself with its distractions, the smell of urine seeped into my nostrils again. I realised I couldn't even sit there for a quick breather as festering in a child's piss was one humiliation too far.

I put my safety-belt on and then started the car. The gears cranked and scraped into reverse.

The over acceleration almost put my car straight into the car on the opposite side of the road. A five-point turn later, and I sped down the residential roads fifteen miles above the speed limit.

I knew if I caused an accident, it would be crucifixion by one of the many newspapers that despised social workers. My career would be over, and they would treat me as a demon worse than the ones I tried to protect children against. Yet, that worry wasn't at all a priority. Instead, my mind fretted about the next task on my ever-growing to-do list; a list that, if looked at mathematically, would be seen to increase at a rate of expansion significantly larger than the rate of completion, meaning its destination was to infinity and beyond.

The traffic light turned yellow, and my foot immediately went down hard on the accelerator. Too slow. As soon as I reached the line, the light went red, but I still went through it and sped onto the roundabout. No car horns chased me, so it at least meant I didn't time it too wrong. I swung my car to the left onto the exit, and it felt as if the rear left wheel cocked up as I went around the corner sharply. I heard a bass-heavy growl of an engine nearby and saw a bright blue hatchback speed pass.

"Bell end," I muttered as I slowly got my car up to sixty miles per hour on a dual carriageway that had a limit of forty.

Even just at sixty, the car shook and shuddered, crying out that it was too old for such recklessness. Suddenly, a hard thud came from the front left wheel, and the jolt went all the way up to my head. I apologised out loud to my tortured machine for hitting the pothole at such speeds and hoped there was no damage. I still did not slow down, that is until I had to.

"Fuck's sake! Move, you twat!" I spat as a tan estate car that drove at thirty in the forty lane in front.

I gave my newfound nemesis a second and a half to comply with my request for it to speed up. This was unheeded, so I swerved to my left to overtake. I saw a middle-aged owl of a lady hunched over her steering wheel, pretending to ignore me as she sped up herself. We reached forty-five by the time she gave up, and I was clear to pass.

Suddenly, I had to slam on my brakes and just about came to a stop at the roundabout for a learner driver with his instructor coming across. I saw a petrified look on the teenage girl and an angry glare from a middle-aged instructor. Once they passed me, I smashed my foot down and sped as fast as I could—which wasn't fast at all—to my exit straight ahead of me.

When I approached a petrol station near my office, the thought of having a cigarette tried to act all innocent, like it had just accidentally made a wrong turn and arrived in my mind. The urge to turn in and buy a packet of the nasty little sticks almost made me forget I was driving as I again had to hit my brakes hard to stop me from going into the back of a van.

I looked in my mirrors and around to see if anyone noticed my near-crash. Fortunately, there was no one other than the white van who was in front. It was a couple of minutes later of tootling along behind it; I turned in left and arrived at the office. I turned left again to head into the pothole-ridden car park. As usual, every spot taken, so I turned around and parked on the double yellow lines near the entrance. No one ever ticketed the vehicles, so it was an area that became full of cars as well, often making it quite awkward when workers tried to leave or enter.

I had already forgotten about being covered in piss, as I was busy thinking about the court reports due this week and next. There were also many other assessments due this week, and the following week as well. I sighed and my shoulders drooped as I visualised the size of the mountain of paperwork I needed to climb.

I knew if I failed these arbitrary deadlines then it was punishment by public shaming and verbal bludgeoning by management. I needlessly locked my dilapidated car—who in the hell would want to steal it?!— and just as I was about to walk to the office, a waft of the kid's piss reminded me I needed a good clean.

Chapter 2

The office was a flat, two-storey and redbrick building that once-upon-a-time was a school. Unsurprisingly, a lot of the school still hadn't changed—as renovations cost money, something which the local authority was always in short supply of.

Some rooms inside still had blackboards on their walls, all of which were used as team rosters to tell others where they had gone. Even the toilets kept their old decorations as the walls in the girls' were bright pink and the boys' were sky-blue.

I swiped my council ID card on the fob at the building's entrance, and a little light on the door turned green. A grunt came out as I pulled the heavy windowless fire door and walked into the reception area lit by obnoxious fluorescent lights. Inside, there were four blue plastic-chairs placed against a thick concrete brick wall. There were also a couple of locked fire doors and a reception covered from desk to ceiling in smash-proof glass.

A middle-aged and thin lady sat inside the reception talking point. She had short curly grey hair and a dour face that was rarely home to a smile. She didn't bother looking up at me as she squinted at her computer screen.

"Blasted thing. I said copy! Why won't you copy!" she spat.

"Hey up, Dawn," I greeted.

"Oh, hello, chicken. Having a good morning? Hope it has been better than mine. This new system is driving me crackers!" she exclaimed without turning to look at me.

"Well, I am covered in a kid's piss. So, I might have you beat on that," I chuckled.

It took her a couple of seconds to register the comment as she carried on with clicking away on her computer. Suddenly, she stopped, tilted her head, and raised it to look me in the eye. Dawn frowned, half stood up and looked down to see my wet jeans. I saw the tiniest upturn in the corner of her mouth.

"How did that happen?" she asked when her eyes came back up to look into mine.

I went through the entire story with manic energy and a grin, as I was certain I proved I was having a worse morning. Dawn simply nodded her head during my recounting of the tale. By the end, much to my disappointment, she only raised her eyebrows.

"I suppose I better let you go, Craig, as you need to get yourself cleaned up," she said with a polite, pursed smile.

I raised an eyebrow as I expected so much more, but then nodded. I edged away slowly at first, turned around, swiped the fob, and then went through the main entrance door. Before the door had completely shut behind me, I heard a roar of laughter come from the reception. *At least I'm making someone happy*, I thought as a smile crept up onto my face.

"Craig, I sent you an email a couple of days ago about a case of yours linked to mine. Please, can we talk about it?" a brash social worker with a dark bob cut bellowed in a posh English accent as I rushed to the toilets.

I've read it, and you can fuck right off! Was what I wanted to say.

"Will do soon. I'm covered in a kid's piss at the moment, so I need to clean myself up first!"

"What?!"

When I got inside the men's toilets, it was empty, which wasn't unusual as the staff in the building was over ninety-five percent women. I naively tried wiping my jeans with paper towels, but it made too little of an impact, and they, of course, still stunk. There was only one other option for me. At first, I hesitated to take my jeans off, but a waft of urine quickly changed my mind.

A minute later, I scrubbed the contaminated parts with soapy water and scrunched up paper towels. That moment, I hoped to whatever deity would hear me that my service director would not walk through the door whilst I stood there in my luminous pink and bulge-enhancing briefs. It was only a couple seconds after that thought that

I froze solid as the door swung open. I was marginally fortunate as it wasn't the big boss but one of the administration staff instead.

It was Rob. He didn't even say a word as he came in and headed straight to the cubicle, shutting the door behind him. The admin worker was a short and quite a slight man whose voice always stayed at the same tone, no matter how excited or upset he was. Surprisingly, I was a touch upset about him not commenting on the fact I was standing near half-naked, cleaning my jeans in the toilet's hand basin.

I then felt the urge to tell him the story, just to see how he would have reacted to it. I was about to knock on the cubicle door and tell him the embarrassing tale but decided not to at the last second, as it would probably have caused him too much anxiety, especially with me being so close and half-naked.

As I dried my jeans under the hand drier, I heard the cubicle door open, and then the toilet entrance open. He had left without even washing his hands!

"Dirty bastard," I muttered when the door swung shut.

I was about five minutes in before I gave up and decided to just let the clothing dry naturally. A quick sniff to make sure they didn't reek, and I put them back on. I gave myself a quick model in front of the mirror above the basin. It wasn't the best sight, especially with the oppressive fluorescent light shining down from above, magnifying all imperfections.

I saw no issues with my hair. It was the same as it always was: short, tight, light brown, and afro-textured on top, whilst I kept the sides shaved and blended. The concern was my visage. Since joining this job, the once cherubic face had become gaunt, greasy, and anxiety had dug battle trenches all over. The cheekbones still stood wide and proud, but now looked like tent poles holding up a tanned circus tent.

The skinniness of my face meant my prominent nose seemed even bigger than it was. I would have tried to grow a beard to hide such a mess, but my facial hair was too patchy to go beyond a small stubble.

The sparkly green irises of my eyes weren't enough to distract from them looking tired, sunken, and bloodshot. I looked at my short-sleeve grey shirt, which hung loosely. It was a top that once fitted perfectly, but missing lunch and dinner regularly changed that.

I stood there staring with a morbid curiosity, half-expectant that my nose or bits of my cheek would crumble off at any instance. I pulled at the skin on my face downwards, let go, and then rasped like a horse. *Is the strung-out crack whore look what you're going for?*

I soon lost interest and coughed to clear my throat and spat out dark yellowish phlegm into the basin. I turned the tap on, turned it off, and then left the toilets. A half a minute later, I was in our team's office. There were only two other social workers sat hunched over their laptops like vultures picking away at carcasses. I looked at the blackboard and saw that everyone else was on home visits or in meetings. I took a piece of chalk and signed myself in with a large and illegible scribble.

"Morning, ladies," I boomed.

They both kept their faces planted at their screens.

"Morning," one grumbled.

"That slag ain't no lady!" the other laughed out.

Taheen lifted her round and young-looking face out of her laptop and raised an eyebrow at her colleague. I saw that her make-up was perfectly sculpted, like always. Her bright red lips turned up into a wide smile on her pale-brown skin just before she guffawed.

"Cunt!"

Nikki's head shot up, and she flicked her long bleach blonde hair off her face.

"Who, me?!" she cried in exaggerated incredulity.

Both chuckled, and then immediately went back to typing away on their computers. I headed to my desk and threw my bag onto it. I went to a nearby stack of grey metallic lockers, flat against the wall, and opened one to take out my laptop; the antiquated technology, which aimed to make our professional lives easier but missed completely by being as obedient as a two-year-old on a sugar high.

The blasted computer often struggled for Wi-Fi connectivity, so much so it would intermittently just give up. It also broke down so often the computer spent at least a week a year in repair with IT.

"Craig, you know getting golden showers from children is illegal," Nikki explained without even looking up from her laptop.

A look of confusion came onto my face as I couldn't understand how she already knew. Then I realised Dawn had probably told them about it. An enormous grin took hold of my face as they needed much more to humiliate a social worker. I told them the entire story of what happened, and they both burst out into near-hysterical fits of laughter. After their cackles calmed down, Nikki got up and came over to me and sniffed the air.

"You did a pretty good job. You only smell a little pissy," she chuckled before she went back to her desk.

"Was the case one of Judith's?" Taheen asked without looking up from her computer.

I connected my laptop to the monitor and powered it on before answering.

"Yeah, it was. I have shit ton to catch-up on as everything is out of their time scales. Also, the case notes, well, they leave a lot to the imagination as there isn't much there at all. Fuck knows what she got up to. To make things worse, I've got a review conference for it this week and it is going to be Sylvia who chairs it!" I moaned.

"That sour cunt! Good luck with that," Nikki laughed.

"Cheers for the sympathy and support."

"HA! You'll get none of that here."

I gave the middle-finger to my bleach-blonde colleague as I double-clicked onto the email icon. When the program opened, my response to the myriad of unread messages was to let out a pained sigh. I knew most of them were pointless as professionals opted to send damn near every morsel of information, no matter how mundane, to the social worker. It was so if newspapers or serious case review investigators ever came knocking on their door, they could kindly say they told the social worker everything so crucify them instead. Every industry needs a scapegoat, and we were *fucking* it.

I waded through the emails to find which needed my attention first. I made quick and haphazard work of assessing them as I followed the philosophy that, if it was truly important, then the sender would try to ring you. It was a tactic that had helped me stay slightly less frustrated and stressed.

Once I had finished with my emails, I quickly logged onto our system, Sense Information—the Robin Reliant equivalent of the Information Systems world. It was the creation of those who knew nothing of social work and only had knowledge of what regulatory inspectors would care about. A few swear words later, and I was finally onto my notifications page.

"Hurray," I muttered as there were no notifications of assaults, overdoses, attempts of suicide, mental health breakdowns, police arrests, or deaths.

I quickly checked my calendar and saw I had a bit of time to get some assessment reports written up before my next meeting. Just before I started typing the first word, a craving for a cigarette slithered up from within, causing my mouth to salivate. Ordinarily, I'd be able to shake it off, but Taheen had to pick that moment to go for a smoke.

The social worker pushed her chair out, stood up, and grabbed a packet of cigarettes out of her handbag. I looked on in envy, as her tall and slender frame hid the fact she had given birth to four children. Not only that, her face still somehow looked younger than the forty years old she actually was, even after the stresses from being a child protection social worker for over fifteen years.

What added more to my jealousy was she chain-smoked, and her skin batted away all carcinogens with ease. A part of me quickly put across a flawed but persuasive logic that if she could stay so vibrant after smoking as much as she did, then cigarettes couldn't be that bad.

"Taheen. I know I shouldn't…but could I nick a ciggy from you?"

"You sure you want one?"

I nodded emphatically.

"Okay."

We both put our jackets on and headed outside. We walked out of the office to a nearby bus shelter where there was a bin that had a little compartment to dispose of the ends. I stayed silent until I had taken my first puff.

"Jesus, I needed that," I moaned as the cool menthol smoke filled my lungs.

My nicotine saviour put her cigarette in her mouth and lit it as well. I saw there was a henna tattoo still on her left hand.

"We went to a cousin's wedding in Bradford yesterday. It was for Amir's cousin, who's such an annoying twat, but at least the food was good," she replied when she noticed me looking.

Before I could further ask about it, she got in first to speak.

"It has been a while since we last smoked like this! You lasted quite a while or have you been having a cheeky cig or two at home?"

"No, I actually haven't. I don't know how, though, as I've been craving them every fucking minute of the day. So, what do you think of the new service director?"

"My friend from Carnston Council had him before and tells me he's hot on stats and a moody bitch. It's another reason to push me to go elsewhere. I know I've said it before but do agency social work. I'll get five hundred quid for a referral fee, and I'd split that with you. They're paying a lot right now, and I think it'll do you good to get away from here."

I took another deep drag, letting the nicotine help me think of a good enough excuse not to.

"I really want to, but I've got to stay to finish the Smith and Khan court cases. I've put so much work into them and couldn't forgive myself if it crashed and burned because I left," I sighed.

Taheen took a drag and then turned to look at me for a couple of seconds. I turned to her and raised both of my eyebrows and nodded, encouraging her to say what was really on her mind.

"You've already done so much, and someone will take over. I doubt the Khans and the Smiths will miss you if you went, anyway! Also, you've got to think about yourself, especially after what they did to you…Sorry, I shouldn't have brought that up. But are you doing all right? I know we all cope in different ways, but we worry about you, you know."

I felt a little moisture creep up into my eyes.

"It's getting easier. I don't really think about what happened anymore."

I stayed silent and took another drag.

"Anyway, I'm actually off out tonight. Going to go to a new Japanese restaurant on Tabith Road with Emma. You know Emma, right?"

Taheen took a drag and stayed silent for a couple of seconds before responding.

"She's your solicitor friend? The one you knew back when you were both in foster care?"

"Yeah, that's her. She specialises in employment law, and she was the one who helped me keep this shitty job. I've not seen her for a while, especially since she had a kid. I've finally been able to wrangle some time out of her."

We both took our last puffs and then put our sticks of burnt tar out.

"So, you're going to eat raw fish?"

I nodded, and my colleague grimaced.

We laughed and joked about one of Taheen's more interesting cases as we both headed back in. It involved a father arrested for allegedly raping his wife's Maltese dog and being caught dressed in her underwear whilst doing so. He still proclaimed innocence and couldn't see why we were preventing him from seeing his children until risk assessment were complete.

When I got back to my desk, I saw a ready-made coffee with a biscuit next to it on my desk. I looked up at Nikki, who typed away furiously as if she was a jazz pianist.

"Three sugars, right?" I asked as I sat down.

"Of course! As if I don't know how to treat my bitch," Nikki exclaimed without taking her eyes off her monitor.

Chapter 3

I checked my phone again as I walked back to the hospital car park. It was clear Emma was ignoring me as there was a blue tick next to my message to show she had read it, but there was still no reply.

"This fucking job!" I cried at my phone.

Initially, the day was going well. I had completed a few assessments, cut a good chunk out of my final court report for a case, and there were no parental spats or arguments in any of my meetings. I also avoided having another cigarette, and, for once, I ate lunch.

I looked forward to going out that evening, but I put such plans on hold when a school decided it was a good idea to telephone in concern about a case of mine at 3:00 pm. There was a mark on a five-year-old boy's forehead, and they said it appeared to be a circular burn. It took a couple of minutes of explaining before they admitted they had identified the possible injury at lunchtime.

By the time they called us, the child had already gone home. I, of course, asked why it took so long and they had contacted us after he had gone home. The best they could provide was that they *didn't know*.

I had to break the news to the parents that we had to assess whether they were sadists of the worst kind who purposefully burnt their kid's forehead. When I saw the child, the alleged injury to me looked like the skin condition impetigo. When I relayed this back to management, my new service director somehow became involved and said the kid needed to go to the hospital for a child protection medical to assess the so-called-wound. I was direct and stated bluntly—probably too bluntly—that foul play didn't cause the mark, and the parents definitely weren't evil bastards. However, he overruled me, even though he was not there and had never met the family.

"Look, Michael, I am right here in front of this kid, and I am telling you it definitely isn't a burn. I've seen impetigo umpteen times before, and that's what it is."

"I hear what you're saying, Craig, but we still need a medical opinion. We've had a strategy discussion whilst you were over there, and we've decided you need to arrange a medical to take place as soon as possible."

"But, Michael, I've worked this case for the past six months. The parents have their issues, but they aren't bad people. They really wouldn't hurt Matthew like that. I'm telling you—"

"You're not telling me, Craig, I am telling *you*. I've decided what you need to do, so, please, do it. Thank you," he snapped before ending the call.

I spent six hours waiting in the hospital with the family before the doctors finally saw us.

They spent two minutes medically assessing Matthew and then came back out.

"It isn't a burn, it's impetigo," the doctor grumbled.

I chuckled to myself and shook my head.

"What's so funny?"

"Nothing, absolutely nothing at all," I exclaimed with my voice cracking like a teenager.

The doctor huffed, puffed, and then stared at me for a couple of seconds.

"Please, ask the parents to come to see me, and I'll get an antibiotic cream prescribed for them."

Without a further thought, I hurried over to the family, gave a lightning quick explanation about the outcome, apologised for all that had happened, and pointed out the doctor that wished to speak with them. I walked away before they could respond.

When I got into my car, I sat there with slumped shoulders and stared out of the window at the orange haze that surrounded a nearby streetlamp. The events of the day ran through my mind on a repeated loop. Eventually I ignored the ruminations and checked my phone. There was still no reply.

I took a deep breath and then let out a roar of frustration up to the heavens until my voice cracked and it felt like the air was flinging razors into my throat. When I finished, I noticed a frightened-looking elderly couple hobbling near my car. They picked up their pace as soon as my eyes connected with theirs. I was about ready to exit the car and try to explain, but I was still sensible enough to stop myself from looking any crazier.

I started my car and headed to my local newsagent in Little Carlton, Senford City. Exhausted, hungry, and emotionally drained, I easily succumbed to a couple of cheap bottles of not so legit looking wine called Shirazaz, a tub of salted caramel ice cream, and a packet of cigarettes. The cashier tried to spark up a conversation with me, but I was just too far gone to understand such inane questions.

"Yeah, yeah, football, kicking it and throwing it, brilliant," I mumbled.

The cashier gave me a look of confusion and gave up trying his small talk and focused on packing my shopping bag quickly. It was only five minutes later that I was in the flat's car park. My car distinctively stood out compared to all the other shinier and newer models next to it. It made me think my physical self probably similarly compared to my vibrant, beautiful, and young neighbours.

As I got out and headed to the building, I nearly trod on a broken glass bottle. I stopped and stared at it and, suddenly, an image of me stabbing it into my service director's throat repeatedly flashed into my mind. As the projection became stronger and stronger, I felt my mouth salivate over such a want. Suddenly, my chest squeezed my ribs tight like a corset as I became paranoid that I'd one day actually commit such a crime. I fought through the screaming emotions and images and stuck my hand into my pocket, fumbled around, and quickly pulled a cigarette out with a trembling grip in hopes the nicotine would help stop such imagery.

"Stop it, Craig. Just fucking stop it," I stammered under my breath before I took my first drag.

The violent theatrics still played in my head, but the nicotine helped lower their volume. As I walked to the entrance of the short and squat five-storey building, my mind soon found itself again filled with worries about the reports still due at work. When I reached the doorway, I put the shopping bag down and inhaled the rest of the tobacco. I looked up at the building, which was a clone like any other modern apartment block, built quickly for maximum profit, bland, and square in design. That didn't stop me from getting a mortgage for one, as they were relatively affordable for someone on my pay grade.

I took my last drag as I stared aimlessly out into the car park, stubbed it out, and then swiped my fob at the front door. It was a heavy door made of a thick grey metal frame and thick triple-glazed windows. It took me by surprise, and I struggled to get it open with the first pull and stumbled forward into the door, hitting my face against the window.

Following a couple of muttered expletives, my second attempt proved more successful, and I got in. I went straight to the staircase as I dreaded the possibility of having to make small talk with anyone in the elevator whilst I was in such a dilapidated state. Three long and steep floors later, I was wheezing heavily and had to sit down on a stair for a couple of minutes to regain my breath before I headed to my flat with aching legs.

After unlocking the door, I pushed it open with my shoulder and barged through. I then switched the hallway light on with my chin and kicked my shoes off at the assortment of shoes that swarmed around an empty shoe rack. I quickly put some slippers on as I didn't want my feet to feel the cold from the light-grey, wood-effect laminate. It was flooring I received a fair few compliments for, and I was quite proud to have it. The cream walls I wasn't so fond of and had been meaning to repaint them since I had bought the property a couple of years ago, but whenever it came to the day, I would instead catch up on sleep because of a hangover or binge on a TV series.

A quick flick of a light switch and the flat came to life. I walked straight to the open-plan kitchen, which combined with the living room.

I rinsed out a wine-stained glass, wiped a semi-dirty tablespoon with a dishcloth, and poured myself a full glass of the Shirazaz. I took a few large chugs, holding my breath so I couldn't taste it, and then poured out some more. A couple of seconds later, I was sitting on my leather sofa in silence, munching on my ice cream and making further quick work of my so-called-wine.

Fortunately, my brain had given up on any serious thinking. There was the occasional feeling of guilt, anger, or fear, that bubbled up, but they all quickly popped as I simply didn't have enough energy for such neuroses. Just as I put my wineglass down after I had finished it, I jumped up in fright when I turned my head to see an ominous figure with deep and empty eyes staring straight into me.

I hadn't noticed, but my flatmate had silently sat himself on a nearby chesterfield armchair. He had dark sunglasses on and wore a thick, burgundy dressing robe with its hood up. His long, bedraggled and part-braided black hair was pushed out by the hood and covered the sides of his face. Further to this, his braided goatee added more cover to his bronze-coloured face.

Only his long and hooked nose with flared nostrils stuck out proudly and uncovered. Even with me making a high-pitched squeal in shock, he didn't move or say a word. He certainly was a peculiar man, but I couldn't complain too much as he always paid his part of the rent and bills. Also, he never left a mess.

I had only seen his face once without sunglasses, and what I saw beneath were sharp but almost sultry almond-shaped eyes that were of a hazelnut colour. His chiselled and angular looks, along with his absolute confidence, seemed to make him taller than he actually was. So much so, I sometimes found that my lanky six-foot-two-frame felt a lot shorter than his five-foot-six.

He was a freelance creative designer who worked from home all the time—not that I was around enough to know if he actually did. I imagine most landlords would have asked such a strange one to leave by now, but perhaps it was the social worker in me that felt I should not discriminate, or perhaps it was because I really wanted to *fuck* him, that I put up with such peculiarity.

"Zee, you scared the shit out of me!" I blurted.

Zee stayed quiet and then turned ever-so-slowly to look at me. His mouth opened, closed, and opened again, but instead of words only a deep exhale of air came out. He then tilted his head and looked straight at my ice-cream. He put his right arm straight out and motioned me to pass over the dessert. I wasn't in the mood for sharing, but suddenly his sunglasses reminded me of empty eye sockets on a skull, and, straight after that, my will buckled.

"Do you want some? There's only like a quarter of the tub left, so you finish it. I'll kill the rest of the wine instead."

Without waiting for him to respond, I passed him the dessert.

He took the ice-cream from me but then pointed at the spoon that was in my hand. It was pathetic, but I felt a brief rush of blood down below because of the prospect of his saliva mixing with mine. I quickly gave him the utensil. Before he munched away at *my* dessert, he pulled out a little plastic bag filled with thick and sticky cannabis buds. The act appeared a great effort for him, so much so the extra exertion caused him to slump further down the chair.

"No thanks. I'm still trying to stay off the drugs."

My flatmate grumbled and dropped the cannabis onto his stomach.

"Yeah, yeah, I know what alcohol is. You know what I mean."

I switched the television on as Zee tried to muster the effort to start his munching on the ice cream. I didn't bother watching what was on, but like a voyeur, I lustfully kept the corner of my eye on my flatmate as he messily ate and licked. Once he finished, shivers went down my spine as he sucked on the spoon and wiped his face with his sleeve.

"Want to know what my day was like?" I announced.

Silence was the weird stoner's response as he sat, staring at me with those two windows into oblivion. Even with the alcohol I had in me, I felt my skin try to wrench itself free to crawl away. To calm my nerves, I took another swig of wine, and then spewed out everything that happened to me that day. As soon as I did, he turned his head to face away to the television.

Zee acknowledged nothing I said or even nodded his head as he just sat there, sunglasses on, facing the television, without a hint of emotion on his face. Eventually, I came to the end of my story and realised I had also finished the entirety of my wine. I went up to get my second bottle and returned. Instead of continuing to talk, I focused my attention on my drink and the television. Time felt too relative as it almost seemed it was only a couple of blinks of the eye until my second bottle had finished. I was still craving for more booze; I had run out, but I knew someone else had some.

"I hate to be cheeky Zee, but can I have some of that whiskey you've got in your cupboard?" I chuckled and slurred to my flatmate, who could have been asleep for all I knew.

A deep exhale was my only response.

"Cheers, Zee!"

I shot up without realising how drunk I was and almost fell over whilst cackling. My oddball comrade stayed silent in response to the clumsiness. I fumbled around his well-stocked cupboard—something I found surprising, as I rarely ever saw him cook—and eventually found the bottle of Irish whiskey right at the back. Half of it was empty, and I felt a tinge of guilt as I realised it was me who drank a quarter of it a couple of nights ago as I had, again, finished my supply of booze.

Such feelings quickly washed away as I lustfully watched the drink rushing into a tumbler. I wasn't a fan of that type of booze, but I found it was most resourceful in helping me seek oblivion. As soon as I picked the firewater up, I gulped a quarter of the full tumbler down. The heat and the bitterness of the liquid angrily lashed at the back of my tongue and throat.

"Argh!" I spluttered as it cannon-balled into me and warmed my stomach.

I hummed out a little tune I made up on the spot and shook my hips to the song as I sauntered back to the sofa.

"What is this utter shite?" I exclaimed as I saw there was a reality show on about rich middle-aged women bitching about each other to the camera.

Zee wheezed, still facing the television. I turned and glared at the oddball stoner. Still, there were no signs of care. He turned his head and looked at me, and that was a good enough signal for me to think he wanted to listen to my alcohol-infused problems.

"You know…you know WHAT! I don't know. I don't know why I work for Senford Council as I hate the bastards so much. SO MUCH. I gave them everything, and they still tried to destroy me because…" I stopped and let out a deep sigh. "They need someone to blame as they can't blame the-the-the system, as that would mean it needs fixing. It's all so messed up, all so messed up. I'm fucking trying to save kids from horrible stuff, really horrible stuff. Stuff people would hate to know about and…and…" I slurred to him before I lost my train of thought.

I frowned as I went deep inside to retrieve my rant from the murky swamp that was my mind.

"That kid. Everyone tells me it wasn't my fault, everyone but these management fucks. Why is it so fu-fu…Oh, I am so bloody drunk. Where was I?"

No response came from Zee, and his face had turned back to face the television. I quickly finished the tumbler off.

"It's cheesy, I know, but I just want to help people. My purpose, it's my FUCKING PURPOSE! Their purpose is to make stats look good for Ofsted inspectors. All they care about, not the kids, just…just their careers!"

I was swaying, and my eyelids became too heavy, and I struggled to keep them open. There was just about enough sense in me to pick my phone up, and switch my alarm on, as I knew it was going to be another night sleeping on the sofa.

I kicked my slippers off and let myself fall sideways onto the furniture with a *thud*. I wrenched the throw off the top of the sofa so it covered me, then I wriggled up to the other end, so I completely stretched out with my head on a cushion.

"It's such a, such a…shit job. Why didn't I trap a rich man or…travel the world and teach English? No, I got to help people. Fucking people who hate me. Why do they all hate me?" I sighed with my face buried into the cushion.

It was only a couple of seconds later when I fell asleep.

Chapter 4

Zee sat in the armchair, staring at the flickering television screen. He paid scant attention to his flatmate, who snored loudly and sprawled out on his back on the adjacent sofa. The long-haired oddball was much too relaxed to bother changing channels and remained implanted in his seat as a reality television show about a spoilt and duplicitous family came on.

He continued to sit there, unmoving, appearing catatonic, and not even when the show turned to one about politics did it cause him to stir. It was a talk show where there was no intention of discussion; it was just a means for the guests to announce prepared quips and tag-lines, which they could use as video-clip advertisements on their social media. The audience whooped, clapped, or booed at whoever suited their own political preference, not caring about if there was any merit in what the politicians said. Even with such tedium playing across his eyes, Zee remained rooted into the chair. Then, like a light switch being clicked on, the stoner realised he was sobering up. He needed drastic action.

It was imperceptible to the human eye, but the flatmate tried to move as hard as he could whilst putting in the least possible effort in doing so. In the end, only a couple of small muscles in his back gave it a good go, but as soon as they realised the workload was being left for only them, they soon gave up.

The long-haired oddball was about to give up, but then the television station wickedly felt it appropriate to air a program about religious hymns. The music zapped a feeling of fight or flight into him, either of which he struggled to do. Soft whines trickled out of his desert-cracked lips as the choir's singing filled his ears. His body still refused to put in the effort needed to get up, so the distressed stoner resorted to lifting his arms up—slowly, of course—and pulling his hood further down to cover his face more. But such rudimentary defences could not protect him from the ongoing auditory torture.

Craig's flatmate groaned and groaned as ecstatic elderly Brits sang about the glory of a type of Jesus that would have caught the worst type of sunburn in the deserts of the Middle-East.

Finally, all his muscles agreed that the cost was too much to bear and worked in unison, pushing Zee up. The stoner's face grimaced as the strain of the act almost sent him back down into the chair.

Craig stopped snoring for a brief second.

"Piss on me?! Well, I'll piss all over you!" he moaned before he started snoring again.

Zee stared at his flatmate for a couple of seconds, raised his eyebrows, and swayed like a grand fir tree being blown about in the wind. Suddenly, behind the snores of Craig, Zee heard a distorted and gargled whine coming from his room. A faint scratching against his door soon followed. The noise turned to whimpers, and then a faint voice.

"Please…please," it whispered.

The stoner rolled his eyes at such pathetic impudence, and straight after his brain finally reminded him about what he needed to do. He let out a pathetic cry as he knew acknowledging responsibility was the quickest way to ruin a high. Much to his dismay, the haze in his mind blew away. The young man took his phone out to check the time, hopeful that perhaps he could squeeze out another spliff and more TV.

It was not to be as it seemed probable Craig would be awake soon, and he had already put the task off for a couple of weeks. He mumbled out unintelligible words of anger as he knew he was going to do the ritual. Zee sighed just as all the lights in the flat suddenly switched off.

The sobering stoner stood in the darkened room, with only faint outlines of himself and the furniture made out because of street and moonlight that intruded through the windows. He stretched his arms upwards and then cracked his neck when he moved it left to right. Without further thought, Zee put his hood down, undid his robe, and let it fall to the ground. Black lounge-wear sweatpants covered his bottom, and a taut, hair-covered and muscular upper-body was revealed. Even with it being so dark, the long-haired oddball still kept his sunglasses on.

He shuffled through the darkness until he eventually reached his flatmate. As the young man stood over Craig, he spent a couple of seconds staring out into space as he tried to remember what he needed to do to start the ritual.

"One coconut, two coconuts," Zee sang under his breath but then stopped as he realised he was going off tangent.

Suddenly, the oddball put his left palm right into his mouth and bit a small part of it hard until he pierced the skin. Blood rushed out down his hand and forearm, but instead of falling and dripping, it threaded together like interconnected rivers, and moved up his arm against gravity. The stoner used his thumb from his right hand and stuck it in the small hole and forced it to go right through the flesh, digging as hard as he could. It was half a minute later that his thumb poked under the other side's skin. He then used his teeth to pierce the skin on the back of the hand. He remained silent as he did such self-mutilation.

Zee took his bloody right hand out from his left, leaving a clean hole right through the palm. Even with such self-mutilation, his face remained as still as a frozen lake. More blood spilt out, moving up him and clinging to the host it came from. Zee then did the same to his right palm, tearing through his flesh, and remained emotionless throughout.

The blood-covered stoner stood next to his asleep flatmate, palms facing forwards, blood pouring upwards, threading all over until the entirety of his body below his face with the streams of blood. Two small threads crawled to the corners of his mouth, and as soon as they did, Zee tipped forward and stuck his long, thick tongue out. The blood streams trailed down and around his tongue until they reached the tip of it and pooled into a globule.

It was a couple of seconds where it stayed like that, and then the liquid finally obeyed the gravity it previously ignored and trickled down right into Craig's agape mouth. The drunken social worker somehow remained asleep and still snored without a cough or a splutter, even with all the blood seeping into him.

It was a minute later of the red lifeforce flowing into Craig that the wounds on Zee completely healed, and the streams of blood all over the stoner slowly disappeared. The flowing liquid that fell into the open mouth soon became droplets, and as soon as the last drop fell from Zee's tongue, he stood upright. He waited a couple of minutes, frozen, and staring into the darkness before speaking.

"I can easily reach down in there and rip you out. If I have to do that, I will take my sweet time in making sure you realise how annoyed that would make me," he snapped in a hoarse and crackly voice.

Craig stopped snoring, then, with his mouth still agape, his eyelids sprung wide open, but only showing the whites of his eyes. Straight after, a thick, rippling, viscous black liquid covered in thousands of tiny hairs, seeped and squeezed out from his tear ducts, his nose, his ears, and his mouth.

It all flowed together in the same direction to drip off the passed-out social worker and onto the same spot on the floor. More and more of the slime wriggled itself out until there was a thick and large globule of it shimmering from the faint streetlight that hit it. As soon as the substance left Craig's face, his eyes closed, and he began his snoring again.

A scent hit Zee's nose, and he crinkled it in disgust.

"Oh, man, you reek!"

There was only silence in response.

"I definitely need another spliff after smelling you. Come on, I'll show you your new home," Zee grumbled just before he shuffled to his room.

The damned oddball turned around and went to pick his robe up off the floor. Just as he did, he let out a deep sigh as the whole affair had sobered him up. As he put his robe back on, the black slime came to life. The viscous liquid slithered and compacted inwards together, writhing like a pit of snakes, and then it slowly etched itself out of the bulbous mass like it was being sculpted by an invisible force.

Soon, a foul creature had formed. It was a couple of metres long and centipede-like. Its skin was a mucus-covered dark brown, and within it appeared small, irregular sized Swiss cheese-like holes, and within each hole were white tendrils that stuck out and wriggled. At the front of the creature appeared a large, serrated, and leech-like mouth filled with sharp, purple, and jagged teeth. On the bottom of the mouth, there appeared another, but this was a painted-on human-like grin. The multitude of legs that sprung out of it were all bright yellow and sharp.

The creature appeared to hesitate to follow its new master, and it turned to face its previous home. It waited for a brief second, and then suddenly scuttled over to Zee, and it climbed up on him and wrapped itself around his body.

"Off!"

The creature quickly let go, fell to the floor, and scuttled back and forth down the hallway as his new master opened the room door. When the door swung open, it revealed an impenetrable darkness that wanted to swallow all those foolish enough to enter.

"Please…please."

Zee kicked hard into the abyss and a squeal then a whimper shot back.

"Don't you ever shut up?!" he hissed as he stepped in, and the door swung shut behind.

Chapter 5

I came to in darkness, and it took me a minute to realise who I was, what I was, and that I was waking up. As soon as my brain powered on a little more, I immediately recognised that I definitely wasn't in my bed.

I pushed myself up to look around, but straight after, I felt a vice-like grip dig into my forehead and behind my eyes that squeezed so much that the pain caused me to gasp. To add more to the discomfort, nausea slithered up from my stomach and caused me to retch. I quickly retreated from the world and fell back onto the sofa. The cold then hit me, and I scrambled for the throw stuck down the side of the sofa. I pulled it up, and its familiar floral smell flooded my nostrils. That was when I realised I had passed out drunk on my sofa from last night.

There was one part of my body that had gotten the wrong orders and didn't realise how much of a wreck I was, as I was rock hard down below. The damn-near-sentient organ was being way too optimistic, and I had to force myself to ignore it. I was quite certain that even if I tried to quench such a thirst with some self-love, I would have vomited all over myself before I even got close to climaxing.

I closed my eyes in hopes this would ease the pain. It didn't. I moved my head a little to the side, and it made my brain slosh violently around like a tugboat in a hurricane. It was after a minute of wishing the pain and nausea away that I remembered it was still a weekday, and that meant work.

"Fuck!"

I tried to find my phone without moving too much and without opening my eyes. I found it under the cushion under my head. I just about opened my left eye so I could see what was on the screen.

6:00 AM

"Why?!" I groaned.

I had two more hours of sleep left, but my body, for some very annoying reason, wanted to wake me up now. I knew it was pointless to try heading back to the land of nod as my brain simply wouldn't allow it. Yet, I closed my eyes, hoping this time would be different. It was perhaps twenty minutes of futile tossing and turning, each movement causing me to feel like my brain tried to squeeze itself out of the side of my eyeballs, and I wanted to spew my guts out. Just as I changed position again, I felt something squashed in my pocket. I reached down and pulled it out to discover a packet of cigarettes.

I waited a few seconds for the feelings of guilt and remorse for losing the battle of wills against such a vice, but there was nothing. I quickly took advantage of this and found a lighter in the same pocket. Within seconds, I was sitting up, throw wrapped around my head and body, and lighting a cigarette dangling from my mouth.

The nicotine certainly wasn't a panacea and didn't cure my hangover, but once I finished it, I found the tobacco stick gifted me with newfound motivation. With the throw still wrapped around me, I launched up and immediately fell back onto my arse.

Take two.

I stood up again, but far slower, and stayed hunched over like I was Quasimodo. I stumbled to the kitchen and grabbed a dirty glass. Rinsed it out and filled it with cold tap water. I then stumbled towards my room, momentarily stopping outside Zee's, listening to his slow stoner laugh and the faint noise of a distorted cry from what must have been a horror film.

"Hur, hur, hur!"

I grimaced and continued my journey to my room, occasionally falling sideways into the wall.

"Fucking whisky." I sighed just before I opened my door, staggered in, almost tripping over the clothes strewn all over the floor. When I got to my bedside table, I almost flung the drawer off its hinges trying to get it open. A quick search, and I had a drunkard's medical pack of ibuprofen, paracetamol, anti-nausea tablets, and indigestion tablets placed out. I took a borderline safe dose of the drugs and lit another cigarette.

I fell back onto my bed, moved the cold duvet to cover me, and puffed away whilst I waited for the drugs to kick in. I put the ash in an empty coke can on my bedside table.

It was 7:00 am when I felt far more human again, and the medicines dulled down the sharp edges of the ailments. I finished my third cigarette of the morning and could get up without falling back down. It was thirty minutes later that I was showered, my sexual tensions were released, dressed, and swaying in front of a frying pan cooking bacon. Next to the pan were two buttered and burnt slices of white bread. I crisped up the bacon, added it to the bread, and put a big squeeze of tomato ketchup on top. Just before I bit into it, I hesitated and thought it might all come back out later, but shrugged and wolfed down the sandwich. Salty meat, fat, sour ketchup, and sweet flavours filled my mouth, causing a groan of pleasure after my first bite. Coffee with three sugars quickly followed.

The hangover-induced morning seemed odd as I kept expecting my usual feelings of guilt and remorse over my indulgences of nicotine and booze, but there was none. Instead of the usual self-flagellation, I spent a relaxed time perusing a casual sex app on my phone.

It was the type of social media where words were kept at a minimum and often risqué pictures were used as a means to determine whether to meet up. I found myself somewhat tempted by some of those on offer, but I quickly realised I had work to go to instead. To prevent any further temptation, I headed to the office early. It was a journey that went with perfect precision as all traffic lights turned green just as I hurtled towards them. I was back in work by 8:15 am.

The car park was quite empty, so I easily found a space—it still took me a couple attempts to park up properly. I breathed in another cigarette in my car before I got out, and I felt ready to tackle the day. However, it went downhill as soon as the fresh air hit me. With each step I took, the more I swayed and the more my brain felt it swam away from me.

As soon as I had got into the building, my stomach dropped so fast it felt like I was going down on a roller coaster. It was rush to the toilet or leave my regurgitated breakfast on the carpet for all my colleagues to see. Fortunately, the reception was still empty, so I didn't have to hide my panic. I quickly swiped my pass to open the office door and sprinted to the toilets. Again, I was lucky I didn't bump into anyone in the corridor.

When I reached the toilets, I shoved the cubicle door open, fell onto my knees to pray to the porcelain gods, and sprayed my offering to them all over the toilet bowl. It was a couple more heaves of spit and bile before I finished. I fell onto my behind and sat propped up by the cubicle as I gulped in breaths of air.

I wanted to stay there for longer than a couple of minutes, but I had to hide the evidence and clean myself up before anyone came in. I pushed myself up with shaking arms, flushed the toilet, and then rinsed my mouth out under the tap. Just as I finished, my headache came back, slamming the door behind it.

"For fuck's sake," I moaned as I looked at the ashen figure that looked back at me.

I took my rucksack off from my shoulders and rummaged around to find a packet of paracetamol. A couple more went down my gullet and were drank down with some tap water. A couple of deep breaths later, and I went to our team's little office. It was twenty-to-nine, and there were already a few others in.

"Jesus Christ, Craig, you look like death!" Amy cried.

I looked at the buxom, newly qualified social worker who had perfect hair, sculpted make-up, immaculate fashion, a body that would have sent me wild if I was straight, and had absolutely no internal filter.

"Cheers, Amy. I think I caught something. A consequence of all the dirty houses we go visit," I stammered.

I saw Nikki raise a knowing eyebrow at me as she was much too cynical about such obvious bullshit.

"How was the medical last night?" Amy asked just as she turned back to her computer.

"It was impetigo, like I said it was, and I didn't get home until around twelve o'clock. It was an absolute waste of time," I sighed as I got my computer out of the locker.

I headed straight to my desk.

"Well, the new service director seems just as shit as Michelle was. I never thought I'd be saying that," I grumbled.

"Morning all," I heard a meek voice whisper behind me.

I turned to see Lisa, a portly young lady who dressed in colourful and mismatching attire. She had a wool hat with cat ears and a rainbow-coloured scarf on. It was another newly qualified social worker. It was a sign of a social care organisation's health, the amount of new social workers they had, and it seemed most our workforce was of that level.

"Morning," I replied as I set up my computer.

A couple of minutes later, I heard a boisterous laugh coming from the corridor.

"Good morning, all!" an enthusiastic voice with a Nigerian accent boomed.

I turned and saw Rose, a squat African woman with long, tied-back beaded hair. Her conservative grey sweater-top could not hide her gigantic breasts, which must have given her backache to no end and probably could be weapons if needed. She had cherubic cheeks that always had a smile or a scowl between.

"Oh, what happened to you, Craig? You look awful!" she boomed as soon as she saw me.

I heard Nikki cackle.

"Just feeling under the weather."

"You look more than that. If you are so ill, stay home."

"Yes, aunty, sorry, aunty, thank you, aunty," I yawned as I rolled my eyes.

"Hey, Nikki, you see this young cheeky man. You think I need to teach him a lesson?"

"I most certainly think you should, as he shouldn't be getting so drunk on a school night!"

I looked up from my laptop at the cackling pair and raised an eyebrow.

"I only had a couple last night. I needed it after that child protection medical."

"Why, what happened at the medical?" Rose asked.

"It was impetigo like Craig said it was," Nikki interjected.

"I was at the hospital until near midnight. The doctors only took two minutes to see him. By the end, I couldn't even look the parents in the eyes."

Rose burst out laughing. It came right from her belly, and it was so infectious that I could not help but smile.

"Oh, these managers, why do they not trust us?! It is like they think we are the enemy."

My eyes went back to my computer screen as I tried to log on but kept typing an incorrect password. Fortunately, on the third attempt, I got it correct, otherwise, I'd be locked out of the system. I logged into my email and quickly sent an update to my service director and team manager.

Hi,

It wasn't a burn, as I previously stated. The doctors confirmed it was impetigo.

Craig.

I wanted to add a few swear words, and I spent a couple of minutes fantasising about doing so. I knew I wouldn't get an apology for what happened the previous night, and I knew such perceived rebelliousness meant it would be another service director who took a disliking to me. As I went through my emails, a new message from my team manager popped up.

Craig, please can you come and see me about the Smith case?

It was safe to say I didn't get along with my manager, as well. I liked to spend as little time as possible interacting with her, so I pretended to have not noticed her email. I felt that if she really wanted me to see her, she would ring me or actually come see me. Just as that thought popped up into my head, my office telephone rang.

"Hi, Craig. I am not sure if you saw my email yet, but I need to see you about the Smith case."

"Good morning, Ann. Is it urgent?"

"No, but I'd like to see you now, please."

"Yeah, okay. I'll head over in a minute."

As soon as I hung up, I gave the middle finger to the telephone.

"Are you all right, Craig?" Lisa whispered.

I looked up and saw those big puppy-dog eyes that were always just a step away from filling up with tears.

"Yeah, yeah, all good. You?"

"I'm just a bit worried about this case I have. The dad is in prison for quite a serious domestic violence offence, and he's being released soon. The mother wants to continue a relationship with him, and she doesn't see the harm he caused the children when they witnessed him breaking her jaw."

Those eyes widened—made even bigger and wider by her jam-jar glasses—to the point it was like two saucers staring at me.

"One of those types of cases. 'He's changed, he's changed,' they always say. Let's hope she realises it's a lost cause before any more bones get broke. You want me to come around and have a look at it for you?"

Lisa nodded. I was more than happy to oblige, as it meant I had an excuse to make Ann wait a little longer. It was fifteen minutes later that I had helped Lisa develop a plan of action and soothed some of those rookie nerves. Just as I finished, I thought she was going to struggle in social work, especially because our manager wasn't the nurturing type.

For supervision sessions with Ann, it was basically a time to jot down a long list of orders. Feelings and professional opinion were irrelevant. Unfortunately, I wish I could say my wage-slave driver was an enigma but, somehow, such autocratic management was quite the norm in a profession that was supposed to be caring.

I went back to my desk, picked up my diary and pen. I spun around in the chair a couple of times to waste a few more seconds and tried to think up another reason to keep her waiting. None came to mind, so I took a deep breath and exhaled before I headed to see Ann.

Chapter 6

I had hoped to have bumped into someone who could have helped me delay or avoid having to meet Ann as I walked through the corridor. I would have been fine with an emergency, anything, just so I wouldn't have to see that sour-faced bitch...ever again.

I'm so sorry, Craig. But your mother has died in a dreadful lawn mower accident! It was horrible, so horrible that someone recorded it and put it up on the internet for the world to see! You're going to need to have at least six months off—all fully paid—to get over such a travesty. The fantasy brought a little pep to my steps.

Unfortunately, I encountered no one, and it was only a minute's walk to the team managers' room.

A couple of metres outside the door was a missing ceiling panel where some loose wiring drooped out. A morbid urge to hang myself on the wires blundered into my mind. I thought at least that would have gotten me out of the meeting. I shook the image off and noticed that my heart thumped just before I stepped through the open doorway.

There were four separate desks, each with a woman sitting behind. I saw Ann in the far-left corner frowning, typing away at her laptop. She was a relatively young woman, early thirties, probably my age or a year or two older. She was so stunning that she could have been model, so who knows why she went into social work.

She was of tall stature, had sparkling blue-eyes, and always wore false eyelashes that were so big they could have been used to rake garden leaves. Her hair was bleached blonde, her unblemished skin was perfectly tanned, and her natural gaze was the very definition of *resting bitch face*.

I didn't get along with her because she had very limited social work experience, had a stubbornly fixed view of how to do the job, only cared about key performance indices, regularly made decisions that weren't in the best interest of the child, and because of the way she treated me in a serious case review investigation.

She was the type who excelled at corporate interactions and was an expert at playing a subservient lackey with upper management, and that meant a promotion would come her way again soon. We, of course, regularly butted heads, and on one Christmas works night out, I told her I wouldn't piss on her even if she was on fire. Which I thoroughly denied when the local authority unsuccessfully tried to enact disciplinary measures against me.

To delay the meeting further, I went across to Sheila's desk instead. She was a manager who was middle-aged, jet-black haired, frumpy and squat to the point she could have come from a Tolkien novel, but was forever happy and excited. She had been through it all as she had thirty years of experience in the field.

"Hi, Sheila. How's it going?"

"Oh, hi, Craig! Just trying to get this computer to work, but like every man in my life, it won't bloody do as they're told!" she chuckled.

I went across and saw she was trying to log on with her caps-lock still on.

"There. Give it a go now."

She guffawed at her mistake.

"You are a star, Craig. Thank you."

"So, how's Rob and Max?"

"Oh, I don't know why I'm still with that arse. Since Rob pulled his back, it has been non-stop complaining. He had the cheek of it to ask me to go over to his house to tidy it up. I told him to sod off, so he hung-up on me in a huff. We haven't talked since, which has done my mental health wonders. Max, well, he takes after his dad, doesn't he, so he just lazes about rather than getting a bloody job!" she laughed.

I couldn't but help to chuckle along. I was about to ask another question when I heard Ann.

"Craig, please, can we have that conversation now?"

Sheila pulled a silly face at me, which made me smile. I took a deep breath and turned around.

My work nemesis looked at me with a gaze so sterile it could have been used to clean hospital wards. I gave a polite, pursed smile at her and walked across.

"Let's go into there," Ann ordered and nodded her head at the adjacent meeting room.

Without waiting for her to lead, I went straight in. It was a dark, damp, and cold room that oddly smelt like a swimming pool. There was one large empty desk that barely gave enough room for the surrounding chairs. They used it for supervisions or other meetings, all of which weren't particularly private as you could easily hear the discussions in the corridor or in the managers' room. I switched the light on and went to the chair furthest from the entrance. Ann sat on the chair closest to the door, which she closed.

"I hope you're doing well, Craig," she said without a hint of sincerity.

"I am doing fine, thank you. I hope you are as well," I replied in the same manner.

We both stayed silent for a couple of seconds as we looked each other in the eyes. She let out a slow and dramatic exhale.

"About the Jacob Smith case. I've spoken with Michael about it yesterday, and we've had quite an in-depth look at it."

"What?!"

"I'll get straight to the point. It's about the father—"

"What, the paedophile?" I interrupted with.

"With Mr James Smith. just to clarify, there are no charges or convictions against him, yes?"

I already knew which way this was going and thought it best I started the discussion swinging.

"No, there wasn't. He clearly downloaded that child pornography, but he played the system and blamed his son Harry, Jacob's half-sibling. Also, the computer evidence couldn't be determined to be Harry's or his. It was a family laptop, and police confirmed it was accessed in various places in the house. Also, when the pornography was downloaded and accessed, it was only at night when both were in the house. The screen name used when he communicated with other paedophiles was Senford United Football Club related, and both him and Harry are fans. Police and I didn't want the poor kid to be charged as we knew it wasn't him but couldn't get enough for the Crown Prosecution Service to bring charges against James."

I waited long seconds for Ann to speak.

"So, where is Harry now?"

"He's living with his mother. You know all this, so why are you asking me?" I said before I ground my teeth.

The ice cold authoritarian paused and pretended to look surprised. Her acting was not her strong point.

"I am just trying to get to grips with the case, Craig."

"So, how many interventions have there been with social care and Mr Smith? Also, does he have a conviction history?"

I let out a heavy sigh.

"No previous criminal history. Harry was subject to child protection for nine months because of James being a fucking paedophile. Ultimately, the kid moved into his mother's care, and James had sought no further contact with him since. Also, he kicked up enough complaints against us and garnered support from the local councillor that management decided to not take it any further. They were happy the kid had moved on and was elsewhere."

"YES! I remember all those complaints made against you. He compiled quite the list of evidence," she chuckled.

"Evidence? It was all just him making shit up!"

"So, ultimately, all we concretely have against him is that one period of child protection planning, which closed because there wasn't evidence against him."

"There was evidence, one thousand images and videos of evidence!"

A grin crept up onto Ann's face as she knew I was not enjoying this one bit.

"So, we have his other child, Jacob, who Mr Smith has not been involved in his upbringing. Jacob is now in care, and the current court proceedings will help determine where he goes."

She paused and stared at me until I averted my gaze, then she continued.

"Since it has started, we have received another complaint from Mr Smith about how we have put no efforts into assessing whether he would be a viable carer for Jacob. He has now found legal representation and is looking to be made party to proceedings. Based on what you have already said, it doesn't sound unreasonable to assess him. Especially as no one else is putting themselves forward for Jacob's care."

Ann leant forward, tilted her head, and stared right at me. She had won, and I knew there was going to be more bad news to come. My shoulders slumped, and I hugged myself with both of my arms. I turned to glare right back into her eyes.

"I imagine this is nothing to do with his current placement costing us four thousand pounds a week?!" I snapped.

Ann tried to stop her lip from upturning and snarling, but could not.

"Don't be so silly, Craig. You're always on your high horse. I am just pointing out the bleeding obvious, which you wilfully ignore because you hate this man. Your petty grievances don't mean you can't be professional and do what you're paid to do!" She paused, letting her condescension to sink in. "Considering your reaction to such news, and considering your history with Mr Smith, we will ask someone else on your team to do the viability assessment to see if Jacob should go into his care."

An image of me wrenching Ann's pen out of her hand and plunging it deep into her throat flashed in my mind. The act played on a loop, causing a hot flush of blood to rush to my back and neck. My hands shook, and the images became even louder when I tried to force them away. I held myself even tighter in fear that I actually would do this.

"Ann, you're making a big mistake. This man is a bloody nonce and a psychopath. Look at his police interview. He was as cold as ice when he tried to incriminate his own son for his crimes. It was disgusting. And now we're considering giving him his other son because of...what? Because we don't want to spend the money on Jacob. That isn't me getting on my high horse, that's just not being a CU—!" I stopped myself before the last insult.

I dug my fingers into my ribs as the violent fantasy of me murdering Ann played even louder in my mind.

"Craig, don't be so petulant. We're only wanting to assess him."

My mouth opened, and I found I wasn't able to say anything more. Instead, I felt tears forming in my eyes, and I started shivering. She, of course, didn't know what was going on in my head and sat with a confused look on her face as I struggled not to hyperventilate. As much as I despised my manager, I knew I didn't want to harm her, but then with such thoughts and urges deafening me with their screams, I became terrified I might succumb.

"Please, stop…not now," I croaked.

"What on earth are you on about?!"

I quickly stood up and squeezed by Ann, yanked the door open, and rushed out. I headed to a fire escape and got out of the building as quickly as I could. There was one silver lining to this ordeal, and that was that I had my cigarettes and lighter in my pocket.

Outside in the cold, I still held myself tight but, this time, it was to keep myself warm. I soon arrived at the smoking spot next to the bus shelter, pulled a trembling arm from my body, got a cigarette out, and lit it with jelly-like hands.

"Oh, God, I needed that," I whispered.

"Yeah, you definitely look like you do."

I turned and saw Taheen dressed in a navy-blue trench coat tied at the waist by its attached belt. She already had a cigarette in her mouth and was lighting it as she walked towards me.

"Properly back on the ciggies?"

"Yeah."

Her long, wavy, and black hair shined in the winter sunlight, and I stared in envy at the mane.

"Where have you been this morning?" I asked just before I took another drag.

"I was at court for a final hearing. Parents didn't even bother turning up, so we got the court order. The Johnson kids are officially staying in foster care. What happened to you?"

"Fucking new service director and Ann. They're pushing for a viability assessment of James Smith for the care of Jacob. Not only that, I think they're wanting it to be positive, which is why I can't do it. That poor kid has gone through enough with his smack head mother and stepdad…now this!"

Taheen chuckled.

"Sorry. I'm laughing because it's so messed up. It's time to leave this local authority, Craig. It's a sinking ship. We both know it will only get a lot worse, especially with the new service director. They brought him in to make the stats look good, and that means the kid's wellbeing will fall even further down the pecking order. Also, you guys are due an Ofsted inspection, and with Michael in charge, the preparation for that will be hell."

I stayed quiet, took the last puff of my cigarette, and flicked the butt onto the road.

"You reckon you will go soon?" I said whilst looking straight ahead at the terraced houses opposite us.

"Yeah. Carnston is offering forty pounds an hour. I worked for them before. They're all right to work for. They've got a lot of spaces going. I think Nikki will probably join them as well."

I turned around and raised my eyebrows in surprise.

"You two going will make it shit. Also, hopefully, they replace you guys and don't just spread your fucking work!"

"Don't worry, Craig, I'll make sure I leave all my cases in a mess for you," Taheen laughed, and then gave me a wink.

She finished her last puff, put the cigarette out, and flicked it into the bin. Without a further word said, we both headed back into the office building.

Chapter 7

The workday was a write-off.

After the verbal castration from Ann and still being stuck with a hangover that didn't even hint of mercy, I found all interest in my work evaporated. Instead of typing furiously at my keyboard to complete reports that were way out of timescales, I distracted my colleagues into conversation.

Like a hunter, I waited for a potential lull in my prey's focus and their guard to come down. When it did, I struck quickly by asking them a question about a subject I knew they were passionate about. For Amy, it was fashion and gigs; Taheen, it was her family and money. Nikki was politics and sex; Rose was eating out and her children, and with Lisa, it was box sets and K-pop. One by one, I distracted them all, and soon, I killed enough time until our shifts were over.

I said my goodbyes and I was quick out of the door, causing it to smash against the wall as I barged into it with my bag with my laptop inside in hand. I hurried to my car, and as soon as I got in, I checked how many cigarettes I had left; only two. Rather than disappointment, I ripped that silver lining out of that big fucking grey cloud that hung over me and made myself feel happy about having some smokes left.

I took one out and lit it in the car, switched the engine on, and then wound the window down. Straight after a couple of meaningful drags—the sort that helps make the world not seem so awful for a few seconds—I reversed out of the space and sped out of the car park at full throttle, causing my clutch to wail in pain from my mistimed gear changes. I breathed a sigh of relief as soon as I crossed the threshold and was out on the public road.

I did well for a Friday with only one car beeping at me on the way back home, and that was because I somewhat purposefully—more like very purposefully—cut in front of it on a roundabout. My excuse was that he was driving pretty damn slow, so I had plenty of time to get by. I gave a wave out of my window at the frothing old man and sped off. I stopped off at the local newsagent and bought a large pepperoni pizza, a pack of cigarettes, and a couple of bottles of real wine, the kind with labels that didn't look like they had been printed on A4 and cut out by child labourers. Tempranillo was my choice, as I felt like treating myself after such a day. When I got back into the flat and switched on the lights, I noticed it was spotless. Such cleanliness always shocked me as I never could imagine Zee having the energy to tidy up, but he always did.

Once my shoes were off, I went straight to the kitchen to get myself a glass. Just as I had poured half a glass, I heard a shuffle, so I turned around and saw Zee sitting in the armchair. A shriek that belonged more to a teenage girl shot out of me in fright.

"For a stoner, you're quite good at sneaking around," I joked and half-stammered.

He sat there, in the same bathrobe and sweatpants he always wore. His hood was down, and his sunglasses, as usual, were on. There was a giant and unlit joint in his mouth.

"You want some?" he croaked as he turned his head and looked at me.

I waited a couple of seconds for a part of me to scold myself with such acidic venom that it would cause my innards to burn for even considering it, but there was none.

"Yeah, fuck it. Let me finish sorting myself out with a glass of wine first. You want some?"

"Nah, m-aaa-n."

I came over with my booze, switched the television on to a program about vets, and fell back onto the sofa. Zee lit the spliff, took the first few puffs, and then passed it to me. I took a long drag and kept the smoke in my lungs for a few seconds before exhaling.

"I've only lived with you for a month, but I've noticed that every weekend you're usually here. Why?" he asked.

I took another drag and then sipped more of my wine.

"I go out…well, I guess just for sex. Like last weekend, I fucked this married guy."

I chuckled as in my head I had already finished telling the story.

"It was awful as he clucked like an actual fucking chicken when he came. It was so disturbing that I became like a deflated balloon right after. I had to pretend I came into the condom and got rid of it as quick as I could. Then for whatever reason, he thought I had become his fucking therapist as, when he turned around, he went on about his fears about what his wife and kids would do if he came out. I wanted to tell him that's the least of his concerns if he orgasms like that. Anyhow, I got out of there as quick as I could."

Zee turned his head to look at me with his sunglasses, and they turned into deep black cavities on a skull that lured me to float into the abyss inside. It caused me to shiver, so I quickly turned away to look back at the TV.

"Yeah, sorry, that wasn't what you asked. I used to live for the weekend as I was a proper rave kid. I had quite a close group of mates I went out with, but one by one, they got married, had kids, or they went abroad to teach English, or they—" I stopped myself and gulped before I carried on. "Now, they're all too busy for me, but I can't blame them as it's just what happens when you settle down."

I raised my eyebrows in surprise that I said something so personal to him. The conversation stopped, and we finished the joint, and I also finished my first bottle of wine.

"M-aaa-n, how about you put that pizza in the oven? I'm hungry."

It was perfect timing as my stomach rumbled in agreement. I noticed I felt so relaxed and light that I thought I was going to keep floating higher when I stood up. I took small shuffles to the kitchen, spent a couple clumsy minutes trying to figure out how to cook the pizza. Eventually, I got the food into the oven and successfully switched it on. Twenty minutes later, we were eating slightly burnt slices of the pizza.

"How about you and I go to a rave tonight? DJ Dethhead is playing a set tonight at the Arches, and I know he will absolutely tear it up. I've got us some pretty decent Es as well. They're crucifixes," Zee mumbled.

I stayed silent and thought for a few seconds. It was odd, as there didn't appear to be any fear of what the drug's comedown would bring, and there were no pangs of guilt for even contemplating the prospect.

"Fuck it, let's do it!"

We spent the next five hours drinking, smoking joints, listening to electronic dance music, and watching people get into accidents on the internet. Even though I spent that much time with Zee, I still wasn't able to get much conversation out of him. I was averaging about two words out of him every ten minutes. It reached eleven o'clock, and we both went to go get ready. I found I was excited about seeing what Zee would look like as I've only ever seen him in his bathrobe.

The dress code for the club we were going to was casual. I put on a simple T-shirt with a psychedelic DJ turntable as its pattern, jeans, and trainers. My mirror showed me mismatching colours and tattered shoes. I am sure if I asked its opinion, it would tell me I was the worst-dressed gay man in the whole of Senford. I sighed as I wasn't always this dishevelled and was once quite the smart-looking guy.

When I went back into the living room, my oddball flatmate's appearance surprised me. It was the first time I saw him with his hair tied up. My face became hot enough to fry an egg on as I quickly looked away when he noticed I was ogling. The oddball stoner wore a tight black T-shirt that showed his biceps off, grey jeans that showed his package off, white trainers, a cologne that made me shiver at the knees and, of course, his sunglasses.

Zee suggested we take an E before we left the flat, and I agreed without hesitation. As I swallowed the drug, I hoped its high would lead to us getting intimately closer.

We quickly made our way to the venue by foot. During our way there, we didn't speak at all, and it didn't feel one bit awkward. His walk was no longer stoned shuffles, but fast and confident strides, and even with my taller stature, I struggled to keep up with him.

On our way, we encountered a drunk group of lads who jeered at us and appeared ready to cause trouble, but Zee tilted his sunglasses down to give them a look. He must have given them a pretty good don't fuck with me glare as they changed their minds and stayed quiet as we walked through the group. My infatuation with him multiplied, so much so I went to the extent of fantasising about what he would look like in a groom's wedding suit.

We reached the venue from the bottom of the queue, and that had already snaked its way to the end of the road and coiled up and down itself twice. I was about to swear as I didn't want to come up on the ecstasy in the queue, but noticed Zee carried on forward.

"Zee, the queue is this way," I called as I hurried after him.

As soon as he reached the entrance, he stopped in front of two very wide and menacing-looking bouncers, both dressed completely in black.

"Hey up, Zee," one said whilst nodding.

The oddball stoner didn't say a word, and the man moved out of his way.

"He with you?" the other asked.

My comrade nodded.

"Hey, Bella, let these two in," one shouted to the kiosk.

My fantasies immediately became far more X-rated. We both walked straight into the club. The bass that was quite soft outside had multiplied to levels where it shook us straight to the bones. The air also suddenly became a lot warmer and more humid.

My crush's pace was still quick, and it was a few more turns in a long corridor and we were finally in the venue. It had changed little since I had last come all those years ago. It was as grimy and dirty as ever, with rusty metal pipes, sticky floors that tried to cling to your shoes, and beams on the ceiling dripping with condensation. Colourful flashes with a dim blue light showed a multitude of faces with clenched jaws, and eyes were wide and cartoon-like with giant pupils.

The bar was to the side of the dance floor, and there was nowhere to sit. The DJ booth was on an elevated stage at the far end of the room, like a totem to the gods and surrounded by spasming worshippers. Colourful and trippy graphics played on a screen behind this musical shaman on the decks.

Zee turned to me and signalled for me to listen, so I leant down.

"I am going to go to the toilet, man. Wait in here for me."

I nodded and moved back to the wall to rest against. I wasn't thinking about the fact that I had taken an E earlier, and spent my time watching people dance, hug, and pant in ecstasy. The lack of inhibition, and the focus on the pleasure of the now, the moment, it was something that I didn't realise that I missed so much. It felt good to be back in the rave scene and the nostalgia was about to bring a smile to my face when, suddenly, my mind touched on the friends that I used to rave with, and then the ones who had passed on.

I never blamed the scene or the drugs, but I knew such things probably didn't help. To me, it was the simple case of having too much of a good thing and having a brain that wouldn't say no. By my early twenties, I had lost friends to overdoses, suicide, permanent psychosis, drug-induced heart failures, and even murder. We weren't terrible people; it was just at that point in our lives, we just didn't know there was more to life than electronic beats and chemical indulgence.

Instead of a morose blue filling me, I felt a warmth grow behind the back of my eyes and realised I had an ear-to-ear grin on my face. At that moment, the rave and my hedonism became a gesture of love to all of my old friends and to all the good times partying we had that come and gone. Before I could become any more saccharine, the ticklish heat spread and moved throughout my entire body, causing it to shiver all over and my jaw to move from side to side. I slumped right back into the wall. My eyes couldn't focus, and my head became so heavy that all I could do was keep it drooped back. I was coming up on the drug hard.

It wasn't long after this first wave of euphoria that I became everyone's best friend, and they were all mine. Perhaps it was because I hadn't had an E for so long, but these crucifixes Zee gave me were like having it for the very first time. I got so high I had completely forgotten about my flatmate disappearing and danced with the utmost of confidence, feeling that every gesture and move was a loving expression of the music that went through me. To someone sober, they probably would have thought my dancing was a symptom of an epileptic fit. If by perfect timing, Zee appeared just as the high came down, and without saying a word, he put another one of the magic disco biscuits in my hand.

I gave him the biggest and tightest hug I could just before I took the drug with a swig of his bottled water, and as soon as the drink went down, he had disappeared yet again. My search for my stoner flatmate was futile, so I spent the rest of the night dancing with my new best friends and also chatted absolute nonsense with them when we were outside in the smoking area.

"Oh my god, it's so amazing that we have this connection! I mean, we have the same t-shirt on so that's fucking destiny saying something isn't it!" A key of cocaine came my way. It would have been rude to refuse, so up it went. "Fucking hell, thanks, man. You're so kind, so special. Why aren't people more like you! WHY GOD DAMN IT?!" I laughed manically. "It's like we're all yin and yang, yang and yin. All fitting together." A snort of MDMA this time. "Oh, god that burns. But so good! Like eating an amazing bowl of chilli or something. Oh my god, you're so nice. It's because we have this connection. That t-shirt! That fucking t-shirt, it's the same as mine!"

During the rave, each time my high diminished, I had the luck of the devil as Zee would appear with another pale blue crucifix, give me it, and then vanish again. A part of me wanted to have him involved with my hedonism but, ultimately, I was too high to care. I was so far gone that a traffic cone could have provided me with hours of delight.

I did stupidly go on my phone to message random people and finally read a message Emma sent me the previous night. She was sweet, sincere, apologetic, and worried about me. I messaged her back an essay about my love for her, how amazingly high I was, how fan-fucking-tastic my new flatmate Zee was, and how it was so great to be raving again.

When DJ Dethhead had finished his last song, the lights switched on, and wide-eyed faces all looked shocked that the fun had ended.

It was over, and based on the gurning faces doing jaw gymnastics, many were still high. Near the end of the set, I had oddly gotten more than a little friendly with a young lady dancing next to me called Lily.

I imagine I focused my attention on her because of the drugs, my feeling exceptionally horny, and my failure in finding any gay men at the club to try it on with. Also, I was in such a state that if Lily wasn't there, then I could have possibly straddled one of the club's pillars and made it mine. I pulled the petite, goth-looking lady close to me and looked down at the young woman who I had only just properly seen for the first time in bright light.

Her slim face was pale, her eye shadow was heavy, her black lipstick painted perfectly, and her sultry eyes clearly said she was sober. She must have been one of those odd and rare ones who went to raves sober and somehow lasted the entire night.

I planted a messy kiss on her. Our teeth bumped, and then our tongues slobbered around each other's mouths. I hate to admit it, but this sexuality wasn't a hugely odd occurrence for me as I had slept with a couple of women before when I was high on E and many other drugs. However, their lack of appendages meant they could only get me so far.

"My friends have gone, and so have yours, so let's go back to your flat," she commanded with a stone face.

I giggled, nodded, and we made our way out of the club hand in hand.

"So, what are your parents like?" she asked during the walk back.

"I rarely tell people much about my upbringing. Well, unless I am off my fucking head, and then it all comes out."

"Well, that you are right now. So, tell me."

I chuckled, was about to lose my train of thought, but then grabbed at the thread just as it was on its way out, and pulled it back into view.

"True, true! Well, it's pretty complicated, but I'll keep it as simple as possible."

I paused for a few seconds to see if any part of me was going to resist such expression. There was no objection.

"I got put into care of Senford council when I was twelve."

"Why did that happen?"

I tilted my head and looked at her inquisitively, and one look from her eyes, I somehow found myself open wide like flipped open book.

"Well, I need to give you a bit of a background so you understand why. My mother, she had some extreme religious beliefs, a couple of serious mental disorders, and many not so delightful lovers. I spent too much of my childhood bandaging her up because of the beatings she took and because of all the cuts she gave herself. I had also become her sponge for all the bat shit craziness she spouted. She was all right when she took her meds but, eventually, she would always think it a good idea to stop, and her crazies would rush out. This one time, she attacked the postman by throwing a cup of her own piss at him as she thought he was an agent of Satan and her urine was holy."

I cackled, but Lily did not join me, and yawned instead. Ordinarily, I would have taken offence to such a reaction, but with this many drugs in my system, I believed the absolute best about her and thought she was just tired as she was not high. Even with that in mind, I still felt it best to finish my history quick for her.

"Long story short, there was a pretty fucked up incident of abuse. It all got found out, and they removed me from her care. None of her family wanted me as she was a pariah to them, and they probably saw me as a representation of her. And I never knew who my dad was, so I spent the next six years in care, which also wasn't a pleasant experience, but that's another story."

Lily tugged on my hand to stop me, and she pulled me hard into a hug. I held her back, thinking she was actually a sensitive soul, but it was only a second later I felt a hand massaging my crotch. I knew I should have at least felt a little hurt at that point, but the high easily washed away such feelings.

"I thought it was big," she teased.

I felt blood rush to my cock as the thought about finally getting it out to fuck played in my mind. A part of me thought about somehow ditching her, and then going to find a guy for some fun, but when I turned to look down at her, the glare she gave subjugated me into obedience.

It wasn't long later that we were both naked in my flat. Because of the E and Lily being a woman, I initially wasn't as hard as I thought I'd be. However, as the drug-influenced my senses, each touch and caress during the foreplay brought a feeling of euphoria, and it was soon that she had me at full mast.

An explosion of psychedelic of colours and patterns appeared in my vision when my eyes closed as we continued with the touches and kisses. Even with my lack of experience with the clitoris, I had her shivering and jutting against my hand in orgasm twice before we even got to the harder stuff.

Lily manoeuvred herself into a position where she sat on top of me, and I sat up against my bedboard. As soon as I squeezed into her wet and tight pussy, trembles took hold all over me, and the drug made me feel like I was orgasming without actually being close to that peak. Each small motion brought the same feeling of blinding pleasure, causing me not to even know or care if my companion was enjoying it or not. That was when she said something that would have destroyed me if I was sober.

"Yeah, fuck me like that. Fuck your mummy exactly like that."

Even the high couldn't hide the revulsion that slithered up my spine like a cornucopia of slugs, yet my body completely ignored it and carried on without abandon. I wanted to say something that would repel her, but an intense pang of pleasure caused me to moan even louder.

"Please, don't say that," I could finally gasp in her ear.

She giggled in response.

"Be a good boy, Craig. Mummy wants to you to fuck her harder," she whispered into my ear, and then bit into it hard.

I felt the shame, pain, and disgust build up inside my chest, and then fire upwards, but nothing in my mind grabbed onto it, and the feelings floated on by into the ether. I wanted to disobey, but I found I still did as she ordered and bucked my hips harder into her whilst maintaining a slow rhythm.

I ordered my hands to throw her off me, but they disobeyed and pushed her down into me at each thrust as our hips gyrated together. I then closed my eyes and kept them shut in hope it would help me get away and become lost in the intense kaleidoscopic visuals, but these visions transformed into the vivid memory of that time my mother raped me.

Each thrust, each euphoric touch, each gasp, and each moan at that moment, was not with Lily but with her. I wanted to cry and wail as it brought me to a pain that had burnt and hollowed chunks out of me all those years ago, but I could not. All I could do was moan in absolute ecstasy and carry the perversion on and on.

Suddenly, I felt a poison that was caustic to the touch bubbling up right down in the dark depths within me. The vision had disappeared, all light had disappeared, and there was only the feeling that I needed to expel this diseased substance out of me. I then heard Lily whisper the same words that were said to me all those years ago.

"Craig, cum into me so I can cure you."

My eyes slammed wide open, and I ejaculated at the same time Lily climaxed. The darkness that had surrounded me dissipated, and it quickly turned into a blinding white light. At that moment, there was a complete acceptance of the cosmic pleasure that came through.

When I finished, I immediately fell back exhausted and slid out of Lily. I lay there staring up into the ceiling without a single thought going through my mind as I was too shocked to do anything else. I then felt her pat me on the head.

"Far more enjoyable than I thought it would be."
She leaned over the bed to her handbag and pulled out four white pills.

"Xanax. If you want to sleep?"

I looked at the pills, and without a thought, I grabbed two of them. I put them in my mouth and chased them down with a nearby half-empty glass of water. We both laid down, under the duvet, apart, and facing away from each other. It was only just before I fell asleep that a semblance of thought returned.

That's definitely the last time I ever sleep with a woman again.

Chapter 8

The pale and naked Lily stared up at the ceiling with an amusement she saved for such sadism as her latest conquest lay near her asleep. He had taken four milligrams of Xanax, so would not wake up soon. She turned over and looked at the snoring victim. She had never turned a gay man before in her long lifetime, albeit she knew it was just temporary because of the drugs, but she still felt a little pride about the act. It seemed, at first, it would be an odious task she would have to persevere through, but it proved most enjoyable, especially the mixing of sex and toying with his deep-rooted trauma.

The seductive sadist moved the duvet cover-up as she had become hot underneath, and she also wanted another look at Craig's manhood. She felt it was a shame that he would waste such a fine tool only on men. She then blew a kiss at her traumatised victim and rolled off the bed. As soon as she stood up, the moonlight from the window shone onto her and reflected off her glistening and smooth body.

Her nipples on her small, pert breasts stood to attention, and she still felt a warmth throb upwards from her clitoris as flashes of the sex and psychological torture erupted in her mind. The twisted seductress's hand reached down, but it suddenly pulled back as her lust soured with the thought she could not further play with the young man because of her master. If she had it her way, she would have fucked him and toyed with him until he was no more. Lily thought it would have been a charitable act, as there were far worse ways to go.

The alluring hellion then thought perhaps she should claim Craig and what she removed from inside him for herself as she did all the hard work. After all, it was this daintiest of horrors who had to pretend to be enamoured by him whilst being surrounded by annoying idiots who shook themselves to the dullest music she had ever heard.

She was the one who had to listen to the bore's tiresome anecdotes and stories about his pathetic existence. She was the one who fucked him into oblivion and collected the nightmare that lay deep within. Lily frowned as she convinced herself more and more she was the one that deserved the prize.

Who cares what HE wants?

The seductress then realised she had entertained the thought too loudly and that he surely would have heard her disobedience.

"No, don't. Please, don't ruin this body!" she moaned and held her neck tight with both hands.

She let go of herself and then gasped in pain.

"Don't you dare! Don't you dare!" she growled in naïve hope that anger would help.

She knew there was nowhere for her to run to and hide, but she still tried. The petite sadist leapt forward and stumbled on the clothes strewn all over the bedroom floor and staggered to the door. Just as she reached it, Lily clutched her stomach so tight the muscles on her taut arms protruded.

"Please, I like this body…"

A distorted and guttural wail erupted from her mouth just as she pushed through the door. Her foot hit the side of the frame, and she fell into the opposite corridor's wall. The dainty horror then slowly slid down the wall and landed onto the floor with her forearms. Frustrated whimpers fled her lips as she dragged and pulled herself through the dark and into the living room.

Every couple of seconds, she winced, and then grunted. As soon as she was next to the kitchen, she let out a banshee howl, turned over onto her side, and lay in a foetal position, grabbing her stomach. Suddenly, Lily flung herself onto her back, with her arms pinned back wide as if an invisible force held her down. The young lady spasmed all over.

Five little nodules rose on her skin on her stomach as she writhed violently. These bulges became taller and taller, and soon, the skin ripped and showed fingers and a thumb sticking out. Another set of nodules appeared on the opposite side of Lily's stomach, and the same occurred until another set of fingers and a thumb poked through.

All the fingers and thumbs then gripped down hard and wrenched outward. A giant gash appeared and then came the sound of creaking wood. A series of bones snapped in quick succession as the ribcage was torn open. Lily stopped moving, and her gaze became vacant straight after.

Inside her agape torso, no blood seeped out, and there was no sign of organs of any kind. There only appeared to be a deep and empty abyss. The hands came out grabbed the sides of the hole in the cadaver to pull whoever was inside up. Up peeked Zee's head, with his hair tied back and, of course, his sunglasses on.

He quickly pulled and then pushed himself out of the corpse. The oddball stoner was soon standing next to the carcass with a joint in his mouth. He took a lighter out of his front pocket and then lit the drug and took a couple of long, deep drags. Zee then sauntered to the armchair, sat back in it, and let out a sigh.

"There really is no need to be so melodramatic."

As if in response, thousands of tiny threads erupted from one side of Lily's wound. Once they had latched on to the other side of the tear, all the threads tightened and, centimetre by centimetre, pulled the wound shut. Then thick viscous black slime seeped over the injury like glue, sealing the wound shut. It was a couple of seconds after that that Lily shot up and gasped for air. She sat with her arms behind her back, taking large breaths. The annoyed hellion knew her master wanted her attention, so she stood, grimacing whilst doing so.

"He isn't yours to play with," Zee explained just before he took another drag.

Lily stuck her tongue out at him, walked to the sofa, and sat on it with her legs crossed, arms crossed, and a pout on her face.

"I wasn't being serious. I would have still followed your orders, so you didn't need to ruin this body for me! It's one of my favourites!" she snapped.

Zee turned to look at her and raised an eyebrow.

"The punishment isn't over yet, you know."

Lily's eyes widened, and her eyebrows furrowed in a feigned anxiety.

"Get rid of it. You don't deserve it anymore."

"No, not that! Please, don't! It's so beautiful, and I've been having so much fun with it!"

Zee let out the type of sigh used by exasperated parents.

"If you behave, and that's a big IF, then I'll let you pick another. You'll have three and a half billion to choose from, so I am sure you will find one you like just as much."

The moody beauty turned her head away and scowled with a jagged-glass frown. The supernatural stoner sat there silently, puffing away at his joint, absently staring at the smoke floating up to the ceiling.

"Fine!"

The woman stood up and moved both of her hands to the top of her forehead. A long and yellow claw grew out of both of her thumbs. With quick and emphatic movements of her hands, Lily made long gashes all over her skin until there were large squares imprinted all over. The subjugated sadist glared at Zee as, one by one, these squares of skin peeled off from her and fell to the ground as if they were nothing but sheets of paper.

This continued until there was no skin left on her body. Underneath were pulsating red muscle fibres, like any other human except, at the head, it was quite different. The only orifice on her head was a mouth, and this was ear-to-ear, lipless and filled with sharp, jagged, and pale-yellow teeth. There were no sockets for eyes or cavities for a nose other than the vicious mouth, and like the body, it was covered with red sinew. The creature sat back down again, legs crossed, and arms folded.

"Now, we can't have Craig finding the skin, can we?"

The creature turned to face Zee for a few seconds, got up, felt the urge to kick the skin at her master, but decided against such desires. Instead, she slowly picked up all the pieces to emphasise her annoyance, and then opened her mouth. A multitude of long and slithering black, forked tongues leapt out of her mouth, grabbed the pieces, and snapped back inside her jaws. Again, she folded her arms and turned away.

"Hur, hur, hur!" the slow and bass-heavy laugh filled the room.

Zee put his joint out on the coffee table, stretched his arms upwards, and stood up. The stoner walked over to the creature, lifted her to her feet by the armpits, turned her around, and then grabbed her by the hips from behind and shoved her so she was leaning forward over the sofa with her rear facing him. Lily put her arms in front to stop herself from falling forward. A deep and bass-heavy growl emanated from the creature straight after. Zee ignored the warning and kicked her legs wide apart.

"Come on. It isn't yours," he cajoled as he moved a couple of steps back behind her.

Both stood there, still, as a couple of minutes went by.

"If you want to not be a rotting torso with no head and limbs for the rest of eternity, you'll do as I say."

Lily growled, but a couple of seconds later, a small hole opened up where the vagina should have been, and black slime seeped out. It slithered slowly down both sides of the legs until it hit the floor and pooled into a little puddle. The creature whined just as the last of the liquid oozed out onto the ground.

The monster quickly stood up and turned around with her hands on her hips. Her master completely ignored the petulance and stood over the gloop, looking down at it. He made a little gun with his hand and pretended to shoot at the substance. Straight after, the slime quickly morphed together and, within a minute, it formed another creature of horror.

Like Lily, this one appeared female and was around the same height as her. Unlike Lily, it was made of thousands of sharp, obsidian-like, and triangular shards that all somehow stayed together with nothing discernible holding them up. All the shards somehow spun around on a different invisible axis and at different rates of speed.

"Damn, ain't you a splendid looking one!" Zee exclaimed.

He leaned in for a closer look.

"I can see how you fucked him up so much."

Both of the feminine figures looked each other up and down. Lily growled at the other, and claws grew from the tips of her fingers.

"Now, now. You two will need to get along as you're going to be around each other for a bit," Zee laughed. "Come on! Let's go."

The master walked by its monsters and headed back to his room.

Lily quickly leapt over the sofa and followed Zee. The newly-formed terror turned its head to look around the living room and tilted its head when it saw a framed picture of Craig's mother. It suddenly sped after the other two, landing its pointed shards into the floor as it rushed into the void that the room's entrance led into, and just as it went through, the door slammed shut straight behind.

Chapter 9

I looked at my phone again whilst star-fished in my bed. Was the device lying or on strike because of the way I treated it? The cracked and greasy screen said it all. Also, the hours of forcing it to show me reams upon reams of porno must have done a number on it. Hell, the thing might dislike cock-on-cock action, but it was its duty to find the most titillating videos for its insatiable overlord, whether it wanted to or not. I pushed such silly thoughts away and stared more intently at the glowing seven and the bright letters that said Sunday. Seconds later, I accepted I had slept the entire Saturday away.

I was glad there were no signs of bodily warmth emanating from the other side of the bed, especially because I remembered it was a woman I slept with. Only vague recollections of what she looked like appeared in fractured shards in my mind. I soon gave up trying to remember the specifics, as I knew instinctively it was a subject should be tackled when I was more cognizant. A rumble of the stomach and a chalk-like tongue scraping against the roof of my mouth informed me how dehydrated and hungry I was.

I gasped and groaned as my legs and body ached right down into every fibrous and knotted sinew. My right eye lost its battle to wake up and stayed shut, but as my left seemed content to do all the visual work, I let it rest. I wriggled like a worm to reach the bottom of the bed and grabbed a bathrobe hanging off the bedpost to put on and armour myself against the sharp winter morning.

I staggered out of the room and went to the thermostat to check that the heating was on. It was, but I still put the temperature up much higher as it was willy-shrinking levels of cold. Shortly after, I had my head under the tap, and I gulped down cold water. I pulled myself up and groaned in pleasure and then went back down for more. Just as I finished my last gulp, I let the water spray onto my face to help wash the grogginess away.

After a wipe of the face, I went on the hunt for a clean mug, finding none that reached such lofty and unattainable standards. I emptied a mug half-filled with stagnant coffee where mould that was creating its own little civilisation on its top. A quick rinse of it and straight after I filled it with instant coffee granules and three teaspoons of sugar. Fortune was with me as there was just enough milk for the drink.

My stomach rumbled as I put the kettle on, so I trudged to the fridge to rummage around. Two fried egg sandwiches with ketchup were the order sent up to my brain. I cleaned the solidified bacon fat off the pan I found hidden under various dishes in the sink. Five minutes later, I sat in the living room, wolfing down my breakfast and sipping coffee whilst the television garbled out words that did not register with me at all. When I had finished my meal, my right eye had got back involved in its duties and opened. I gulped down the rest of my coffee and went back to the fridge, grabbed a litre carton of orange juice, and finished it all.

A wipe of my mouth with my forearm, and I felt ready to tackle the day. Suddenly, a panicked thought shot into my mind that the woman I slept with could have robbed me. I hurried into my room and went to check my wallet. All the bank cards were there, and even some cash. I then checked my work rucksack, and found my laptop remained.

I momentarily stared at the computer, grimaced, turned my head away from it, and puffed as I decided it would not steal the weekend like it often did. I rooted around my jeans, found my packet of cigarettes, and did a little celebratory dance as there was one cancer stick left. The cigarette lasted me a couple of minutes, and just as I finished, a bell noise dinged from my phone.

I fell onto my bed and had a look. It was a message from Emma. Much to my horror, I saw I had sent her an essay of a text when I was high on Friday night. I read that first and the soppiness of it caused me to cringe and turn away. It took a minute before I built up the courage to turn back and read the rest. Emma's reply was brief and to the point. She asked me if I wanted to come over for a coffee. Her husband Miguel had taken their daughter out to a local petting farm and a day out, so she had a couple of hours free after eleven o'clock. I messaged back saying I'd be there.

Aside from feeling groggy, I didn't feel awful. Even when my brain had finally put the pieces back together regarding the sex I'd had and the awful roleplay that occurred within it, I oddly didn't feel fazed. Even when my memories touched on that parental abuse that was expelled by the ordeal, my response was remarkably flat. It was as if a herd of elephants in the room trampled on by and I couldn't even bother shrugging my shoulders.

Instead, I treated the memory as an uneventful thought and focused on the awful Sunday morning television that was on. I ticked over into zombie mode, and my brain was quite content staying that way. When a dull as dishwater cooking program finished, I realised it was ten o'clock. I rushed and stumbled to the shower and got ready. More than usual effort went into my appearance, so I ironed a white fitted shirt—well, once upon a time it was fitted, now it was baggy.

Once out into the cold world, I hurried to the local newsagent and bought another packet of cigarettes. Straight after, I went to my car and I speedily joined the Sunday drivers. I was more than happy to overtake their meandering whenever there was an extra lane. Sleeping for twenty-three hours seemed to be quite an excellent health benefit as I found my mind had become sharp, although those who beeped their horns at me probably disagreed. I found it was one of those pleasant drives where I just about got through all the traffic lights when they went yellow before they went red.

It wasn't long until I was on the hilly outskirts of Senford, where the views of the city became quite spectacular. The downside was my car had to stay in first or second gear and travel fifteen miles per hour max, just so I could make it up those hills. Eventually, I reached a red-brick end-of- terrace house. The front of it had a well-groomed front garden filled with flowers. It took me five goes of parallel parking into an embarrassingly wide space before I left the car and went to the house. I knocked on the door, but there was no answer. So, I gave a policeman's bang on the door, and I heard Emma shout. "Coming!"

I heard feet pattering down the hardwood steps. The door swung open, and a short, tanned, freckled woman with a red-haired bob and a masculine jaw appeared. She wore grey yoga pants and a flowery zip-up hoodie.

"Hello, handsome!" she cried.

"Hi, beautiful!" I beamed back.

Emma leapt forward and hugged me hard. I reciprocated, and we stood there quietly holding each other.

"Come in, come in. You're looking very dapper. Sorry, I look like a scrubber. These days,

I'm just too tired to put on anything nice, and if I do, you can bet that Hayley will spill something on it."

"You really don't. You look amazing," I chuckled.

I, of course, didn't say the truth that I had long since noticed that she had let her appearance go since she had her daughter. We both walked through the bohemian and stylish household interior where assortments of scattered toys oddly juxtaposed against such hip décor.

"So, honey, how's the job?" she asked as we went into the kitchen.

Emma put the kettle on and went about making me a coffee with three sugars. I sat myself down on one of the bar stools at the kitchen counter.

"Same old, same old. There has been a lot of court work. At the moment, I've gotten myself down to two families in court proceedings, and they are both stressful."

"When are they ever not?!"

"True. Well, one case is more worrying than the other. It wouldn't be so bad, but management is really trying to take control. As fucked-up as it sounds, I feel like they're wanting this kid to go live with his likely-a-paedo father. It's disgusting really."

"Yes, they're quite the shit bags at Senford Council. I wonder whether it was the best of ideas for me to help you stay there. They've been treating you awful since I've helped. Also, my lovely, the fact that they tried to blame you for that death shows you the type of people they are," she said as she poured the boiling water into the mugs and stirred.

Emma passed me a pink polka-dotted mug and kept one for herself.

"You're not on the ball this morning. We're missing—"

"Ha! One second."

My bosom buddy spun around, went to the cupboard, and took out a tin of biscuits.

"Hobnobs, of course."

We both took a biscuit each out of the tin and nibbled on them.

"I know, I know. I need to leave, but it feels like they win if I do. But I'll do it, I just have to finish these two court cases."

"Honey, you said that six months ago," Emma said with a raised eyebrow.

I quickly finished the biscuit and took another. My friend looked at me for a few seconds and then took a deep breath.

"I know we don't get to see each other as much as we want to. I have Hayley now, and since becoming a partner at the firm, well, I have a lot less time. And then there is you with child protection social work constantly stealing you away."

She took another deep breath.

"Even with me seeing you less, it's obvious it's getting really difficult for your..." she paused for a second. "head. We both know what happened last time when you got like this. And now, you're back on the drugs again, Craig. So, I'm worried."

She only ever used my first name when she was serious.

"Please, don't worry about me. I know I look like a used-up crack whore, but I've actually been feeling quite good. The other night really was amazing, and it really has helped with me de-stressing. I know the drugs are a worry, but I won't be getting into them like I did before. Also, things that used to bother me before don't seem to anymore. I admit I'd wouldn't bat an eyelid if I slit Ann's throat with my own bare hands, but…"

My friend's eyebrows both went up in surprise.

"Wait, what?"

I frowned and then raised my eyes in surprise as I realised what I had said.

"Sorry, I meant I probably wouldn't bat an eyelid if Ann died. Harsh, I know, but she is horrible."

An image of me with cutting into my manager's throat flashed into my mind, and I felt my mouth salivate. Oddly, there wasn't the usual fear of such violence, and the scene more than willingly played in my head as I tried to get back to the conversation.

"You okay, Craig?"

"Yeah, sorry, randomly realised something I needed to do for work. I promise I will get help if I get bad again, and I will make sure I'll tell you, too. Also, I will definitely leave Senford soon and get a new job elsewhere. Okay?"

"Good," she replied with a blatant scepticism I could see in her eyes.

We both sipped on our coffees and munched on our biscuits. The scenes with my work nemesis being hurt in my head did not stop, and I became hotter and hotter.

"So, how's the wonderful world of protecting the downtrodden employee?" I asked.

Emma went through the ins-and-outs of her new role as bloodthirsty scene after scene with my manager flashed in my head, all of which I kept trying harder and harder to force out of view. She spoke about a new class-action lawsuit against a local authority she had a lot of input in. From what it sounded like, she was making a lot more money, and they were going to use this newfound wealth to help with a move to even leafier suburbs of Senford. Then she went on about Miguel's promotion, these new friends from his work they'd made, and a new car they were looking to buy. On and on she went about how *fucking* perfect her life was.

Suddenly, the savagery that was forcing itself into view of my mind's eye changed from Ann being the focus to Emma, and I gasped, almost making myself choke on the biscuit.

"Are you okay?"

I got off the barstool and nodded as I spluttered.

"Just going to go to the toilet."

As soon as I got into the toilet, I locked the door, leant over the basin, and washed my face with cold water. I told myself I should be happy that she was doing so well, but such thoughts felt hollow. I tried to tell myself that, even though we were both raised in the care system, it was just a simple chance the dice roll had favoured her.

It was only seconds later that I found rage boiling up into my mouth, making me want to scream that it was so unfair she had got this amazing life, a beautiful kid, buckets full of money, and the manliest husband with washboard abs. The best I had was a one-way infatuation with a stoner flatmate who was stranger than an army of frogs wearing top hats.

The love I felt for my best friend evaporated with such heat it scorched my back and innards. My fists and jaw clenched as an eerie calm suddenly came over me. I left the bathroom and went back into the kitchen without a thought in my head. I stood just across from her and glared at my friend, who focussed her attention on a biscuit.

My buxom buddy looked up and immediately saw that something was wrong. Even in the face of such blatant aggression, she gave me a look of such concern. It caused my rage to falter, and that was just enough to get me to realise what I wanted to do. With this much anger in me, I knew I had to do something, so I scrunched my face and stuck my tongue out at her.

"Eh? What's wrong?"

"What's wrong?! What's wrong?! Well, what ISN'T wrong?! That's the fucking question. Coming from Little Miss Fucking Perfect with her perfect fucking life, with her perfect fucking husband, who has a perfect fucking cock." I paused, Emma's mouth fell wide open. "Yeah, I've seen it. When I borrowed your phone ages ago, I snooped and looked at your pictures. Anyway, you skanky bitch! That's right, I'm calling you a bitch, because…because…" My bottom lip trembled. I had lost my flow, and I did not know what I was going to say next, so I was about ready to run out of the house.

For whatever strange reason, Emma's face wasn't one of hurt. Instead of mirroring my rage, she opened her arms.

"Aw, baby, do you need a hug?" she soothed.

I stared at her with a face I kept like stone for only a second. Straight after, it all cracked, and I was bawling.

"You god damn cunt. Why do you have to be so fucking nice?" I whined as I rushed over to her, stooped down, held her, shoved my face into her shoulder, and wept.

I choked and sobbed as she held me tight and stroked my head. It was a few minutes before I even made sense of why I was in such a state and that the jealousy I felt was just a guise.

"W-w-why wasn't I able to protect him?" I cried into her shoulder.

"What? Who?"

"Who do you think?!"

"Oh, I see."

Emma then kissed the top of my head before she stroked it again.

"There was nothing you could do, Craig, nothing at all. You did everything humanly possible," she soothed.

I cried into her shoulder for a couple more minutes, and I mistakenly thought I had calmed down a bit as I lifted my head off her shoulder, but then plunged it back down into it to bawl again, wiping all my snot onto her.

"The things they said about me, like I was the one who killed him!"

Emma held me tighter and continued with her soothing.

"It was all bullshit. If it wasn't, then they wouldn't have so easily backed down when I got involved…There, there. Come on, let it all out."

It was five more minutes of me crying and my friend comforting me before I lifted my face off her shoulder. As soon as I did, I noticed a big wet patch and slug trails where my tears, mucus, and drool had soaked in.

"I'm sorry about that."

"No, no, don't apologise. You know I prefer it when you open up like this. Come, let's sit," she said as she took my hand and led me to the living room's sofa.

We both fell onto it, and I sat with my head cradled on her lap as she stroked it. When I looked up at her, I saw she gave another look of such concern I thought I was going to bawl again, but I held it back.

"It wasn't your fault. They were cowards for trying to blame it on you, as they're so scared of what the inspectors or what the media might say. What happened was shit but, sometimes, children will die, and there is nothing we can do to stop it. In the end, the only people who should be blamed are the ones who actually did the harm, his parents."

I sniffled and nodded.

"I know, I know, but I just couldn't stop feeling guilty about it. Especially after I gave every bit of me I had for this fucking job. I still give it my all, but all I get back is that I'm told how shit I am and how I keep on messing up their precious stats!"

My friend tilted her head and looked at me for a few seconds.

"I am getting the feeling there is even more that has gotten to you?"

I frowned at her at first, then looked away into the distance, turned back, and nodded.

"When they suspended me, I read my old case file they had on me for when I was in care. I know I told you I wouldn't read it, and that I had thrown it away, but I just wasn't able to and kept it under my bed all this time. It was fucking horrible, Emma. They kept on calling me a problematic child that was a high risk. Like that was all that mattered and there wasn't anything else to me. I wasn't some downtrodden kid who was struggling to find out if he even had any dreams or hopes, I was just a burden and a piece of difficult fucking work!"

I took several deep breaths, stared down, frowned, and then looked back at her.

"You remember the Hunters, one of the foster carers I stayed with?"

Emma nodded.

"They had a meeting about being worried about me staring at their daughter funny. They told the social worker it worried them I was going to rape her because I didn't act *normal*! Then there were all the stupid complaints they had about me. Once they moaned about me always shaking my leg when sitting down as they thought I was doing it on purpose to annoy them. Do you know what the last reason was for why they kicked me out?!"

Emma shook her head.

"It was because I slammed the door in the middle of the night. So, they said I had to leave. They got rid of me like that, like I was nothing because I got upset and slammed the fucking door. I didn't hurt anyone, didn't even swear at them, and I was never breaking my curfew, yet they fucking hated me. I always thought what my social worker said about why I had to leave was bullshit, and I was right." I huffed and puffed out my frustration. "Considering all that happened to me in care, I don't know why that was what really got to me."

I frowned and then thought for a minute.

"I think maybe because it really made me really feel like I was nothing but a fucking stain they wanted to clean away."

Emma bent over and kissed my forehead.

"Oh, honey, you never were and that still applies. You've got so much to give. You've made such an amazing impact on so many people, you need to remember that. I'll admit we did some pretty awful things when we were young, but I think we've definitely made up for it and given back to society a hell of a lot more in return."

She paused and looked at me with eyes that turned moist for a second.

"I think you should get rid of those files. I've used mine for a bonfire long ago. As soon as I read the court report about why they removed me, I just knew I couldn't go any further. Get rid of it, Craig. Don't hurt yourself anymore."

I nodded as I knew she was right, and we stayed silent for a minute. I felt a lot better, so I got up off her, stretched, and leaned back into the sofa.

"I'm feeling parched over here, Emma. Oh, and a few more biccies, please," I chuckled with a grin on my still wet face.

"Cheeky twat! Okay, I think we have time for one more before Hayley and Migs get back," she laughed.

I wiped my face and nose with a tissue as Emma went back into the kitchen. She soon came back with two fresh cups of coffee and the biscuit tin tucked under her arm.

"Before I tell you about the funniest thing Hayley did the other day, make me one promise."

I raised my eyebrows to encourage her to speak further.

"Promise me you really will leave that awful place and get a job elsewhere before it destroys you. Okay?"

I sighed, looked back at her, and nodded.

Chapter 10

It wasn't until I was back in my car that I realised I hadn't had a cigarette the whole time I was at Emma's. To make up for such good behaviour, I immediately lit one, and then wound the window down. I smoked it as quick as I could, and then immediately lit another.

As much as an emotional detox seeing her was, I needed the sweet nicotine to soothe the nerves after such a mental exertion. When I took some time to think about it, I realised that was the first time I had cried since Michael—or Child M, as they called him in the serious case review—died.

A turn of the ignition, and I was soon darting in and out of the city's traffic again. A quick stop off at the supermarket, and I had to play hide and seek. Inside the store and before I had bought anything, I had nearly bumped into a dad whose children I had removed from his care a couple of years ago. Fortunately, I noticed him before he noticed me, and I literally dived into the cereal aisle, causing a middle-aged woman to yelp in fright as I flew past her and landed on my arms.

The removal really wasn't a surprising result, but he thought it was. He didn't quite understand that repeatedly breaking the bones of the mother of his children and making her black and blue was harmful to their development. Also, as the mother refused to leave this horrible bastard, work with professionals, and to put minimal care in for her children, there was no alternative but to enact court proceedings.

At the court, he turned up drunk, wore shorts and a T-shirt, and called the judge a cock-faced nonce. All of which didn't benefit him and made it far easier for us to do what we needed to do. Even after all that, he still blamed me and wasn't particularly fond of me or my welfare.

I found the possibility of getting caught by him quite exhilarating. Fortunately, I didn't get to find out if such fun would last if he saw me as I made a stealthy escape, much to the confusion of bystanders who couldn't understand why I was sneaking about in such a manner.

I was lucking out, as at the next supermarket I went to, I bumped into another family I used to work with. Like the one before, and the great majority of families I supported, the primary issue involved domestic violence. Somehow, these people never received the nationwide memo that it's not okay to beat the shit out of your partner. However, the result for this case was positive, and I didn't close that one as an enemy.

The mother called my name and ran up to me to give me a hug from behind. She was a young, mixed-race mother who, like me, had a black father and a white mother. Police referred her family in because of her relationship being exceptionally violent, and she struggled to leave it. Fortunately, I could dedicate a lot of time to her as my other cases at the time were as calm as the eye of a hurricane.

With such time and persistence, I could convince her there was far better than her then partner out there, to get her the right mental health support, and to get her moved away into a new home that was safe. That being said, even after all this, I had forgotten her and the children's names.

"How are you and the kids?" I said to a beaming face.

"They're lovely. They're with nana right now whilst I am doing the weekly shop."

We talked for a few minutes, and I felt I could ask good questions without having to use any of their names. From what she said, it sounded like life was going well for her. The forgotten parent had started a college course and she had a plan to get herself into nursing. She said her parents supported with the kids, and that she was really enjoying the single life—with a wink.

It was good to see she looked a lot smarter and fresher since I last saw her. As soon as we said our goodbyes, I went about trying to guess her name. By the time I finished shopping, I still couldn't figure out what it was and gave up when I got outside.

I came back to my car to find some twat parked very close to me on the passenger side. I left my shopping at the driver's side—I still hadn't fixed that door—and then went about trying to get in through the only entry of the vehicle. It took a fair bit of effort to squeeze myself in through the passenger door. Even with me being rakish thin, I still had to suck in my stomach. Finally, when I got in, I reached over and opened the driver's side door.

Next, to get to my shopping as I thought it would be too difficult to get back out the way I came in, I crawled over the handbrake and driver's seat to slide out of the driver's door face first—I could open it from the inside. As I pushed myself up, I saw the driver of the other car that was next to me patiently waiting and standing there humming a tune whilst looking away.

"Sorry, mate. I'll just get my shopping," I chuckled nervously.

The middle-aged man moved out of the way, I grabbed the bag and rushed back into my car. I got out of the space as quick as I could, which was quite slow as I needed a couple of attempts at reversing out as I was worried I'd scrape the car that was right next to me on the passenger side. The middle-aged shopper who waited with his arms folded near my car didn't help with my concentration. As soon as I was out of the space, I zoomed away as fast as my little engine could take me. It was only ten minutes later that I returned to my flat.

When I got in, there was still no sign of Zee. I knocked on his door to see how he was, but there was no answer, so I went to the kitchen to make myself some lunch, which was oven chips, baked beans, and a mound of grated cheese. I went to eat it in the living room and started my hunt for a casual encounter on my mobile phone. After the sex on Friday, I felt I needed a decent fuck to help get the experience out of my system.

During my hunt for a fling, I didn't even bother typing any words as I had a copy and pasted introduction message all lined up. If they responded favourably, I would send and request risqué pictures, and if that led to a favourable response, then it was usually an agreement of hooking up. It was far too easy for my own good, and there had been days I'd come back home and collapse in bed as I had fucked too much that day.

A couple of people replied to me, saying we already had slept together before and they wouldn't mind doing so again. For the life of me, I couldn't remember them, and I felt that that doing it again would be awkward as they'd have a level of expectation. I ignored those messages.

It was an hour later that I had a successful catch. He was a very muscular and macho-looking young man. Although the beefcake wasn't well endowed, it did not bother me as he had a rear end that I felt deserved a thorough punishment. We arranged for me to pop over to his place later that evening.

I put my phone down, laid back on the sofa, and then switched the television on to kill some time. Any programs that became too serious and weren't mindless enough, I changed. I ended up watching quite a lot of cooking shows and realised I should probably try to learn from what I saw. It was something I always wanted to do, but I put no genuine effort into doing so. The best I could make was burnt steak, soggy chips, and some sautéed vegetables.

Before I knew it, the sun had gone down, and it was pitch black outside. I had dozed off for what must have been just a couple of minutes and when I opened my eyes, I realised I wasn't alone in the room. There sat Zee on the armchair, unlit joint in his hand, the same clothes he always wore, and sunglasses on.

"Hey, m-aaa-n," he croaked.

"Hey, Zee. The other night. What a night. It ended pretty weird, though," I laughed as I excitedly sat up.

I frowned as a flash of movement burst into view at the left corner of my eye. When I turned to look, there was nothing there, and when I turned back, I saw the scariest looking thing curled up on Zee's lap. It appeared to be a giant centipede with sickly white hairs sticking out of it.

I shot up, leapt over the sofa, and pointed at the creature.

"WHAT THE FUCK IS THAT?!"

My flatmate stayed quiet and turned to look at me, keeping his face stone still. I turned to run but bumped into something that felt immovable, warm, and sticky. I turned around to see another monster. This one was just as disturbing. It almost looked like a human with no skin, except its head had no orifices other than a giant, sinister mouth with sharp teeth that went across its entire head.

The foul beast opened its mouth wide, and many black tongues leapt out, wrapping around each other and writhing apart like snakes. I fell back onto my bottom and scooted backwards until I bumped into the balcony window. I reached down to feel my butt, and the small positive was that I hadn't shit myself. My mind immediately went back to the creatures that looked like they didn't mind dining on a human or two.

Then I saw that where I had just been sitting, a feminine figure that was made entirely out of thousands of pieces of swivelling obsidian sat with its legs crossed, looking at the back of its fingers on its right hand. I tried to process what the hell was going on, but before I could, I felt a fiery breath coming from the side of me. I turned to see a gaunt, long, grey human-like face with slits as a nose, empty black sockets for eyes, and a toothless mouth on a tiny and frail human body.

"Please. Please!" it moaned at me.

I screamed and swung a backhand at the creature. It let out a howl, whimpered, and crawled frantically away on what appeared to be four stumps in place of its arms and legs. The creature headed straight to Zee. My flatmate kicked his foot up into the creature's body, and it whimpered in response and scampered away to hide. The long-haired stoner then shoved the centipede off his lap.

"Zee, what the fuck is all this?! Jesus fucking Christ…have I completely lost it, have I?"

"Chill out. No, you haven't gone insane. They are real, and I guess in your world you'd call them demons. I call them a pain in the arse," he chuckled.

The centipede went to crawl up my flatmate's leg, but he smacked it away with the back of his hand, and it scurried off to be close to the small grey creature, which peeked from behind the sofa and gave me a toothless grin. I curled up into a ball whilst I sat pressed against the window. No words came to mind, and all I felt was that I was hyperventilating because of the sights before me.

"You need to calm down, Craig. Here, take a puff. This is even stronger stuff than before, and it'll sort you right out," he drawled as he gave me a grin so friendly I found myself powerless to say no.

My flatmate came up off the chair and reached over with the lit joint. I grabbed it and took a couple of deep drags. He was certainly right about the weed being effective as I found I had calmed down to where I could think and speak again. However, I remained curled up and frightened that those evil-looking monsters would devour me.

"W-w-why are there demons here, Zee?" I stammered.

The stoner sat cross-legged on the floor next to me as I took a couple more drags of the joint.

"Well, three of these ugly bastards came out of you. The other one with that mouth filled with teeth. Well, she's different. Let's just say she owes me big time."

My eyes darted around, looking at each demon, all of which appeared focused on me.

"Zee…who are you, really?" I whispered as he took the joint off me.

A wry grin crept up on my flatmate's face just before he took a few drags of the spliff himself.

"That's quite the philosophical question, but I'll keep it at a level you will understand. Zee obviously isn't my actual name, it's Beelzebub.

As you can see, I'm not the angry pitchfork waving type. That's all hyped-up bullshit, something made up by the bored and power-hungry. I'm actually quite the helpful sort of dude. Like, for example, I've saved you from a complete mental breakdown."

He gave my shoulder a slap.

"W-w-what? The Devil? Stop fucking with me, Zee."

The alleged Lord of Darkness let out a deep-bellied stoner laugh.

"Craig, man, just look around you. Do they look like they're heading out to a fancy-dress party?"

I quickly assessed each demon. I had been to many a Comicon, so I knew my costumes, and they all definitely did not look like they were dressed up.

I sucked up enough courage and looked him into those bloody sunglasses that seemed like windows to an endless abyss. A second later, I did not know why, but I felt powerless to question his fantastical claim. All reason, logic, and scepticism had fled from the horrors before me, and even if he claimed to be the resurrection of Gandhi, I would have chosen to believe him.

"Yeah, I suppose you being the Devil would explain all these scary things." I paused and took several deeper breaths to calm my frazzled nerves a touch more. "Sorry, but my head is all over the place, and I don't know what to think. Wait, what, you said three of them came from me. How?"

Before he could answer, I instinctively grabbed the joint from his hand and took another couple of puffs. I saw him raise an eyebrow at me when I gave it back.

"Hur, hur, hur! They are the physical manifestations of your unresolved and repressed traumas. Every human grows them, but most people's psyches operates like a healthy ecosystem where such species are kept in check by your psychological immune system or destroyed by other internalisations. For you, it is different. These sufferings, or inner demons if you like, were about to become the dominant order of your mind, and if they had, then the result would have been catastrophic for your mind and, ultimately, your life."

Beelzebub took another drag of his joint until it was at its end and then stubbed the roach out on the floor. I, of course, didn't complain.

"So, they came from me…Why would you, the Devil, save me from them? Also, don't you have Hell to run or something?"

"Heaven and Hell, aren't really like what you think. Hell isn't like a place for me to run like some weird hotel of the damned. Why I helped you, well, it's because I like you, Craig, and didn't want to see you in the gutter."

I found myself astounded that the pointed tail and horned one had an interest in me. I wasn't too sure of whether that was a compliment or a profound worry.

"I know you say you like me and all that, but I feel there is definitely more to you wanting to help me out."

"You're rightfully cynical. I know you think these ugly mugs are horrifying, but to me, well, I find them pretty interesting, and some of them have their uses. You never get the same one from people, they're always so different from each other, so I enjoy them like people who collect pets." Zee then sighed. "To get to the point, I've needed someone to help me with my collecting for quite some time, and I've found the right person to do this. It's you."

"You mean you do it like Pokémon, except more fucked-up?"

"HUR, HUR, HUR!"

I didn't think the joke was that funny, but Beelzebub carried on with his slow and methodical laughter.

"I need you to help me as I've got the God squad and others always on the lookout for me, so I can't spend too much time out in the open looking for who's ripe for the picking. So, I need someone a little more inconspicuous and someone whose got an expert eye in spotting the darkness within others to help, and that's you."

The Devil stopped, frowned, and stayed silent. I simply stared at him, waiting for him to continue.

"M-aaa-n, I'm so baked right now. Yeah, I need to tell you about the perks, as there are a few! You'll live as long as I want you to live, and that could be until the end of time. Also, you'll get to smoke the best weed ever grown, it's Biblical stuff."

I had turned to look at the obsidian demon and turned back to see Beelzebub with an already rolled joint being held by his teeth and being lit.

"But there's more to it, something I know you'll definitely want. It'll be a way to save others, like how I saved you. Not that I care, but you'll be helping me purify human souls, and with that, you will prevent so much more pain from being caused by these corrupted and hurt people."

I sat there staring at him, not knowing what to say as he took a few drags, and then blew smoke rings that morphed into upside down crucifixes.

"Think of all the times you struggled to reach parents who were just too far gone, and you had to use the most draconian of methods by removing the kids from their care. Instead, with my help, you can actually give the families a fighting chance!" he exclaimed with a clap.

An image of my mother flashed in my mind, and it made me stop breathing for a couple of seconds. Beelzebub took another couple of drags of his joint as I mulled over the matter.

"What if I say no?" I eventually replied.

The alleged Lord of Darkness did his slow and deep stoner laugh.

"What makes you think you can?" he said before he tilted his sunglasses down and winked at me.

Chapter 11

"Just use your imagination about what could happen if you said no to the Devil." He paused and gave me a stare so intense that it caused my skin to want to crawl right off me and hide. "Here, have some more of this, m-aaa-n."

He then leant over and passed me the joint. I was more than happy to have more of the weed as I felt a panic rise again. I gave the spliff back to him after a few puffs but kept my gaze averted from his.

"So, clearly, I don't have a choice in this fucked-up matter. So, what's the catch?"

"I'm hurt that you think there's a catch! If you can't trust Satan, then who can you trust?!" He laughed and feigned offence.

"Yeah, you're right. There is more to it. With those you choose, you'll get to decide whether they will be purified and live on, or be purified and die, and by die, I mean become food as my demons got to eat!"

"Oh."

I then felt a bit perturbed as a pleasant warmth slithered into me as the prospect of being able to choose whether people lived or died was oddly arousing. I quickly forced in the thought that all chosen must live as that was what was moral and right. *Wait, a second, you're going along with all this madness?* The clarity of thought shattered into pieces and scattered like a disturbed flock of pigeons as my gaze caught the muscle-sinew covered demon. *Fuck's sake, I don't want to die. I don't want to die!*

"So, how do I do the picking? Also, Beelzebub is quite a mouthful, so can I still call you Zee?"

"Yeah, definitely call me Zee. Beelzebub is way too pretentious. As you've probably gathered, the best and strongest demons come from, let's say, people with a lot of issues. You regularly work with these types of people, so you'd do the choosing whilst you carry on being a social worker. I'll tell you how you do that once we get this one, last thing done."

I let out a deep sigh and closed my eyes for a couple of seconds. *So, I'm doing this. I'm actually doing this. You'll get fed to those things if you don't. FUCK!*

"Fine, what do we do next?"

Zee turned away from my gaze, pursed his lips, and then turned back.

"Yeah, you won't like what we've got to do. We're doing it because I need you to be game ready to take this role on. Also, you've got a demon still in you that I want. You've got this big, grotesque, and utterly mean son of a bitch in you. You know, what I am on about, it was making quite the racquet and encouraging you to kill your best friend earlier on."

My mouth dropped open.

"It's always angry, always raging, and the moody bastard is pretty powerful as it has grown in you since you were a little kid. What makes it worse is that you don't know how to handle it and just keep on feeding it. I want it out of you, and that won't be easy."

"Wait, what do you mean it won't be easy?"

Zee did his stoner laugh again. I leant forward and took the joint off him as I knew I wouldn't like what he was going to say. I took a few puffs just before he settled to speak.

"Yeah, for you to understand, I must explain a little about demons first. Although I've got a knack in getting most of these ugly bastards out of people and subjugating them, with the more stubborn ones, other demons are actually much better at exorcising them than me."

He paused and sat there staring at me with those empty-skull-socket sunglasses. I quickly gave back his joint, turned away, and waited.

"So, if you haven't guessed it yet, Craig, these guys are going to help me get this mean dude out of you. Once we've done that, you'll be suitable enough to work for me."

The thought of being the Devil's employee did not sound right in my head. It didn't have a nice ring to it, and it wasn't a job title I could put proudly on my job resume. Yet, I knew I had no choice, so I'd have to accept whatever horribleness came my way. As soon as Zee stood, I realised what he actually meant and what was going to happen next. Panic gripped my chest hard, trying to squeeze every drop of breath from it.

"You mean, these scary fuckers are going to remove a demon that's still in me? How?" I whispered.

Beelzebub had sauntered away and sat on the sofa's armrest.

"Yeah, m-aaa-n, probably best I don't tell you how as it'll freak you out," he drawled before he shrugged.

"I'M ALREADY FREAKED THE FUCK OUT!"

Suddenly, all the demons rushed at me. It was only a couple seconds later that they had my writhing and struggling body pinned to the ground. It was the centipede-like creature that then crawled to my face. The feeling of it and the excrement-like smell of it caused me to retch. As it reached my head, it bared its leach-like mouth and ghastly teeth at me.

I screamed, and just as I did, it somehow forced its way down into my mouth. I felt and tasted the foul slime of its skin as it wriggled in. As soon as it got all the way down into me, all the other demons let me go. A pang of intense nausea hit me at first, and I dry-heaved hard and tried to vomit out the foul beast.

A minute later of me trying to expel the demon and feeling intense nausea, a slicing pain stabbed out from my chest into the entirety of my body. My vision went completely white after that, and my body shook violently and juddered.

I couldn't say how long it took, but the centipede demon wriggled out of my mouth, and something stone-like and scorching quickly followed. The stone burned with such an intensity that the pain became all I felt in those long moments. Every little part of me screamed in terror as the blast of heat consumed me. I lost all concept of any other feeling or even that I was alive.

Instead, there was a searing pain that went right through me. When the suffering ended, my vision returned slowly, and I saw a monstrous, seven-foot-tall beast that had a skin of glowing stone and swirling magma. Its head comprised of a half-sphere of lava that sat on a broad, square, and humanoid body. I wanted to move as far back as possible from the creature, but the balcony window trapped me.

I saw that the magma demon had the tail of the centipede creature in its hand. The insect-like demon lunged and tried to sink its teeth into its captor's upper arm. As soon as its teeth hit the stone, they shattered, causing the creature to let out a high-pitched squeal that forced me to cover my ears. Without a moment's hesitation, the magma demon grabbed the head of the centipede creature with its other arm and pulled until it ripped the creature into two. The giant insect's innards spilt onto the floor and its lifeless corpse dropped a second later.

To emphasise its victory, the magma demon beat its chest and it sounding like the thunderous smashing of rock. It then let out a bass-heavy roar that caused the whole flat to shake. The magma demon turned to face Zee, who still sat on the sofa's arm with one hand over his mouth as he yawned.

The fiery demon had taken one step towards its antagonist when the small grey demon scuttled over and threw itself at the gigantic monster's legs. The little creature turned into a rubbery and viscous substance that wrapped itself around both legs as soon as it hit. A few seconds later, I saw the heat and energy from the fire monster being drained away by the grey mass that clung to it.

The magma demon turned downward to rip the creature off its legs, but found its arms became tied and wrapped around from behind by the obsidian demon's arms, which had become thick obsidian ropes. More of the energy and heat from the molten monster drained, and its head solidified to grey stone.

Suddenly, the muscle and sinew covered horror ran up and jumped at the trapped enemy.

It swung a punch and struck right onto its rocky forehead. The sinewy monster's fist broke through the rock and went right into the head. The magma abomination let out a groan and then fell to its knees as the demon pulled its fist out. At that moment, Zee, who was smoking a joint whilst he watched this spectacle, stood up and sauntered across to the growling and defeated beast.

"Sometimes, you need to do a little more to control the more rebellious ones," he said to me.

My flatmate lifted one hand, and a glowing neon blue-collar appeared. It floated across to the magma demon's neck, opened, fitted itself on, and then vanished. As it did, the creature let out a soft groan. Zee's joint went out, so he took it and used the small heat left over from the magma demon's head to relight it. My satanic flatmate then took a few deep and long drags of his spliff.

"You lot can let the grumpy one go," he ordered.

The obsidian ropes loosened, and then the viscous grey substance fell away and transformed back into a demon. The magma demon slowly heated again, but stood obedient and still.

"Make yourself a lot smaller, this flat isn't that big. We can't have you cramping it all up!"

A split second later, a flash of orange light, and in the demon's place was a small, floating rock about the size of a tennis ball that was on fire.

My flatmate went to the floating ball and inspected it as close as he could get to it without setting his long hair on fire. Zee then put his index finger near it. Some flames leapt onto it, and set his digit alight, but this didn't seem to bother him. He then flicked the fire at me and it leapt straight into my agape mouth. I coughed and spluttered as I felt the flame shoot straight down into me as quick as it could.

"What was that for?!" I cried.

"I can't be working with someone who's too prim and proper. That'll be enough to give you an edge."

I stared at Zee, flatmate and supposed Lord of Darkness, and then exhaled quickly. I then realised that if Zee was telling the truth, then the rage in me that I had feared and coveted since I was a child had allegedly dissipated. If that was the case, then perhaps he did save me, as it was a part of me that always seemed to be a couple of steps away from taking over to make me do things I knew I'd regret.

I mulled over such thoughts and then felt I'd have to wait and see if I actually was free from such a beast. Rather than further dwell on the matter, I turned to look at the dead centipede creature near my flatmate.

"How about that one?" I said and pointed.

Without looking, Zee clicked his finger. The little grey demon rushed to its fallen comrade with a giant, toothless grin on its face. It could only get its mouth around a leg and rip it off before the sinew-covered demon kicked it away. The little one howled in pain and scampered off, opting to gum and suck on the foot that it had taken. The sinew-covered demon leant down and ripped into its dish with its myriad tongues and sharp teeth. It was only a minute later when it consumed the remains.

"I've got to feed them something," Zee laughed.

I stayed quiet as the act quite repulsed me. Watching lions dine on a zebra on a documentary made me squeamish enough, let alone bloody scary demons feasting on their own with the grossest of appendages.

"They only eat meat and aren't picky about where it comes from. So, if you decide to choose a person to be eaten, well, that is pretty much how they will go. The good thing for someone with your stomach is that you won't have to watch the act. Unless you get all dark on me and want to."

Finally, I pushed myself up and out of the ball I was curled up in. I frowned as I realised I had neighbours, lots of them.

"What are we going to do if the neighbours have called the police because of the crazy fucking racket that you made?!"

"Don't worry about it, Craig. I made it so they couldn't hear any of the commotion that went on. You know, I'm Beelzebub with spooky powers and all that," he drawled before he rolled his eyes.

I avoided eye contact with the remaining demons, headed over to the couch, and sat on it with my head in my hands. As I had calmed down a little, I noticed Zee's drug in me a lot more and realised I felt pretty floaty and spaced.

"So, what do we do from here?" I groaned, my head still in my hands.

"Well, I think you need a bit of time to process all that has just happened. So, I reckon you have some fun tonight with that guy you've set-up to meet. When you come back, and if you're struggling to fall asleep, well, just come and knock on my door and I'll let you have a smoke. That'll be sure to knock you out," Zee chuckled as I felt him squeeze my shoulder.

Chapter 12

Ever the polite soul, I sent a message to the bit of fun I had arranged to meet to say I would not be meeting up after all and gave some excuse about food poisoning. I instead had opted to stay in my room so I could think about the insanity of what had just happened, and so I could somehow process it all. Well, that was the hope as how in the hell do you get to grips with demons, the Devil, and being made an acolyte of Big Red himself? I lay there on my bed, face staring at the ceiling in absolute silence.

Initially, when Zee and his demon pets had all gone back to his room, my first instinct was to contact Emma. I rushed into my room to tell her all that had just happened, but I quickly realised she would think I had lost my sanity again and force me to get psychological help. This inevitably would lead to me becoming sectioned, placed in a mental health hospital, and pumped full of anti-psychotics. I thought I would probably get the same result no matter who I told. It certainly was not a place I wished to return to.

Without being able to tell anyone, all I could do was ruminate, so I let such thinking run rampant to see where it took me. What came to me was the worry that I had already become quite insane. I tried to analyse the supernatural events repeatedly to see if there were any clues or metaphorical representations of a broken mind, but I could not identify any.

Next, I conjured up memories of the time and stressors that significantly influenced my being forcibly sectioned into a mental health ward all those years ago. The involved factors were my taking lots and lots of drugs, a couple of traumatic events where good friends died, a dash of long-term unemployment, life brutally chiselling its mark onto me during my upbringing, and my genetics. Like an orchestra, each played an essential part that led to my mental disintegration.

At first, I thought such history was not repeating itself, but then changed my mind. It might be different instruments being used but, ultimately, it was the same melody being played. It wasn't nice to realise that after all these years, my life wasn't faring much better. One of these new players in my destabilisation was my repeated social isolation. Another was a British favourite, alcoholism.

I couldn't even remember the last time I drank less than two bottles of wine a night. I guffawed as I realised I had somehow convinced myself that, as it was wine, drinking that much wasn't that bad at all.

Then there was my job, but I dwelt little on that as it was an obvious issue with a giant red target sign over it, and I didn't want to sour my mood any further by thinking about it. There was also insomnia and lack of sleep, something my alcohol intake had lost its ability to solve. Then there were, of course, the intrusive thoughts which had got louder and more violent again, a clear-as-day sign that my mind was not faring so well. It became abundantly clear I was crumbling apart, long before Zee came into my life.

The prospect that I might be insane again caused me to shiver all over and tears to form. I curled up into a ball and was just about to wail when a realisation of one significant difference in my present and past mental states wriggled through. That was that this time around I was aware of my own mental fragility and its destabilization. I immediately calmed down and frowned as I went deep inside myself to further contemplate the matter.

During my previous experience of psychosis, I initially didn't think my mind was sick at all and carried this belief, even after being thrown into the ward kicking and screaming. This time, there was a palpable fear I could taste in my mouth about whether I had fallen to such levels again. I realised the positivity of this fear, this sense of awareness as being proof that I still had some sanity left in me.

I next moved onto realisations that I had actually felt better since Zee came into my life, even when he allegedly and somehow removed demons from me. With my rage, if most of it did definitely leave me, then it wouldn't be long before I'd be able to tell, especially when I returned to work as that was where most of its fuel came from.

Next, the whirring cogs in my head sent my mind to the possibility I was actually living with the Devil as my scepticism had returned. I had never been a religious person, so the prospect of Zee's theological claim to fame was difficult to believe. I tried to come up with a logical deduction about the matter, but I just got flashes of the demon fight I had just witnessed and my exorcism.

I rolled onto my shoulder, kicked my feet against the duvet, and then sighed. I thought even if the Bible wasn't true at all, in this circumstance, the alleged Satan had all the power and held all the cards. Ultimately, what was concrete was he actually helped me, and because of this, I owed him a significant debt, which he was collecting on. I also, feeling a bit of life down my pants, found that I was still infatuated with him!

I rolled over and looked at the two crayons he had given me on my bedside table. One red and one black. One decided a reborn life, and the other decided a gruesome death. Apparently, that was how I was going to pick the targets. Zee said that once I had chosen someone, I would need to go into their household and draw an upside-down crucifix anywhere inside with one crayon. I asked why inside and why not just draw one on the outside of the home, and he explained:

"The crucifix allows me to enter their home, through the shadows if you will. If my demons and I appeared outside the home, the homeowner would need to invite us in or we would need to break through a sacred barrier. I'm sure as Hell that no one is inviting me in because of the way I look, and about the latter, it would cause such an

*almighty racket that Heavenly forces would
probably hear and come looking for me.*"

It sounded a simple enough task, especially
with much of my job involving going into people's
homes. Zee didn't give me specific details of what
would happen next. He just said that the events
would go as described, depending on what crayon I
picked, and that no one would witness the matter.

It tempted me to write on some bits of paper
with the crayons as nothing seemed magical about
them at all, but I lost my nerve when I reached over
to pick one up and moved my hand back. I stared
at them for a few minutes more and then decided
that moving forward with what Zee wanted was
the only way for me to see if all that was
happening was real and not some fantastical
delusion.

With that last thought, I felt a reprieve from
the pressure of my ruminations and sat up. I
glanced at the time on my phone and saw there
were still a few hours to kill before it was a good
time to go to bed. I wasn't hungry and, oddly, I
didn't have the urge to drink any wine. That meant
there were only a couple choices of things left I
could do, and as I had opted to not have sex that
evening, it meant I naturally decided on
pornography.

It was a couple of hours and many used tissues
later that I was all spent. There was absolutely
nothing left down there, and I had exhausted it into
complete submission. I suppose it was quite a good

thing it had given up, as what I watched increasingly got weirder and weirder. By the end, I was onto a peculiar porno about a muscle-bound man purposefully—and poorly—disguised as a sheep, just so he could seduce a randy and exceptionally hung shepherd who only seemed to go for such furry beasts.

As soon as I climaxed, I knew it was time to give up on the wanking, otherwise the next thing I would have watched would probably have been even more disturbing.

Even though I felt exhausted, I did not feel I could fall asleep. Just as I had fallen back onto my bed and grunted in frustration, I heard a soft knock on my door. My head shot up, and I listened intently. I heard feet shuffle away, then Zee's door open and close.

I leapt off my bed, with only a T-shirt on and nothing on underneath, quickly pulled on some underwear, and then pressed my ear against my door to listen. Only silence was my response. The door creaked opened, and I peeked my head around. No demons, so I breathed a sigh of relief.

I was just about to shut the door when I noticed something just below on the floor. It was a thick, pre-made joint. A smile erupted onto my face, and I quickly grabbed it. Not long after, I had lit the spliff and was taking in puffs of smoke.

I flung the used tissues onto the floor and grabbed my laptop. I soon had some trip-hop and chill-out beats playing in the background as I lay on my back, puffing away until the drug was all gone.

My eyes became heavy, and a manic grin crept from both corners of my mouth. Soon, all of my worries shrank so small that my mind easily shooed them away. The music brought about a slight euphoria and warmth. It wasn't long before random psychedelic visuals crept up into the vision of my mind's eye as my body felt itself melt into the mattress. None of the visuals were nightmarish, which was peculiar, considering what had happened earlier on. Instead, they were filled with intertwining colours, fractals, and the smiling faces of various twisted-looking animals that all meshed and transformed as the music progressed.

I pulled my duvet up, and the cold of it touched my face. I moaned and took a deep breath in as the familiar musk filled my lungs. That was when I conjured up the magma demon in my mind, except a miniature cartoon version who tried to kick my leg but fell on its bottom. A chuckle that was as slow as tar fell out of my lips.

"Jesus, this is some powerful shit," I groaned just before I fell asleep.

Chapter 13

"You're looking quite chipper and raring to go, Craig. Did you have a pleasant weekend?" Dawn boomed through the reception's security window.

"Cheers, Dawn. Yeah, I had quite the blow-out and feel nicely de-stressed. How about you?"

"Oh, it was housework, and then a quiet night in with a bottle of prosecco or two! Quite a relaxing one for me. I'm glad to see that spark in you again!"

I chuckled and headed to the office entrance, swiped the fob, and walked in. It surprised me how good I felt, considering all that had happened. I even got a normal night's sleep the night before, albeit with the help of the Devil's weed. Also, earlier on, I'd even cooked up a full and hearty English breakfast of two eggs, four rashers of bacon, two sausages, two slices of buttered toast, and a cooked tomato. For my drive to work, I didn't even get beeped at once; I didn't swear at anyone, and I arrived at work on time. When I went to the toilet just before I went into my team's office, as I felt that good, I half-expected I was going to shit out rainbows. I, of course, didn't.

"Morning all," I proclaimed to all as I walked into the team's room.

Only half the team was in and everyone but Nikki greeted me back.

"You seem cheerful," Nikki muttered without looking up from her computer.

"I suppose I am. I suppose I am. It was quite a cathartic weekend."

I headed to my desk and unpacked my laptop.

"So, who's the lucky guy then?"

"It actually isn't that. Surprise, surprise, I didn't get any cock over the weekend. I went to a rave, and I think it helped me blow off a lot of steam. I have been feeling quite good ever since."

"The drugs were that good that they've lasted this long?"

I chuckled and felt my neck heat a little.

"Or are you just happy because Ann is off today?"

"Get in! No, I didn't know that. Please, tell me she caught a deadly variant of gonorrhoea!"

Nikki looked up from her computer and squinted at me, so I gave her a warm smile and a wink back. Clearly, such positivity from me was much too abnormal for her. She then shrugged and went back to focussing on her computer. A couple of minutes later, my computer finally logged on and I went through my cases.

I wasn't thinking about the actual work I needed to do. Instead, I tried to figure out which was the lucky parent that I'd decide to be marked for the Devil. I paused for a moment as such a prospect still felt unbelievable. I told myself that this first one was just an experiment to see whether I was indeed mad. I didn't have to deliberate for long before I had the perfect choice for this experiment.

I actually had an appointment booked with the potential mark. It was a father I was going to assess to see if he was a risk to his children. We found out about this man when the police visited them because of the neighbours reporting a lot of shouting and screaming. They arrived at the home where the mother had sustained several injuries and both parents were, as the officer told me, "reet fucking pissed."

The mother was happy to tell all, but did not wish to press any charges. Although police dropped the matter, social care had instructed he move out whilst we assessed the situation and identified what we could put into place as both parents wanted the family to remain together. We placed his children on child protection plans because of all the punching and kicking of their mother that the dad had exposed them to.

The father had a long and colourful history, which involved a lot of assaults against previous partners, several public disorder offences committed whilst drunk, and a multitude of low-level thefts. I had briefly spoken to him on the telephone, so I knew how he was going to play himself off, and that was going to be that nothing was his fault and everyone else was to blame.

I knew he would be the perfect test to see what happens with him and my supernatural friend. A part of me hoped nothing would happen once I drew an inverted crucifix in the father's home as, although that meant I'd need serious help, it also meant I wasn't having to work for the two-horned and pitchfork holding one.

My risk assessment session was due to take place at three o'clock, and I had nothing else booked in before. So, I took the time to clear a lot of my paperwork. Even though I had finished many pieces of top priority work, I still had a lot more left to do. I've always wondered what would happen if I completely gave up on my paperwork, whether nothing would happen to the families I worked with, as most of what we wrote was only for other professionals and regulatory inspectors. I had the strong feeling that the percentage of my workload that mattered was in the minority in comparison to the utter bullshit made for my bureaucratic and corporatized overlords.

Later on, I gave myself a break for lunch and ate a bland shop-bought ham sandwich with a packet of crisps. Not the eating at my desk whilst working kind of lunch break, but the rare one where I sit on a park bench and worry about all the work I'm not doing.

The clock quickly reached two thirty, so I headed out for the risk assessment and to see the sacrificial one. It was a short and pleasant countryside drive before I arrived at a small, four-storey block of flats. I purposefully parked a minute walk away to keep my car relatively safe from any objects hurled out of windows, which has happened before due to people not being so fond of social workers.

The block of flats was out of place. They were next to a row of small semi-detached houses that had stone cladding, and all had quaint gardens at the front. There wasn't a single piece of litter to see until I walked into the flat's car park. On the large front door, there were small bits of spray-painted graffiti dotted all over.

"Who is it?" a crackly voice snapped from the buzzer.

"It's Craig, the social worker."

"Oh, you."

A couple of seconds later, the door buzzed obnoxiously and the lock clicked. I had to go by the stairs as the elevator was out of order. As soon as I reached the stairwell, a warm waft of urine charged into my lungs. I took one step back, composed myself, and braved the sensory onslaught. My poor health didn't help with the matter as my quick exhaustion made me gulp in the ammonia-filled the air. I had to rest for a minute whilst I wheezed like an emphysemic eighty-year-old chain-smoker. I fought off the temptation to smoke a cigarette to help me feel right again. Well, that was what I thought until I realised I had one in my mouth and was lighting it.

"For fuck's sake, Craig."

Cigarette smoked, I ventured into the corridor. There were only four flats on the top floor, two to the left of a hallway and two to the right. I guessed his flat was on the right and got that correct. I knocked on the white composite door hard and to a little musical rhythm. The man who opened the door really did not look like how I thought he would. The dad was a tall bean pole, bug-eyed, buck-toothed, and goofy looking. He wasn't the most attractive, and he seemed quite shy. He wore a plain grey T-shirt and black tracksuit bottoms. *The perks of smoking, not being able to smell properly,* I thought as a blast of hot air came from behind him and hit me.

"Hi, Dave, I'm Craig."

"Yeah, come in," he mumbled whilst turning away.

I walked into the studio flat. There was a separate bathroom, but everything else was in the same large room. Empty cans of lager littered the kitchen countertop, and there was a bowl full of cigarette ends on a coffee table near a leather sofa which had probably once been cream but had since become darkened by grime. A single bed was in the corner. It was quite the tip with empty food cartons all over the floor, something you'd expect from someone in their late teens, not their early forties.

"Have a seat, mate," Dave grumbled.

I put my bag down at the end of the sofa, took my coat off, and sat down. The furniture damn near sucked me right in, and I thought that was not so good if I needed to make a quick escape as I could imagine myself floundering as I tried to get up. My sacrificial pick perched himself against the kitchen countertop with his arms folded.

"Glad to see you found somewhere and have gotten settled."

He just looked at me and grunted. I tilted my head back and stared back for a couple of seconds, but then turned away.

"I know I have already told you over the telephone, but I can explain to you the purpose of this risk assessment again. Is that something you want me to do?" I asked as I took my notebook and pen out.

"Nah, mate, I remember. Let's get it over and done with."

I nodded. *Yeah, lets. You woman-beating piece of shit.*

"So, an important part of this assessment is getting an understanding of your version of events, as this assessment is, of course, about understanding you. Also, there's more than one side to every story. With that in mind, I hope to start off talking about the most recent incident that led to your children being put on a child protection plan."

His eyes suddenly lit up.

"Look, mate, it's all bullshit. Claire made up a lot of what she said just to get back at me because we got into a silly argument. It was about me messaging another girl, who was just a friend. If you ask her, she'll tell you the same. It was just a silly petty disagreement that got heated, nothing more," he blurted.

I raised both of my eyebrows. A bit heated. *You stomped on her head, you twisted cunt.*

"The police reported and identified several injuries Claire had sustained from this incident. So, how did she—"

"The bruising around her throat, that was just rough sex. What can I say, she likes to get choked whilst we fuck. The black eye, as I said to the police, she was getting ready to make tea, and when she opened the cupboard, a tin of beans fell out and hit her eye."

Honestly, how stupid do you think we are?! I then felt an urge to laugh in his face but repressed it and simply nodded. We went over the ins-and-outs of the event. As predicted, none of it was his fault, and he felt there had been no wrong committed at all.

"I've had a couple of chats with your kids, and they have all said you and Claire argue a lot, especially after a few drinks. They haven't been too specific about what happened other than they hear you guys getting angry, things get broken, and that your partner would scream and cry. Why do you think they say that?"

Dave huffed and then puffed.

"They're lying."

"Why would they do that?"

"It's probably because I didn't get them a fucking Xbox for Christmas, so they got upset. Also, they've got this one friend who has a social worker, I think he's in care, and he gets all sorts. So, they probably believe if you get involved, you'll get them an Xbox."

I took a deep breath in and out. I again went over his children's statements, prodding and prying with various other questions, but all his answers still amounted to the children were lying, and he had never exposed them to domestic violence. The rest of the risk assessment was more of the same—deny any incriminating evidence and pretend that absolutely nothing wrong occurred within the family home. I went into his history of offences and his previous domestic violence incidents, but again, he had an excuse for them all, and he had committed no wrong.

"A part of the risk assessment is to understand your willingness to change. So, would—"

"Change! Why would I change when I did nothing wrong?!"

"Well, it might help you if you attended some courses, like a domestic violence perpetrator course. I think—"

"A fucking perpetrator course? I said I've done nothing wrong. The police didn't charge me for that bullshit with Claire, so I don't need to do a course."

"I'm just saying that—"

"Nah, mate. Stop chatting shit. I am not doing any fucking course. I've been good and worked with you guys so far when I should have told you all to fuck off as you've got nothing on me and you have done nothing for me. So, sorry for saying this, but you can stick your course up your arse," he ranted, with veins protruding on his neck and his arms still folded.

I raised an eyebrow and sighed.

"Fair enough. I think that's enough for one day. We can organise another session later on the telephone, okay?"

Dave grimaced.

"Before I go, can I quickly use your toilet?"

He stared at me for a few seconds, frowned, but then nodded.

"Cheers."

The toilet was cleaner than I expected. It was quite sparse, and there was no bog roll or soap at the sink, but at least the porcelain throne wasn't stained with piss and littered with skid marks. I had purposefully not gone to the bathroom all afternoon so I could use Dave's. As I let it out, a faint moan of relief came out of my mouth.

After I finished, I balanced on one foot and flushed the toilet with the other. I rinsed my hands, and then had a quick look around, and found the best spot to draw the upside-down crucifix. The bottom corner near the door's hinges.

Use the black one. He's a right bell end and deserves nothing better. I raised both eyebrows in surprise at the thought, but easily brushed it away and drew a small upside-down crucifix with the red crayon. A few seconds later, I was out of the toilet. Dave was still in the living room.

"See you, Dave."

"Yeah, bye."

I was quickly out of the flat and rushing down the stairs as if I had just stolen from the dad. There was a big Cheshire Cat smile on my face, which quickly evaporated as soon as I got outside. By the time I reached my car, I doubted that anything would happen, and that perhaps it was best to check myself into a mental health hospital instead. As I sat there with my shoulders slumped, I took a couple of deep breaths.

"Fuck it, Craig, let's just see what happens first."

I stared at myself in the rear-view mirror, nodded to give encouragement, and then drove back to the office.

Chapter 14

"Fucking get off the telly, you Jew cunt!" Dave roared just before he chugged the last few drops of beer.

He crushed the finished can and threw it into the kitchen as he sat and watched an elderly Jewish lady walked off shot. In his head, he told himself he'd pick the can up later, but he didn't tell himself that later was probably in a couple of weeks. It didn't seem like Dave enjoyed watching television as, more often than not, it led to the device being screamed at about how the liberal elite had purposefully brought about a plague of culturally different people to destroy this once proud nation from the inside. Such ranting and raving had even somehow come about after watching a child's cartoon show about a pig and their family.

"God damn muzzy yid bastard..." he trailed off just as the visit he had with the social worker popped up into his head.

Dave wasn't too happy that it was a *darkie* who saw him, but told himself he could put up with him as the social worker could speak English like how it should be spoken. However, the rage-filled dad wouldn't have admitted it that, even if the social worker turned up in a dashiki, a kippa, and singing Hindu chants, he would've still acted exactly the same.

The father thought back to the risk assessment session and thought he did well with his answers as he didn't give any admissions of guilt or further evidence to show he did indeed significantly assault his partner. Suddenly, his thoughts flitted to the fact he definitely wouldn't have let the social worker in if he was a Slovakian.

In the past few years, on Dave's *who I fucking hate* list, the Slovakians had quickly climbed the rankings to the top spot. This was because all they allegedly did was spend their entire time drinking alcohol, claiming unemployment benefits, and causing trouble. Yet, through all such supposed parasitical indolence, they also somehow stole all the jobs he never bothered applying for.

"Fucking diseased cunt," he muttered to himself as his thoughts went back to the time a young Slovakian lady rejected his drunken advances.

The man suddenly realised that was the last beer he had just finished. He quickly pulled his wallet out of his trousers and checked but saw there was no money left. The drunkard growled and then threw his wallet against the wall as he wasn't due a benefit payment for a couple of days. An idea came to him—not an original one, as he did this every time he ran out of money. Dave pulled out his phone and sent a message to his partner, Melissa.

Was on way 2 shops 2 buy soming 4 kids and lost me last 20£ it must av fell out of pokit. I need 4 food as well, so can u send me another 20? Cheers.

He was quite confident she would send the money, as she always did when he asked, as she knew what saying no would mean.

The boozer's mind went back to the risk assessment and the social worker. He guessed it would probably only be a couple of weeks before they allowed him back into *his home*—the tenancy was under his partner's name. Living on his own was much too boring, and as much as he would deny it to his friends, he missed the kids.

The woman-beating drunk missed hearing their laughter and patter of feet. He missed their wide, curious eyes as he told them stories about all the fights he won. He even missed the silly faces they pulled when he tickled them until they cried. Tears formed at the corners of his eyes as he thought more and more about them. Soon, he found that all he really wanted to do was give them all a hug.

"Fucking bitch, it's all your fault," he growled as Melissa's image popped up into his head.

Dave promised himself that when all this was over, he would have to make sure she understood never again to tell the truth to the police as they'd just pass it onto social care.

"Bloody child snatchers. Doing it just to get their bonuses to remove kids, it's disgusting. No fucking morals," he muttered to himself.

As the man's attention turned back to the television, the shadows in the flat's kitchen flickered and shimmered like water. Suddenly, a human hand reached right out of the darkness next to the kitchen counter. The hand moved up and then grabbed onto the luminated part of the kitchen floor. Another hand and arm followed to do the same. Both arms pulled, and out of the shadow came Zee. He had a joint in between his teeth, his long and tangled hair flowed down light a waterfall filled with tar, and he wore sunglasses. Instead of his usual bathrobe, he had a black T-shirt, black jeans, and white trainers on.

Zee stood up straight and then reached up to stretch. Dave was none the wiser as he faced away from the kitchen, fixated on the new program that had scantily clad celebrities salsa dancing. The supernatural being leapt over the sofa and landed onto the cushioned side bottom first.

"WHAT THE FUCK YOU DOING HERE, PAKI!?" Dave roared and tried to leap to his feet.

He only got up a couple of centimetres before two muscle sinew-covered hands pushed him back onto the sofa. Dave turned his head up to see an enormous mouth filled with sharp, yellow teeth. It opened and roared as a host of tongues came out to slither around and onto his face. He immediately urinated onto himself and fainted.

"Hur, hur, hur! Craig, you've picked well. Don't you think, Lily?"

The demon ignored him, and saliva from its tongues rained down onto the unconscious man.

"He isn't for eating. Don't worry, though, I'll let you have some fun with him first before we get the good stuff out of him."

Without facing Zee, Lily's hand moved up, and a sharp claw grew out of her index finger. She immediately jammed it into Dave's ribs, and his eyes shot open as he shrieked in pain.

"GOD, please, stop, please, fucking stop!"

"I'm definitely not God, but for you, right now, I might as well be," she giggled in a deep woman's voice that echoed and came from a mouth that oddly moved to enunciate the words.

She let him fall to the ground, and he tried to move backwards whilst he was still on the floor but ended up bumping into the coffee table. To flee, he spun around and crawled underneath the furnishing. Lily grabbed his leg and wrenched him out from underneath, causing the terrified abuser to squeal.

"Please, don't hurt me!" he begged as she flipped him over.

Lily picked him up by the throat and lifted him into the air. She opened her mouth again to reveal the myriad black tongues that slithered all over his face as he slowly choked. Just before he was about to black out again, she threw him onto the coffee table, causing it to crumple. The demon stood over the semi-conscious and whimpering man. Zee let out his stoner laugh and clapped his hands just before he lit his joint.

"Lily, I'm just saying this as it might help you with your fun."

The hippy-looking home invader got up and sauntered over to Dave.

"Well, this guy, apparently, he's very much into his rough sex. So much so that his missus will end up quite black and blue afterwards. It's the excuse he keeps giving to the police and social care. Coincidentally, isn't that the type of sex you're into, Lily?" Zee chuckled as he grabbed both of Dave's cheeks and squeezed them inwards with one hand.

The supernatural stoner stood back up, headed back to the sofa, and fell onto it to watch the entertainment. Shrill laughter came from the demon as the abusive dad burst into tears. Yellow claws grew out of all the fingers on her left hand and, suddenly, she swiped a few times at Dave's clothes, causing him to wail each time her hand swung by. With her other hand, she wrenched off the ripped piece of clothing to reveal a pasty, pot-bellied naked body covered in shallow scratches that dripped blood.

Dave tried to crawl away again to the flat's front door. Lily let him get a metre to the exit before grabbing him by the ankle and yanking him back to the middle of the room. The demon then sat on him, straddling him just above his crotch. Her mouth opened and again the tongues came out, except this time one went deep into the his mouth and throat.

The demon let out a guttural moan, and she briefly dry-humped the chosen victim. With one hand, she moved down to feel his small and flaccid penis. Straight after came a laugh that flitted from high-pitched to deep and bass-ridden. By this point, Dave closed his tear-filled eyes and waited for what he thought would soon be death.

Instead, she stood up and tossed him over again, and then stuck one claw deep into his lower spine. This caused the drunkard to feel a pain like no other he had ever felt as it stabbed into his nerves, causing the feeling of little glass shards to cut into every part of his body. The man screamed, squealed, and then cried. Rather than cause paralysis, it had done quite the opposite, and Dave confusingly felt an organ of his somehow become hard. Lily flipped him over again and straddled her toy again. As she leant near his ear, he felt copious warm and gooey slime leak onto him from where she straddled.

"Rough sex, yes, I like rough sex as well," the monster tittered just as she dug the claws from both of her hands deep into his upper back.

Zee opted to watch the news as Lily had her fun with her new plaything, as that level of torture wasn't his cup of tea. The television showed a story about Catholic priests in Belgium molesting and raping children over many a historical year. It talked about how these supposed men of God moved around with the help of the Catholic Church as soon as their deeds became too public. It had caught the stoner's attention, so much so that he almost didn't notice Lily was about to kill the man as she raped him.

"Oi! None of that. I don't want him dead," he scolded.

Zee went back to see if the authorities arrested any of the perpetrators or the Cardinals who had ensured such crimes continued unpunished. It appeared neither took place. Such villainous behaviours from the church and these priests was now publicly known, yet the Vatican still stood proudly and unharmed in its adorned garishness with over a billion followers ignoring such crimes.

It baffled him that so many of these followers still believed that it was an organisation of good. He felt the church were the types who took a message of peace, love, and forgiveness, and then turned it into means to accumulate and abuse power. These human actions did not surprise him, but the Vatican's hypocrisy and the outright lies they told did.

Just as the news piece finished, Zee fantasised he would one day make sure they paid for their crimes. Somehow, he would right the wrongs, he thought, just before he turned his attention back to Lily. He saw she had finished with her torture, as she stood facing her master with her hands on her hips. Below her, curled up in a ball, weeping softly and covered in blood, was their victim.

"Dave, my man. You need to toughen up a bit here, as this is only just the beginning. We can't be losing you before we're all done. What is it you like to say after you knock your son about, and he cries? Ah, yes, quit being such a little bitch!"

Chapter 15

It shouldn't be normal to feel nothing when you break a child's heart. Yet, for me, it is. I knew it should be sad, it should move me, but the office printer being jammed would have gotten me feeling more than I did at that moment. I want to think it isn't because I've become a sociopath but more because I've done it a hundred times before.

"That's why you can't go back home," I explained to the wide-eyed six-year-old in an empty classroom.

His big blue eyes stared at me for another second, and then there was the briefest of flickers where I saw what I said had registered, and it hurt right down to his core, but before he processed such pain, the kid had buried it down deep within. It might be later today, or it might be years away, but it would come back up, barbed, sharp, and hurting.

I thought perhaps I had just planted a seed of a demon of his own to grow. The supposed rescuer is just another on the long-list of people who had fucked the little tyke up. I don't know why, but at that moment I wanted to feel some sort of emotion, but still I felt nothing.

To remind me I was still human, I thought about a recent removal of a couple of children from the care of their parents and recollected how it did just about get a reaction from me— those screaming and crying faces as I took them from the ones they loved, and also the ones who had hurt them the most. Straight after, I wandered about the day when even that didn't cause a stir.

"Okay," he said.

The six-year-old went back to smashing and squashing the Play-Doh family we made earlier.

When he looks back at this moment, will he remember me as evil, or as someone who rescued him?

I sat back down onto the floor and watched him play. I then looked at each part of him, from his mousey brown hair styled into a little mohawk, to his chubby soft cheeks, and then his grinning face. He was a cute kid, but it felt as if my motions, my statements, and my play with him were all being done out of habit and simply because it was my job.

I had never noticed this before as I realised I always had my rage to steal my focus. There was always something that brought my gaze outward. Injustice to the family, against the child, against me, or my team. A system that tried to force corporate and political values onto a human-centred job.

All such fuel kept the fire going so I would stay staring into the flames and not look at what was around me. Now that this fire had lost my attention, I could see I had lost so much of my compassion. I wondered when this had happened. When did I stop caring about those I tried so hard to protect? A hot flush of shame crept up my back and neck. I knew what would come next, so I quickly finished our session.

"Look at the time! Come on, I'm afraid we've got to pack up. Because you've been such a star, I'll let you pick any sticker you want!" I said with energy, but each enunciated word rang hollow and felt acted.

He pouted at first, but then quickly complied. The boy picked a large sticker of a comic book superhero. I walked him out, holding his hand back to his classroom. I then rushed out of the school as quickly as possible.

"Craig, please, can I have a word with you?" I heard the head teacher call me from the reception.

"Afraid it has to be some other time. I've got to get to a meeting. Sorry!" I yelled back as I left the building.

I hurried to my car and quickly got in. As soon as the door shut, I frowned and tried to push down the emotions trying to break in. I tried to think about why I felt this upset, and then Michael's image flashed into my mind. After that, I felt ready to burst into tears, but then nothing. It was as if the shame and guilt suddenly fell off a cliff and disappeared into the abyss below. I looked into the rear-view mirror and saw a face that was serene.

"Fuck."

I knew I needed to cry. It would have been normal to, but there wasn't any semblance of such emotional expression left. I imagined myself falling into a fit of wrenching sobs. Mucus, tears, and drool dripping onto the floor and my legs as I rested my forehead against the steering wheel. Instead, I sat there with a look of constipation on my face.

I stared into the rear-view mirror again and then cracked my face into one of despair. I tried whining and mewling, but then I quickly stopped as there was still no sense of moroseness in me.

"Well, if you're going to be like that, I'm going to force you to think about Michael, you heartless prick!" I spat at the mirror.

The first thought in my head was, *Did I actually care that Michael died, or did I just care about people blaming me for his death*? I winced in pain as I found I couldn't answer.

Memories of the face-to-face work I did with the kid came up, all of which reminded me that I hadn't thought of him as a child. Instead, he was just a timed task I had to complete within forty-five working days. I knew I'd done a thorough job in assessing him, but I couldn't let go the feeling that, before his death, all he was to me was a target that needed completing.

My memories went to when I started off as a social worker all those years ago and being so keen to help and save those who were young, defenceless, and suffering. Then at some point it changed completely, and I only cared about wanting to show I excelled so my bosses would promote me.

You're upset because you've found out you're not Jesus and you have a selfish side?! Stop being so pathetic.

Such a thought caught me off-guard, and my immediate reaction was to growl at my reflection in the mirror. Straight after, all the chatter in my mind went silent, my eyes went wide, and a couple of long seconds of silence later, I broke out into manic cackles.

The laughter flooded out of me so hard it hurt my sides. The more I laughed, the funnier the absurdity that was me and my life became. It all ended abruptly when I slammed my hand down hard and accidentally hit the horn. I shot out of my mania and realised I was still in the school car park and looked around to see if anyone had seen my episode. Fortunately, no one had.

I put the key into the ignition and zoomed off back to the office, leaving behind all my previous dour musings at the carpark, excited about trying to contact Dave. I would have called him then and there, but my work mobile had run out of power and I had tried calling him loads of times earlier that morning, but there was no answer. So, I left a couple of messages and a text saying it was about booking another risk assessment session. I, of course, only wanted to see if there was any change since yesterday.

What added to my need to know was last night. I knocked on Zee's door to find out what was happening, but he didn't answer. When I went to open his door, I noticed a pre-made joint balanced perfectly on the handle. I took the spliff as I assumed it was for me, and then tried opening the door but he had locked it. At that point, I checked my mobile phone and realised I didn't have a phone number or email address for him.

That night, before at my flat, I started to question whether Zee actually existed. Perhaps he was all imagined, and I was the one leaving joints, but then I thought that wasn't quite possible as any spliff I rolled was embarrassingly awful. I then thought that perhaps a trick was being played on me, especially if he was the supposed to be the Lord of Lies. What if the crayons were simply crayons and I was getting myself excited about absolutely nothing? I had to remind myself there was only one way to find the truth, and that was to speak to Dave.

As soon as I had got back to the office from the school, I rushed through the reception. I quickly said hi to Dawn as I hurried by. I marched straight to my team's room. Everyone sat at their computer, I mumbled my greetings, didn't wait for a response, and then went straight to my office phone. I dialled Dave's number, but again it rang out and went to answer message. I slammed the phone down a bit too hard as Lisa looked up from her computer at me.

"Are you all right, Craig?" she whispered.

"Yeah, yeah, all good. I just need to contact this dad."

"What about?"

I looked at her for a few seconds and ignored the question.

"How's that case we went over the other day?"

"A lot better. It really helped that. Thank you. I hate to be a bother, but if you have some more time, can you help me go through another case later?" she said whilst averting her gaze.

"Yeah, sure. How about in an hour?"

She nodded vigorously. Straight after, my office phone rang, and I wrenched it off the receiver.

"Hello. Senford Children's Social Care, Craig speaking. How can I help?"

"Yeah, Craig, it's Dave," a voice trembled.

A full smile, baring all teeth, exploded onto my face.

"Good to hear from you, Dave. How are you?"

"Yeah, I'm feeling...I'm feeling..."

I heard him then break out into a little sob, but he then held it back.

"Sorry, mate. I didn't answer because I was in hospital earlier."

"Oh, how come you went to the hospital?"

The phone stayed silent.

"Hello, Dave, are you there?"

"Yeah, sorry. I fell down the stairs, so I needed a few stitches and ended up with a few fractures. Nothing life-threatening. I've been doing a lot of thinking, and I want to come clean with you," he sighed.

"Okay, so what has changed?"

The phone stayed silent again, but this time I waited, saying nothing.

"I want you to know the reason I am telling you this is that I want to do right for my kids and Melissa. I want to be with them as soon as possible, and I will do anything you guys ask me to do so I can," he stammered.

"What do you want to tell me?!"

I heard another deep sigh from his end. Dave then went and told me the truth about the domestic violence incidents with Melissa and how they were his fault. He told me about the guilt he felt for doing things that horrible and must have said at least ten times he was going to make it up to her and his children.

He implored me to put him on a domestic violence perpetrator program, and he promised to do whatever work was needed. I was ecstatic about the change in attitude and immediately felt relief as it was a good chunk of proof that Zee was real, his claims did have a level of authenticity, that I wasn't insane, and that this was a genuine opportunity to make people's lives drastically better.

"With the perpetrator program, you can self-refer. I'll text you the telephone number and you get yourself on to it today, okay?"

"Yeah, yeah. I will do it. Believe me when I say I'm going to prove to you lot I have and will change," he affirmed.

I bobbed my head from the left to the right to an imaginary beat.

"I'm really glad to hear that, Dave. Just so you know, I will have to double-check to make sure you do the things you say you will do. So, when you refer yourself onto the program, I'll need you to tell them you consent for me to speak to them. Is that okay?"

"Yeah, yeah. No worries. Oh, before you go, this might sound like a stupid question, but is an Anglican church still Christianity?"

"Yeah, why do you ask?"

"Well, just thinking about popping around to this one that's nearby. Anything else you need me to do?"

We booked our next session to take place in a couple of weeks and gave our farewells. As soon as I hung up, I pumped my fist into the air.

"You seem happy?" Lisa said.

"Yeah, I suppose I am. It's just good when a case goes right for once! Got a good feeling this dad is actually going to change for the better. He's got a lot to prove, but I feel quite optimistic about him."

I turned back to my computer and looked at my caseload.

"Who's next?" I whispered.

Chapter 16

The badger scurried through the dead leaves and mud on the forest floor. Its swagger was like a short and belligerent drunkard that took little care in the noise that it created. It knew that anything in these woods would have to get out of its way unless they wanted a few sharp teeth bitten in them.

Even with the full moon out and its light trying to slice through the canopy, the woodland floor remained pitch-black. An occasional conversational coo of an owl cut through the silence of the night. Soon, the badger came across the sound of rustling from another animal further down the path. A few more footsteps forward and a fox, which was busily scouting for its next prey, came into view. The badger took no consideration of the other animal and carried on towards it as if it didn't even exist. The fox raised its head and saw the grumpy denizen trundling towards it. At first, the crafty beast considered standing its ground, but then the scar on his right hind leg reminded him what happened the last time he got too close to a badger. A low growl from the chubby thug, and the bushy-tailed foe ran away.

The black and white hooligan carried on its grumpy way back to its sett, but it was not long after the whiff of blood and death crept down into its nose and stomach. There was a split-second deliberation, and the beast decided it was hungry again. As it barged through the woodland, causing further obnoxious rustles, it soon found where the smell was coming from and saw a deer's head ripped off with its spine still attached. Something had cleaned off most of the meat around the backbone. Fortunately for the belligerent beast, the head was intact.

Without a care in the world, the little animal went about taking the carrion apart. Suddenly, the creature found itself jerked up from its feast, feet dangling in the air as a hand held it by the scruff of its neck. It angrily hissed and tried to bite and claw at whoever had grabbed him. It landed a couple of its attacks, but the arm still held on.

The assailant moved the badger close so it could see who its enemy was. Even though the black and white thug knew, deep down, it didn't have a chance, it continued trying to flay the arm that held it up. Lily giggled at the prey that would not give up. She then slowly opened her mouth wide, with her lower jaw reaching back until it touched her neck, and gave a roar that was even more bass-ridden than a lion's. The badger stopped for the briefest of seconds before returning to its attempts of mauling its attacker into submission.

"Let's hope you have some taste to you, my grumpy little catch," the demon sniggered as she moved it closer to her mouth and wildly flailing tongues.

"Oi! No! Put him down. It was bad enough you ripped Bambi's head off, but now a badger? No chance. I like those fuzzballs, so put him down!" Zee scolded.

Lily swung to face her master and hissed.

"This angry little fat thing? What is there to like?!"

The stoner swung around to glare at her. She soon complied and dropped the critter, which scurried quickly away from the demon and disappeared into the night's darkness.

"Come on, it's this way."

Lily and the obsidian demon followed without issue. Their master had no issues in navigating through the darkness, even though he had his sunglasses on.

"If you weren't such a coward, we could have used the shadows to arrive there by now!" Lily hissed.

Zee sighed and contemplated biting, not because he cared what the demon thought but more because it might have been entertaining. Undeterred, Lily continued with her goading. She let out a rumbling chuckle.

"So afraid that your brother and your father would notice your movements without the noise of the humans make to cover your tracks. It must be so embarrassing that you have become nothing like your brother, a true leader. You are nothing but a degenerate and a little weak speck compared to him. Then there is, of course, what your father thinks of you."

The long-haired ringleader stopped in his tracks and let out the type of heavy-gut laughter that belonged to a supervillain on a Saturday morning cartoon show. It echoed throughout the woods, but then as quick as it came, it stopped.

"Lilith."

The demon froze. The urge to lunge at her master from behind and stick her fist right through his back and into his heart, and then to rip it out so she could dine on the organ whilst it was still beating, fired into her mind.

"You ain't brave or strong enough to do that to me, Lilith," Zee drawled without turning back around.

A silence that was much too long for Lily's liking. Her master yawned as he stretched his arms into the air.

"You know what, I will not punish you. As I know you'll still do as I say."

This agitated the demon to no end as she didn't know how to respond, confident passivity was not something she'd had to deal with before. Seconds later she could feel that the comment, like acid, was eroding bits of her ego. With no vicious reprimand, the truth that she hated to acknowledge became all too glaring and insufferable.

It only took a couple more seconds of the shame scorching her before she ran and then lunged at Zee, fist first. The supernatural being didn't bother turning around, and as predicted, the fist only went as far to touch the hair on the back of his head.

"You shouldn't have mentioned my brother and my father. Below the belt that, Lily. Now, if you behave, I might let you earn some of your pride."

As soon as the dishevelled leader finished speaking, he carried on walking through the woodland bramble, crunching dead leaves with each step he took. Lily growled and sent a roar up into the heavens that curdled the blood of every animal in the woods. The demon then spat on the ground and followed. The obsidian glass demon was the last in the line and stayed the silent follower.

They all eventually came to a small opening in the side of a cliff face. The surrounding stone was slippery and green with moss. However, the party were all able to maintain their footing as they slowly meandered through. They all bent down as they scooted into the cave entrance. It took a minute more of walking in a small, dark tunnel before they reached a large, empty cavern. They could hear only the dripping of water inside, and they encountered no creature as none ever dared enter it.

Zee put his hand into his front pocket, pulled out a rock, and tossed it into the air. Rather than hit the ground, it floated.

"Wakey-wakey."

The magma demon lit up, and the light from its fire illuminated the entire cavern, showing dark red Hebrew and Arabic inscriptions all over the walls. When the light soaked into the scripture for several seconds, it glowed to a neon red. The dry dirt ground was littered with a myriad of oddly shaped bones. Zee headed over to a boulder, kicking the odd bone out of the way, and pulled out a book from his back pocket just before he sat down.

"Come here and hover behind me," he ordered the rock.

It was a book about evolution, biology, and atheism. Not that he didn't understand natural selection and people's opposition to antiquated theological belief systems, it was more just a fascination of what humans were presently believing. Zee chuckled to himself as he thought his father would be upset over his creations' lack of belief—not about natural selection, as that was fact, but about his existence. As Zee slowly and methodically read his book, Lily paced around the obsidian demon, who stood in the centre of the cavern.

"Are you not going to tell her?" Lily snapped at her master after a minute had gone by.

"Oh, yeah, completely forgot," he laughed as he put his book down on his lap.

"You might have noticed that most of the demons I collected have disappeared recently. I get rid of them when they no longer serve a purpose, and by get rid, I mean that greedy cow eats them," he said as he pointed at Lily. "I don't know why, but it has only been recently that I've gotten bored with you demons a lot quicker than usual."

The sinew covered belligerent swung around and hissed at her master. Zee took a deep breath in and exhaled slowly.

"You talk too much!"

The master ignored her as his brow broke into a frown with the pressure of heavy thought.

"I'll be frank. I'm also realising that you beasts cause more issues than you solve. There is also the minor fact that Lily just loves to fight all the bloody time, and I've got to keep her entertained somehow or she'll go kill a few thousand humans when I'm not looking. Also, I hate to admit it, I do like to watch her battle as it's pretty damn cool. Anyway, we've come here for such entertainment, so we don't bring any Heavenly attention to ourselves. So, much appreciated for serving your purpose, but I'm sorry to say you're going to have to die."

The obsidian demon immediately turned to face Zee.

"Lily, please, do your thing."

As soon as the scruffy overlord finished his rambling, Lilith charged at the obsidian demon and launched a fist right at its face made up of tiny shards. It perfectly struck and sent chunks of obsidian flying, but as soon as the fragments flew a half-a-metre away, they somehow shot back to the body where they came from. Lily sent another punch, then another, and another, all aimed at her opponent's head. It was the same result after each strike.

The obsidian demon tilted its head inquisitively and then made its arm morph into a spiked mace and swung it at its foe, catching her straight in the chest and sending her flying across the cavern. The sinew-covered beast skidded a couple of metres before she leapt back up onto her feet.

Blood dripped and poured out of the wounds on her hands and chest. A second later that the blood solidified around the injuries and the bleeding stopped. Both eyeless creatures stood ten metres apart and faced each other as if they were assessing each other for weaknesses. Suddenly, the obsidian creature flicked her arms out at Lily, and these limbs morphed into long rope-like whips made of the slicing material.

Lilith dodged the initial blows and rushed forward, avoiding the crackling attacks that followed. She just about ducked a rope that aimed to decapitate her and went hurtling forward with a punch that went straight through the torso of her enemy.

Lily's momentum sent her skidding by as her arm and shoulder ripped through her glass-like foe completely, and she had just about turned around when another obsidian rope came at her. She brushed it away, but it still took a chunk out of her forearm. The whip swung back but accidentally hit the ceiling. As soon as the weaponised limb touched the scripture on the cavern's roof, it ignited and disintegrated. Lily saw what happened, and grumbled as she realised what she needed to do to win and that she could not kill in her most favourite way, with her fists.

The muscle-sinew monster immediately charged at the obsidian demon. As soon as she got close, she leapt forward to tackle it, but before she could make contact, she felt herself get launched upwards. One of the obsidian demon's legs had morphed into a long spike that shot up and extended right through its foe. It lifted the impaled demon and then flung her down onto the cavern floor. Lily was straight up off the floor with a gaping hole right through the centre of her abdomen. Suddenly, she felt an obsidian rope wrap around her throat and begin moving so it serrated deep into her neck.

She paid scant attention to her injuries and instead grabbed the part of obsidian rope that wasn't wrapped around her throat to stop it from moving. Even though it cut into her, she coiled her opponent's weapon around her arm. Lily's other arm shot up and blocked the other obsidian rope that swung down at her. The sinew-covered demon quickly maneuvered that arm to wrap the other rope-weapon around her other wrist.

"You are too young and too weak to beat me," she taunted in a bass-heavy voice.

Lily then snapped herself around, using the obsidian demon's ropes to swing it into the cavern's wall, causing the being to become immolated and incinerate into dust. The ropes became lifeless without a master, and so the demon easily snapped and broke the ropes wrapped around her and then threw the remaining pieces against the cavern walls. The victor turned around as she heard hooting and clapping.

"That was so cool! It was like a badass Marvel fight-scene!" Zee exclaimed.

Just as Lily faced the stoner, he went into his pockets and pulled out his sticky weed and rolling papers. He then tried to roll a joint on top of his closed book. The demon stayed quiet whilst her wounds healed rapidly.

"Man, that was a such a good fight. Usually, it's so bloody one-sided with you. I've got to give credit where credit is due. You know what, I think you deserve a reward for that."

"I want to have a new skin to wear," Lilith stated without hesitation.

Her master licked and finished his newly rolled joint before he spoke.

"Fine, fine. Take your pick of whoever you want."

When he finished, he turned his head and stared at the demon who stood with her hands on her hips and arched his eyebrow at her.

"You know, sometimes, it would be nice to get a little appreciation of the fact that it was me who saved you from certain death," he teased.

The demon growled and spat black slime onto the floor.

"Saved me? I am now but a lowly slave," she growled.

Zee raised both eyebrows.

"A slave?! If I didn't treat you the way I treated you, you would have killed half the world by now!" he exclaimed with incredulity.

"Half of the world deserves to die!"

The demon master stared at her for a couple of seconds before bursting into his deep, stoner laughter. The merriment quickly subsided, and he then lit his drug. He then blew smoke rings that morphed into upside-down crucifixes as he looked up and stared at the inscriptions.

"Perhaps you are right, Lily. Perhaps I should just allow you to fuck, murder, and consume that many. Many of them certainly deserve it."

There was silence, so he turned to look at her. She sat on the ground cross-legged, moving her head from side to side as if it was only just loosely attached to the neck.

"I wonder what skin I will pick next. Shall I be South Asian, or maybe Native American, as I have never been one before? But where would I find a native American in England?"

"I suppose you don't care about why I feel the way I do?" Zee grumbled, and then turned to the floating burning rock.

There was no response. He sighed just before he took a long drag. The supernatural pothead then pushed himself off the boulder, sat on the dirt, and then laid onto his back as he smoked the entirety of his spliff.

"All you do is smoke your drugs, it is pathetic. You have all this power, and you waste it on collecting and killing a few weakling demons!"

"Here it comes," he yawned.

"Instead of all this toying and murder of demons, let us raise an army instead, and we can then conquer all. With me as your general, I can assure victory against all who oppose us!"

"Like I have said many a time before, and then what?"

"I have thought about that. It is easy, we find new worlds to conquer!" Lily roared.

"And what do we do with all these conquered worlds?"

"Why do you ask me such a stupid question? I fight, I do not shepherd and tend to flocks."

Zee guffawed and then chuckled.

"I do not know why you laugh when it is an idea that makes far more sense than what you are doing right now," Lily snapped.

At first, her master ignored the statement and lifted his left hand up to look at it. First, he looked at the back of it, then he stared at his palm, and then it was the back of his hand again.

"You're probably right. What the actual fuck am I doing?"

Chapter 17

I stood at the top of the stairway thinking about how stupid I had just been as I gulped in and wheezed out air that felt like shards of glass scraping against my throat. My excitement had gotten the better of me and I ran up the stairs to my floor. However, I had somehow forgotten that I was a chain-smoking loafer who, given the choice, would opt to spend the rest of my life horizontal.

As I breathed in, I felt the phlegm covering my throat congeal. I coughed and hacked up the sticky grime, looked around to see if there was anyone around, and then spat it out into the corner of the stairwell. It took a couple of attempts to rid the substance from me as a thick, long trail of the viscous stuff stuck to my tongue and dangled tauntingly out. When I eventually got it all out of me, I quickly smudged it around into the hard flooring with my shoe so it looked less like the disgusting stuff it actually was.

"I need to get healthier," I muttered, knowing full well I had no intention of doing such a thing.

Once I had recuperated, I walked to my flat. Halfway down the corridor, I had to stop as a tendon around my knee twinged. I grumbled a couple of expletives, slowly kicked my hurt leg out twice, and then hobbled the rest of the way back home. Once in, I kicked my shoes off and headed to Zee's room.

I hesitated to knock on the door at first, but then did so as, although I felt frightened and in awe of him, I knew deep down he would not harm me unless there was a significant provocation. An impatient sigh fled my lips. I still hadn't seen him since he'd removed that rage demon from me, and it had also been a couple of days since Dave had changed miraculously into a person who I didn't hope would die.

"Zee, are you there?! Zee!"

Still no answer. I tried his door handle and found that he had locked it.

"For fuck's sake."

I went to the living room and slumped myself down onto the sofa. I took my phone out without even thinking about it and went on my casual encounters app. There were many messages and propositions, all of which I had put off as I wanted to see and talk to my unholy flatmate first. It was silly, but it worried me that if I organised some fun, I'd miss out as he'd turn up when I wasn't around. I moaned in frustration as I stared at my potential flings. It had been too long since I last had sex. Well, there was, of course, the weirdo from the rave, but she didn't count for obvious reasons and because it was too damn traumatic.

I cycled through my list again. There was one that I really wanted to meet as I had seen a lot of him already through the pictures he sent, and I saw that he definitely ticked all the right boxes—he was ripped, well hung, in his early twenties, and seemed desperate for me to have my way. However, through messaging, I found out that *Sub-donkeyD72* was already in a relationship with a woman.

Emma had scolded me enough for encouraging infidelity, but I had quite a thing for fucking those who were in the closet. It felt like something I shouldn't do, that it was taboo, I shared in their shame and all those reasons turned me on to no end. Unfortunately, sometimes this aroused me too much, and before I knew it, the carnality would be over in less than a minute. Many apologies and excuses would follow, and I'd leave their flat quicker than I lasted in the bedroom department.

I looked at his pictures again, all of which showed him in provocative positions, and then immediately thought of how Emma would likely tell me off. She'd definitely bring up how I would be helping to break the girlfriend's heart. It wasn't long after that I was questioning myself about whether I was in the wrong. However, straight after, like high-priced lawyers without a shred of morality, my tried and tested rationalisations came out to defend such behaviours.

This wasn't the first time I had considered such deliberations, and I imagine it wouldn't be the last. Ultimately, if the closeted cheater was going to get cock from somewhere, that was an inevitability. The harm would still exist and my lack of involvement would not change this, so I felt I might as well have my way and enjoy it.

I scrolled through the pictures again, hoping Zee would turn up soon, otherwise I might just have to go out for this shag. I spent a couple of minutes deliberating, and in the end, I went to my room and let my hand do the deed instead to quiet the mind. The sun had retreated from the sky by the time I'd had my release and cleaned myself up.

When I opened my door to go back to the living room, I heard the television. When I got there, I saw Zee was sitting in the armchair with his back against one armrest and his feet hanging over the other. He was in his bathrobe and as scruffy as ever.

"Hey, m-aaa-n, long time no see," he croaked.

I stayed frozen, even though I felt the urge to rush over to embrace him and spew out all that had happened to me.

"Come over here, man, I ain't going to hurt you."

I didn't need to be told twice and hurried to the sofa. I sat down, perching on the edge, leaning towards him.

"So, did you get demons from Dave?!"

"Yeah, m-aaa-n. You picked well. He had a lot to extract out of him, and he was a lot nastier than you thought," he said without turning to look at me.

I giggled and clapped my knees.

"I spoke to him, and he said he was going to make all these changes. You know what, he has actually done what he said he would do. It's a fucking miracle!"

"That it isn't," Zee mumbled.

His reticence to speak surprised me as I thought since he had revealed his ungodly self he would be keener to interact, but it was as if he was the same oddball stoner he always had been.

"Man, I am parched, and I'm pretty wedged in here. Could you sort me out with a cup of tea?"

Thinking that it might loosen his tongue, and also because he was inhumanely powerful, I did as requested.

"How many sugars?" I called as the water boiled.

"Four, please."

Even though he said much of what the devout masses said about him was a lie, I found it strange that the Devil would ever say please. I made myself a coffee at the same time and slowly brought both over. He lifted his hand up for me to place it in it.

"Careful, it's hot."

"Ha!"

The Devil grabbed the drink and sipped it. I sat there, leant forward, and waited for a cue to speak.

"Go on, ask what you want to ask," he chuckled.

"Yeah, I've got a load of questions. Just tell me to shut up if I talk too much." My hellish flatmate nodded. "I'll start off with an easy one. Is being gay a sin?"

"Neither God nor I give a flying fuck about a guy fucking another guy. One of the stupidest things to have come out of the Bible, but what do you expect when people who were so damn sexually repressed wrote it." He yawned.

I laughed and then shifted nervously.

"In Genesis—"

"Great big crock of shit. Big bang and evolution are how it happened, but you can't blame the Bible for not knowing that as people were so damn stupid back then. Not that much has changed in that department for you guys."

"Noah—"

"M-aaa-n, are you serious?"

194

I turned red and felt my neck heat.

"No, sorry. Of course, he didn't exist. Well, how about Jesus?" I stammered.

I could feel the air become thicker with the tension after I asked the question.

"What about that prick?"

"Did he exist?"

Zee stayed silent for a minute before responding.

"Yeah. He was just some idiot who naively believed in the betterment of humanity. He had some jazzy powers, tried to help a bunch of people, and eventually got stabbed in the back by them all. That's about it really," my flatmate sighed.

The unholy stoner pushed himself back against the armrest until his head hung back far enough that he could see me and stared at me until I did a nervous giggle.

"My turn. Do you believe in good and evil?" he asked.

"I suppose I do," I said with such indecision that it sounded like a question.

"I don't, but you might think it is natural for the one and only Beelzebub to say that."

My flatmate stayed there with his head upside down as his frown dug deep trenches into his brow.

"Have you heard of the jewel wasp?"

"No, what is it?"

"It's this wasp that has an interesting way of reproducing. It does so by finding a cockroach, stinging it with mind control venom, guides it to a nest, and then lays its egg inside its new obedient slave. Then the eggs hatch and eat the cockroach inside out, leaving its nervous system last so it feels every damn thing. Would you say that is evil?"

"Yeah, that's pretty fucked-up. But isn't that just nature? It's just what happens as innate behaviours develop, and there isn't good or evil to be derived from it."

Zee took a deep breath in and then sighed.

"That's how I now see so-called good and evil human acts. They are simply behaviours derived from a hodgepodge of genetics and learned reactions to random environmental factors. Albeit the behaviours are far more complicated than the jewel wasp's, but to me, it's still just cause and effect. There isn't anything evil or good in the actions."

I raised my eyebrows, his nihilism taking me by surprise.

"You said *now* that is what you believe. So, you didn't used to?"

"Yeah, I didn't used to be like this. I used to believe what my dad preached. That good and evil actually existed, and it was a choice, but then if he actually believed humans were so free to make such decisions, then why did he decide to kill a load of them because he didn't like the way they acted?"

Zee groaned and it soon turned into a loud growl of frustration.

"I suppose there's also a selfish reason for me to believe that there is no free will in humans. I have to so I can stay sane."

I stayed pinned to the spot and dared not move as I listened. Zee ever so slowly changed his position in the armchair until he sat in it properly, and turned to face me.

"If there isn't good and evil, then the pain and suffering I feel from every human on Earth loses its meaning and becomes just a simple consequence of cause and effect. It is like a lion ripping into a human being, it happens not out of evil but because that is its nature, something of which evolved from an extremely complex system of cause and effect. Just rain drops falling onto puddles and ripples flowing out, m-aaa-n. That is how I have to see it with humanity."

I noticed my breathing was shallow. It wasn't as if I hadn't heard such pessimistic views before, but I think the discomfort of hearing it was more due to it coming from someone so much more powerful and knowledgeable than me.

"S-s-so do you need such nihilism?" I quavered.

"I hear every bit of pain from everyone on this planet. At this very second, I can I hear the screams of a beaten woman. I can feel the tears come from a man as he is being stomped to death by another. I can hear the whimper made as a child is raped, and thousands of the like every fucking second. If I didn't perceive such suffering as just predictable consequences derived from logical actions, then I could not cope as it would be all too much for me to feel."

I looked away from Zee's gaze and listened to his deep breaths.

"It seems I am cursed to live, watch, and feel humanity harm each other until the end of time. Especially, as you cockroach-like bastards are probably going to last that long," he laughed.

I let out a deep breath. I didn't quite know what to say, and whilst I thought on what to do next, the stoner had already gotten a joint out for me. He lit it, passed it to me, and I sucked in lung-filling puffs. I waited for the weed to slow my thinking and anxiety down. My confidence to speak with him returned.

"If there is no good or evil, and right or wrong, why don't you just end it all? You know, kill all humans. I won't lie, a part of me thinks we deserve that fate," I stammered as I passed him the joint.

"M-aaa-n, it's because deep down I still like you apes, and even if I wanted to, I think my dad would stop me."

We stayed quiet and passed the spliff back and forth until we finished it. It was probably another fifteen minutes of staring mindlessly at the music videos on television before we spoke again.

"Do you think you collect demons and cleanse people because you still care?"

"Huh?"

"Like, because of the good that follows," I croaked.

Zee raised both his eyebrows.

"Nah, I don't think so. I think I do it out of boredom." He frowned. "Actually, maybe just a bit. It's difficult to be a total heartless cunt, as it takes too much effort."

I raised my eyebrows in surprise, but I was far too stoned to carry on the conversation. As speaking and listening became a struggle, I volunteered to get snacks from the kitchen. I shuffled my way to my cupboard, opened it, and then stood staring as there was far too much choice. Eventually, I powered through the haze and picked something.

"Chocolate bourbons. Bourbons. B-ooo-urbons. B-b-b-bourbons. Bourbons," I mumbled as I held the large packet of biscuits in my hand.

I went to the fridge next and took the whole four-pint bottle of milk out with me. I shuffled back and fell back into the sofa. Soon, we were munching on the biscuits, drinking the milk, and watching a classic comedy about a false messiah. I had never seen Zee laugh so much or so hard. Twice, he spluttered milk onto himself. Once the film finished, I noticed I had sobered up a little and felt more able to talk.

"M-aaa-n, that was some funny shit. Never seen something like that before," he said.

"Yeah, yeah, it was. I am surprised you've never seen it. So, with the demon collecting and all that, are you still good with me choosing people to cure? Just because I thought you might have changed your mind because of what you were saying just then."

"Yeah, yeah. Of course, didn't I already say that Dave was a good pick? Man, there was a lot that came out. No wonder he was such a dick!"

"Yeah, I think you've already said that? I can't remember. Anyway, I need to go to bed as I've got work tomorrow, is that okay?"

"Of course, it is. Night night, m-aaa-n," he replied.

It took me a couple of tries to push myself up off the sofa. As soon as I turned around, I saw the sinew covered demon standing just behind the sofa with her arms crossed.

"WHOAH! What the fuck?!" I shouted.

"Chill, Craig, chill. She's just wanting to check up on you and me. She's protective, you see."

"Man, she scares the shit out of me," I giggled in a high pitch.

"Don't worry, man. She's a pussycat, really."

"Okay, okay. I'm still good to go to sleep right?"

"Yeah, yeah. Of course. Take this. Might help after that shock."

He held out another joint, which I grabbed as I tiptoed around the demon to leave the living room.

"What's the matter? You don't want to stay for a bit of fun?" an oddly familiar voice sniggered.

I shuddered and thought it must have just been the weed that messed with her voice. Then I realised the thing actually spoke, and grimaced. I didn't bother ruminating on the matter and rushed to my bedroom, shut the door quickly, fell onto my bed, and lit the spiff Zee had given me. All my anxieties and worries melted away as I smoked and stared at the ceiling.

It soon felt like I was sinking into a pond of marshmallow. When I finished the joint, I put it out on the bedside table and wrapped myself up in my duvet as strange and fantastical images played in my mind. I saw a giant figure with the body of an Egyptian mummy, a triangular head, filled with little holes with eyes, quite a horrifying figure, but because it was raving and throwing shapes with ever-morphing and colourful fractals behind it, I found it quite amusing. More strange monsters became involved in the rave, making me giggle, and then I fell asleep.

Chapter 18

"Please, tell me you didn't invite her!" I groaned.

"I didn't! She just somehow forced me to tell her what we were doing," Lisa blurted.

Her eyes darted from left to right.

"I don't think she's going to come, anyway. She didn't sound enthusiastic at all."

I sighed just before I took a gulp of cheap cider from a pint glass.

"Well, if she comes, I'm going to fuck off, as I will probably push her into moving traffic after another one of these down me."

"Craig, put your claws back in. Look, once we all finish, and if she hasn't arrived, we'll go to the Cross and Thorns for a drink. If she calls after we leave here, we'll just ignore her or say we've already gone home," Nikki insisted.

I pulled a face and stuck my tongue out at her.

"As it's your and Taheen's leaving do, we'll do as our majesties command," I conceded.

"Yes, it's our leaving do, and we didn't invite her," Nikki sighed, and then gave a stabbing glare at a sheepish Lisa.

I took another couple of gulps of cider to speed others up in their drinking. As I couldn't smoke Zee's joints out in public, I had to resort to alcohol to calm my nerves. I was already on my second pint when everyone else was only halfway through their first drink. We were all still in our work clothes and sat around a large square wooden table in a chain value-pub in Senford town centre.

The floors were sticky, the clientele wouldn't think twice about head-butting your face, the toilets were so bad they might have well just been trenches in the ground, but the place did one thing spectacularly right—they served dirt-cheap drinks.

"I didn't realise you were such an alky, Craig," Amy teased.

I put down the pint just as I had finished another gulp.

"HA! Rookie, this is just what happens when you do social work for too long. Nikki isn't drinking as much as me as she's a booze snob. How much do you drink when you get home after work, Nikki?"

"Me, a snob? How dare you! I only have a little tipple of one bottle or more of the French stuff a night. I wouldn't call it drinking as red wine is so healthy for you."

I again took another gulp and was down to the last dregs of the cider.

"Who says addiction and alcoholism is a bad coping mechanism. Oh, wait, we do all the fucking time to the families we work with," I scoffed.

I shot a suspicious look at Taheen, and then raised my eyebrow.

"Fuck knows how you cope with your teetotal ways?!"

Immediately after, she pulled out a pack of cigarettes.

"This is how! Ciggie anyone?"

I quickly snatched at one and joined her outside. We threaded through the packed pub and as soon as we were outside, we went to stand under the shelter provided by the bar's balcony to hide from a lecherous drizzle that tried to seep into every crevice. We took our first drags and both sighed in unison.

"So, how come Rose isn't coming out?" I asked.

"Lambert has try-outs for Senford United's youth team. He's apparently shit hot at football, and she's supporting him. She said she couldn't do that with a hangover."

I raised my eyebrows. It seemed like they had a family of talented children as Rose's other son studied Economics at the University of Oxford. I blamed her massive tits, as all that good milk from breast feeding must have done wonders for their brains and bodies.

"Jesus. I was getting high, partying, and fucking anything that moved at his age," I said, trying to conceal the jealousy.

"So, not much has changed then!"

"HA! True, true."

"You seem better and are looking less stressed, especially over the past few weeks," Taheen said, looking out at the busy town square filled with scantily clad women and men wearing T-shirts two sizes too small.

"Yeah, I am feeling better. I think it's because I am finally processing all the nasty shit that has happened with the job," I lied and then sighed.

I had a powerful urge to tell her the truth of why during the past couple of weeks I had become far less anxiety-ridden and a touch happier. I wanted to tell her all about Zee and how through such horror, I had found meaning again through the exorcisms I helped with. There was also the otherworldly cannabis I was smoking to levels that would have done Cheech and Chong proud, but I was not drunk enough to let something stupid like that slip. I knew I couldn't say anything, as she would not believe me, and it wouldn't be long after that I'd be back inside a mental health unit.

"I'm still planning to leave after I finish my court stuff, Taheen. Senford Council is just so fucked-up, and it somehow keeps getting worse and worse."

My comrade turned to look at me with a gaze I knew she saved for the families that she became cynical of. Suddenly I hacked as the smoke tickled my throat and I felt the urge to spit out the phlegm but swallowed it instead.

"You looking forward to work for Carnston?" I asked.

"I wouldn't say I am looking forward to working there. They're probably in deeper shit than Senford…but, hey, they're paying forty pounds an hour. I've already got my mortgage down to eight years left on the repayments. Hopefully, I can bring it down to four or even three after a long stint over there."

We took another couple of drags.

"I wish I could do what you do. I'd probably be happier, but I wouldn't like to move jobs so often. Then again, that's probably the most attractive part about working with an agency. Not being attached to these fucking robots in local authority," I muttered.

"Well, if you ever join, join the agency I am with. Tell them I referred you, and we can go halves on the five-hundred-pound referral fee, yeah?"

I nodded, took my last drag, and flicked my cigarette out onto the pavement. Taheen did the same and we headed back inside. We got back to the table halfway into one of Nikki's stories.

"…he was covered in poo, and when I say covered, I mean covered. He even had somehow gotten it in his fucking hair! I had poo all over my hands because he had grabbed onto them. I was just in shock, not knowing what to do as my little shit monster had just come at me from nowhere, and everyone around us was just staring!" Nikki cackled like a Shakespearean witch.

"She's talking about when one of her boys somehow pooed on himself in a portaloo, then slipped on the poo that had gotten on the floor and fell into it at Glastonbury," Lisa whispered to me just as I sat down.

"Oh, Poo-geddon," I laughed before I downed my drink.

Lisa gave me an inquisitive look.

"It's the name we gave to the story."

"We had to go back to the portaloos as I thought I could at least get some of it wiped off. We had to wander through the crowds, and when I finally found one, I quickly discovered that using toilet paper was like bringing a broom to Chernobyl to clean up. So, he was still covered in poo, and so were my hands. The smell was gut-wrenchingly awful, and as there was still so much of it, I realised we needed to get to a water point to get him cleaned off. We spent the next fifteen minutes trying to find one, walking through crowds and getting given a wide berth like we were fucking lepers! One young lady with a white dress on wasn't so with it, walked into Kyle, and didn't even notice. I didn't dare say anything and kept my mouth shut as she walked on by with a shit-print of a boy on the side of her dress!" Nikki ranted just before the shrills of laughter came.

"Finally, we found a water point! I unhinged the tap and hose from the fence, had him strip off naked, and used it to clean him and my hands. Good thing it was sunny, as it would have been freezing. Anyhow, whilst I am doing this, these two big, brick-shit-houses of security guards came up to me and asked what I was doing. As soon as I explained, they jumped back and buggered off as quick as they could into the crowd!" Nikki paused and took a swig of her gin and tonic. She waited for the laughter to die down a little before continuing with her story.

"So, at least we're less covered in shit. I just think, sod his clothes, leave them there, and I then wrap him up with my hoodie and T-shirt so he isn't stark bollock naked. This means I'm just in my bra and shorts. We then both head back to the campsite, with every bloke we walk by ogling my tits, and find some soap and a change of clothes so I could wash him up properly at the campsite showers. Fortunately, after telling people at the front of the queue for the showers what happened—and they could also obviously smell what had happened—they let us cut in at the front."

Nikki downed the rest of her drink as we all laughed.

"Where were Ted and Vicky?" Amy asked.

"They had fucked off to go watch some silly dance show. Tell you what, I'm never taking the kids to a festival again until they're at least teenagers. Knowing my luck, even then, one will probably still end up shitting all over himself somehow!" Nikki exclaimed before a chorus of giggles.

"Come on, let's move on before Ann gets here," Taheen said just as everyone had quieted down.

The two rookie stragglers both downed their drinks. We all stood up and then shuffled through the pub's revellers to get out. Lisa, Amy, and Taheen were responsible and had brought umbrellas. I purposefully picked Lisa's to go under as we headed to the Cross and Thorns. I put my arm around her upper back and waited a couple of seconds before going straight to the point.

"How's your court viability assessment going for Jacob Smith's dad?"

"I've got the last session with him in a couple of weeks. I should be able to write it up soon after that," she stammered.

"So, what do you think of him?"

Before she could reply, I felt a hard thud into my shoulder, so I turned to scowl at the group of staggering and cackling women who had barged into me.

"He's very charming and knows all the right things to say." I opened my mouth to reply but she added more. "But I just get this uneasy feeling about him, especially knowing what has happened before."

"He's a nasty piece of work, Lisa. He also hasn't been in Jacob's life at all. God knows what a man like him would want with the kid. Has Ann been telling you which way the assessment should go?"

Lisa's mouth opened, but no words came out.

"She's a nasty piece of work as well. I don't see how people like her come and do this job."

"She keeps on telling me he wasn't convicted of anything, and we have nothing concrete on him."

I immediately turned my head to assess her, but she kept her gaze forward.

"I'm not saying I am going to side with him. It's my first ever viability assessment, and it's a bit of a tricky one for me. Please, be patient," she mumbled.

I turned my head away and rolled my eyes so she wouldn't see.

"Look, I will not force you to write what I want. You've just got to put down what you feel is right from what you've seen and what you've read. But you need to remember, Jacob has gone through an awful lot, and we want to make sure he has the life he deserves."

I shook Lisa slightly as her shoulders slumped, and she seemed dejected, so I hugged her tighter from the side, kissed her on the top of her head, and jogged away to see how Taheen and Nikki were doing.

It was a couple more minutes and a cigarette later that we were in the pub. It was a lot quieter as it was further out of the town centre. Unfortunately, the drinks didn't have the bargain-basement value attached to them and were more known to suit boozehounds who liked to think of themselves as sophisticated—that is until they're puking up into the gutter outside on the way back home. It was a quaint and homely pub in a small stone cladded building. Inside, there was a wood fire, comfortable seating, dark wooden beams, burgundy patterned carpet, and dim orange light.

It was quite the relaxing atmosphere, but too comfort-inducing for a leaving do night out as it felt we might end up wanting to fall asleep in there. The table we sat on had two quicksand-like sofas that sucked you in on either side of an oak and steel coffee table. When I bought the first round, the barmaid raised her eyes in surprise at me, as I must have made quite the grimace when she told me the price.

There were more stories from Nikki, and a few stories about Taheen that showed me a side to her I never knew she had. My tea-totalling colleague told us she used to be quite the stoner when she was young and a bit of a tearaway. Then motherhood came, and as she grew older, she became a touch more appreciative of her Muslim heritage.

As she recounted some of her own youthful escapades, I felt a sadness pulling from within as I was going to miss them both. It had been quite a while since I felt this way about anyone leaving the team. Especially with the quality and personalities of the previous agency staff that joined our team—some of the social workers that were sent across, a cardboard box with a smiley face drawn on could out-charm them.

"I'm going to miss you two! Also, just to add, you know I am going to be getting all your shit cases," I blurted at Taheen when she finished telling her story.

"I'll miss all of you as well."

"I won't miss you lot! I've been looking forward to this day since I started," Nikki cackled.

That caused me to spit out some of my cider onto the table, which caused us all to giggle. We stayed there for a few more drinks and, fortunately, no one received a phone call from Ann. We agreed we'd head to Throne as it was a bar with a dance floor. Taheen said she needed to go as she and her family were going to a wedding tomorrow and they had to drive to London for it. I found that when I gave her a hug that I didn't want to let go.

"You take care, Craig. Don't let the job eat you up! Stay in touch," were her last words to me.

We both knew that unless we came across each other professionally, we wouldn't be seeing each other again. It was a quick stagger back into the town centre and to the swanky bar. We were all merry and laughter followed us all the way there. As soon as I got in, I recognised someone I knew.

"Hey, Nikki, look over there. The guy in a white shirt with the size six blonde in a tiny black dress," I shouted in her ear because of the music.

"What about him? Is he a service user?"

"No. I had some fun with him a month back. He's deep down in the closet, and that's his wife. He could not get enough!" I laughed.

Nikki giggled as well, but I could also see a pained expression on her face. My past conquest then saw me staring at him, and he quickly averted his gaze. His shame caused me to feel a little aroused. We all ended up at the bar, downing a round of shots, and then took our drinks to the dance floor.

Unfortunately, I don't think I could describe what we did as dancing; it was more like flailing our arms, staggering, and struggling to stay up on our feet. A couple more rounds and shots later, I noticed my past conquest going into the toilet by himself. With no thought, I immediately followed.

I saw that the urinals were empty as he headed into a cubicle. He was just about to close it when I shoved the door open and came in.

"What the...Oh, it's you. Look, we can't—"

I interrupted his pleas with a kiss straight on his mouth and pushed him back into the side of the cubicle. At first, he tried to push back but quickly gave in. As I kissed him, I put my hand down his trousers and felt that he was hard. Suddenly, I felt a violent push back and I went right into the wall.

"Look, I can't, my wife is here!"

"Come on, you want it. I felt you want it," I slurred as I shook the hand that touched his crotch in his face.

"What the hell! Just because we fucked doesn't mean you can just barge in here and try it on with me like this."

"What are you on about? You loved being fucked by-by...by me! Look, I will be quick, and she won't know," I rambled, then grabbed his cock and went in for another kiss.

That was when I saw a fist hurtling towards my face, and then it all went black.

"You all right, mate?" I heard a gruff voice bark.

"Yeah, yeah. Shine-sun, I am sure am!" I mumbled.

"Come on, get up. Your friends are waiting for you outside."

I responded with a moan. I felt myself being gripped and lifted onto my feet.

"What happened?"

"From what it looks like, someone clocked you right on the chin. You've got a bit of swelling and a cut around there."

"I need a drink!" I exclaimed, barely able to keep my head upright and leaning on whoever had saved me.

"Not happening, mate. You've had way too much, and they sparked you right out. So, you're going home, and your friends are taking you."

I turned to look and saw a bald head with a stone face that seemed as if it had been chiselled into being by punches. I nodded and knew there was no room for argument with the bouncer. He carried me through the busy dance floor and took me outside where Nikki and Lisa were.

"Amy?" I slurred.

"She's headed off with some guy," Lisa laughed nervously.

"What the fuck happened, Craig?" Nikki cried as she and Lisa took me off the bouncer's shoulder.

"This guy. I only tried to kiss him, and he punched me."

"You daft git."

I was in and out of consciousness on the way back in the taxi. I remember at one point the taxi driver had stopped and hurriedly got me out with the help of Nikki so I could vomit on the side of the road. Next thing I remembered, I was being tucked into my bed by her.

"I love you, Nikki. Don't go, please, don't leave me," I whined.

I heard her speak, but none of the words registered, and I passed out for the night.

Chapter 19

"It's really nice having daylight again. Especially with the winter we've had. It has been awful, hasn't it? It was constant rain, and that has been awful for my garden. It also hasn't done my car any good. I think I am getting a lot of rust around the brakes. Not that it matters, my car is still in warranty, and I could easily get it repaired. Yes, daylight just seems to make me feel a lot better. I do wonder if I have that disorder that people have because of the weather. Um, seasonal appearance disorder I think it is…" Julie droned on and on, seemingly without taking any breaths.

I wanted to head-butt my desk as listening to her was becoming too painful. Even with such ongoing auditory torture, I still nodded politely and pretended to pay attention. I couldn't understand how she just kept going on and on when it was clear I wasn't enjoying the lecture— it wasn't a conversation as I had barely got a word in. Unfortunately, there was no one else in the office to rescue me or replace me as a victim. In the end, I just said I had to go to the toilet and quickly left.

I sighed to myself as soon as I left the team room as I felt a longing for Nikki and Taheen to come back. Unfortunately, the agency replacement was just the one worker, Julie.

It was fortunate there was no one inside the toilet as, otherwise, I'd have to pretend to use a cubicle. Instead, I stared at myself in the mirror and noticed I still had the crack whore look going on, but at least I appeared a well-rested crack whore. It was quite wonderful getting a regular night's rest, and I hadn't felt this sharp for such a long time. I gave myself a cheeky smile, spun around on the spot, and then gave myself a wink. I thought I'd need to waste another minute before heading back, so I killed that time by splashing my face with cold water.

As I headed back to the team's room, I went as slow as I possibly could without looking as if I was acting quite silly. I hoped that by doing so, Julie would have completely forgotten that she was talking at me and not bother trying to subject me to further inane natter. There was a less kind part of me that hoped she would have gotten the hint that I find her intensely boring. Fortune shone favourably on me, as when I returned, she didn't even bother looking my way.

I went back to my computer and rather than go into my emails, I looked at my caseload, the majority of which were going exceptionally well since Zee's interventions started a month ago. In fact, he'd been involved in nearly all my cases, except when it came to Jacob Smith's parents. This was because I wasn't allowed to do the viability on his father, so I didn't have a reason I could use to get close to him to mark him as someone to be cured by the Devil.

My mind soon went to thinking that I needed to find someone to pick soon as I didn't want to disappoint the unholy one, but also because I didn't know what he would be like if he didn't get what he wanted in a timely fashion. I didn't want to find out as I could easily imagine his ugly, muscle sinew-covered demon getting involved.

To try and keep the flow of people for him to collect demons from and cleanse, I had resorted to helping co-workers on their visits so I could mark them for Zee. However, recently, it had become difficult to create excuses for me to tag along or for me to do my colleague's visits, and it had reached the point where they politely made up excuses to reject me.

I soon found myself looking at my actual work to distract myself from the problem. I looked at my key performance indices and saw I was behind on half of them. Some were in yellow and too many were in the red. This was because since I started to work for the unholy stoner, I felt I was making a bigger impact with him, so I focused on that, and not arbitrary targets made by directors who had long since forgotten what social work involved.

Before Zee, the poor performance would have grated against me hard, but I was finding that these days I simply didn't care, even though I knew I would soon be brought in to meet with management about such failing statistics. Suddenly, an email came in from our manager, Ann.

Hi all,

As you are aware, I am working from home. However, I have misplaced my charger and I have left it in the office. Please, can one of you come and drop it off! I need it as a matter of urgency.

Ann

I chuckled because I knew if us lowly peons were in her position we would have had to simply drive to the office. I was about to say an expletive or two and delete the email when I suddenly got an idea of who could be Zee's next mark. I quickly typed a group email back to the team and Ann.

I'll bring you the charger. I've got a visit soon, so I can drop it off before it. It'll be no bother.

Craig

It was twenty minutes before I got a reply.

Okay. I live at The Morscroft Cottage, Lower Fields, Senford. See you soon.

I imagine my voluntary help came to her as a surprise. I smiled to myself as the fact that I was coming to see her, and her home would aggravate her to no end. Pissing Ann off was something that always had helped lighten my mood. In fact, I was so happy that I half-danced and shook my hips as I went to leave the building.

"Oh, you seem ever so happy, Craig. I think I need to have whatever you're taking," Dawn laughed as I went by her at reception.

I turned around and gave her a wink before I left. The traffic was light so I could have gotten there quick, but I decided to stop off for a takeaway coffee first and parked at the cafe's carpark. I didn't want to be too timely as I wanted to make her wait at least a little while, so I sat in my car sipping away whilst I scrolled through potential casual flings for that night. With work becoming less stressful, my libido had rocketed to the point where I tried to meet up with people at the very least once a night.

As I scrolled through my potential prospects, I saw a young mixed-race guy who eerily looked like me when I was young. I knew straight away that he wasn't eighteen, sixteen at best, and that meant he reminded me of my time in care. I wanted to message him and tell him that this medium of perversion wasn't the right place to explore his sexuality. I wanted to tell him that he was too young and he'd twist himself by getting involved in this depravity at such an age. Then I saw it on his profile:

DM me for bookings.

It really was a younger me, except I didn't have the means of social media to utilise for prostitution. I wondered if he was in care and had a social worker as well, someone I could contact. I quickly realised that was a stupid idea

222

as even if I did somehow find out who he was, how could I explain to the local authority how I found him? Anyway, not that social care could prevent him, as I remembered they couldn't stop me and Emma when we got up to our trouble.

My mind soon turned to my time in social care. In a way, Emma and I were too clever and were far too able to play the system. It wasn't until we ended up with Neville as our social worker that it all changed. I laughed at the memory of this muscle-bound meat-head with police banging on the door of a drug den me and Emma frequented, and Neville threatening the drug dealer by picking him up by the neck and pinning him against the wall.

It was safe to say he was quite unorthodox and certainly wouldn't have gotten away with his ways these days, but it was such methods that somehow convinced me and Emma there was much more to life than the hedonism we followed.

My mind broke free of the nostalgia and was back to thinking of how I could discreetly intervene and help this teenage prostitute but, suddenly, he logged off and disappeared into the ether. There were no further means to message or contact him, so all I did in the end was let out a little sigh.

I finished my cup of coffee, put my phone down, and then drove to Ann's house. When I arrived and saw it, I became instantly envious. It was a beautiful five-bed cottage in the countryside that was built with large stone bricks, and it had an elaborate front garden I imagined would be soon filled with flowers when spring finally came.

The sun was shining bright and it only added to the fairy tale effect of the home. On the driveway was her sports car. Although I didn't know that much about Ann, from gossip I heard that her elderly husband was a director in some conglomerate, and he was often away on business. At that moment, I thought perhaps that finding a rich old man should be what I should aim for.

The front garden's gate made a slight *creak* as I pushed it open and the fine gravel path made a crunching noise as I walked along in. A large ornate metal knocker was stuck to a composite door that had been manufactured to look like oak. A few knocks and ten seconds later, the door swung open.

"Hi, Craig. I hope you are well," Ann said with a smile that appeared to pain her.

"Hi Ann, glad to see you. I've got to say, your home is quite amazing," I replied with a full grin.

The warmth of my response appeared take her by surprise as her eyes widened. There were a few seconds of silence before I spoke again.

"Am I okay to come in?"

Ann frowned and appeared to think deeply for a moment.

"Yes, yes, come in, Craig," she sighed.

Inside was just as charming as the outside. Thick, rustic wood beams were seen around the roofing and walls. The walls and ceiling were painted in dark reds or dark purples. Brightly coloured furnishings sharply contrasted against such a backdrop, and each one appeared quaint and homely in their own way. My envy overflowed, but the reason why I was here was enough for me to easily ignore such resentment.

"I really am impressed, Ann. You definitely have an eye for decoration!"

"Yes, yes, thank you," she mumbled as she led me to her home's office.

It was a small room that just about fit in an oak pedestal desk which faced a spectacular view of Senford's hilly countryside. I put my bag on the ground, opened the zip, and pulled out her charger.

"Just in time as I only had four percent battery left," Ann said.

She quickly grabbed it from my hand and plugged it into the socket and her computer.

"Is there anything else you want, Craig?" she asked with a straight face.

"No, well not work-wise," I beamed and then took in a deep breath. "I simply wanted to apologise for how I have acted with you before. I am hoping we can start again with a clean slate as I've had a change of heart recently and realised I have been unfair to you," I enthused.

Ann raised both of her eyes in surprise.

"I'm glad you have said that. Because, to be quite honest, Craig, you have been difficult to manage."

She then stayed silent as she looked out of her office's window at the view.

"Let's just move on from here and hope we can work better together, yes?" she asserted without turning to look at me.

"Of course," I said and nodded vigorously.

She then turned to me and stared at me for a couple of seconds.

"Good, good. Anything else?"

"Just one small thing, please. Can I use your toilet before I go?"

"It's the second door on your right. I'll see you back in the office tomorrow. Goodbye," she stated as she sat down at her desk.

I headed to the toilet, which was really quite different from the rest of the house as it was quite modern and well-lit. I struggled to find where I could draw a cross as I felt Ann would surely notice. In the end, I opted for right behind the toilet on the wall. I was just about able to get the cross behind the toilet so that it wasn't going to be seen by Ann or her husband, that is if he was going to be back tonight. I flushed the toilet to make it sound like I had used it and washed my hands.

As soon as I opened the bathroom door, I saw Ann waiting at the front door. She opened it for me and just as I walked by, she spoke.

"Just so you're aware, Lisa has completed the viability on Jacob's dad. He has been assessed as a positive carer for Jacob. I will be submitting the paperwork to court later this week."

"No worries. I think it was probably good to get a fresh pair of eyes on it. She probably saw something different than I did," I blurted straight after, and then reached down into one pocket, and then to check my other pocket before grimacing. "I think I must have dropped my phone in your bathroom!" I exclaimed as I barged past her before she could respond.

I quickly ran to the toilet, pulled the black crayon out of my pocket and coloured over the red cross. As I came out, I giggled and feigned embarrassment.

"Found it. Cheers, Ann, and see you!" I boomed as I brushed by her again.

I didn't look back as I strolled back to my car, my breath slowly going in and out. I pulled the black crayon out and stared at it, expecting there to be feelings of guilt but, instead, I only felt a cold stillness within and no thought of condemning what I had just done. I didn't want to dwell on the matter so I rummaged for my car keys.

I started up my engine and drove back. No one beeped a single horn at me as I kept it slow and precise. My attention was fully on the drive itself. I felt the clicking of the indicators echo in my head, the plastic of the steering wheel in my hand, the slight judder of the car as I changed the gear, the scraping of metal from within my gearbox. It wasn't long until I got back to the office.

I sneaked in without Dawn noticing me hurry by and came back to an empty team room, which was fortunate as I wasn't in the mood for talking. I spent the last few hours of the afternoon clearing the backlog of reports and assessments, still without worry or concern. If I hadn't been so dulled in my emotions, I imagine I would have been quite proud of the amount of work I had done. As soon as the clock struck five, I left the empty room and headed straight home. Again, my drive was slow, precise, and mindful.

When I parked up at my flat, I felt a vibration in my pocket and heard the ding of a message. When I looked at my phone, I saw that I had a message from Lisa.

Hi, Craig. I've been meaning to chat with you, but I haven't been able to as it has been so busy. Not sure if Ann has told you, about what I am going to recommend for the court assessment for whether James Smith should care for Jacob. She kept on trying to persuade me to say yes for Jacob's dad. I haven't told her (as she's scary!), but I am going to recommend he doesn't get to care for Jacob. I wanted to make sure you knew as I know how much you care about the case.

My eyes shot wide open as I realised what I had done. I swung my car door open, grabbed my stuff, slammed the door shut and ran to my flat. As soon as I got through my front door, I collapsed onto the floor and swallowed in gulps of air as I lay on my back. I took a few more breaths and crawled on my hands and knees to Zee's door. I knocked on his door. No answer. I knocked on it harder again. No answer. I tried again and again, to no avail.

"FUCK!" I shouted up to the ceiling as I lay on the floor.

It was obvious he wasn't in or didn't want to see me. Once I had got my breath back, I pushed myself back up onto my feet and swayed for a couple of seconds. I headed to the living room and saw three perfectly rolled joints lined up next to each other. I sat on the sofa and told myself I wasn't going to smoke any until I spoke to Zee. That promise lasted about three minutes.

Within half-an-hour, I had ordered a takeaway pizza, and my thoughts about Ann were barely staying afloat in my mind. By the time I had finished the last joint, I was sprawled out completely on the sofa, fighting to keep my eyes open, as I knew as soon as they shut then that was it. It was a battle I lost quick.

Chapter 20

I fantasised about swerving my car onto the pavement and driving down it past the standstill traffic. It was small enough to fit and there were only a group of male teenagers walking with chins up to the sky and their legs band-wide as if they were cowboys. Would anyone call the police if I actually ran them over? I guffawed at the silly thought. Then, as predictable and as frequent as the rainy English weather, my mind went back to social work.

My shoulders hunched as I thought about a court report that I had finished a few hours past today's deadline. Well, I say today's deadline, but it was already two days late. I sent it to our legal team with profuse apologies, which were written out of politeness and not because I actually cared. It was a report that had the arbitrary due date of a month before the court date, while all other professionals could hand theirs in a week before. Why? So they could copy all the good bits from mine and pretend they actually did something. *Twats*.

I will admit it was paperwork that I had left to the last minute, as since placing Satan's mark on Ann yesterday, I had become racked with guilt. I had hoped that perhaps because I used the red crayon first, it meant that nothing bad had happened to her. Fortunately, just after lunchtime, I found out she had telephoned in sick. That immediately killed off all my worries and I could focus on the ever-growing mound of paperwork.

I was daydreaming about what the exorcised demons from Ann would have looked like when a car horn beeping from behind shocked me out of such imaginations. The traffic in front had long since moved, so I went to drive off, but I accidentally lifted my foot up off the clutch too quickly and caused my car to stall.

The horn behind me beeped again as I fumbled around my car keys to restart the engine. I thought I must have pissed the car gods off somehow as in the anxious rush to try again, it yet again stalled. More beeps and horns followed. Fortunately, the third time proved the charm and I sped off with beads of sweat erupting all over my forehead.

A minute later I drove by a two-car accident, both looking like certain write-offs—one front bumper was caved inwards and the other's rear bumper was just as badly damaged. The police had moved the wrecks to the side of the road. Even with such clear warnings, I continued at fifty in the thirty zone.

Ten minutes later, I parked up and rushed into my local newsagent. I bought a couple of tubs of ice cream and a couple of pizzas, but quite unlike me, I didn't buy any wine. My copious booze intake had significantly dropped as Zee's weed was far more effective in alleviating any of my anxieties, and it was absolute magic for helping me sleep.

When I reached my block of flats, I noticed that one of the car park's streetlamps was off, and it was right next to my space. A part of me—the part that was so used to being attacked as a social worker—thought that my neighbours had somehow done this to my spot, just to hide my derelict of a car so they would not have to see it. Without the light, it meant I had to drive into the space incredibly slowly to get between the parking lines. As I hurried back to my flat, I noticed my armpit's dampness because of the cold air making them cool to the touch.

I looked up and saw a couple of people smoking out of the second-floor window. As soon as their gaze came close to mine, I turned away and walked even more quickly to the building's entrance. I swiped the fob, swung the door open, and rushed inside.

Aside from always fucking hurrying wherever I went, I also wanted to see Zee as I had yet to talk to him about what had happened with Ann. He usually gave me some sort of explanation of the exorcism after I had placed a mark on someone—to do this, he used words rather sparingly, as the talk always seemed to require so much effort for him that it would cause him to deflate and collapse in on himself completely like a punctured blow-up doll. Even though I was quite keen to get back home, I opted to wait for the elevator.

Unfortunately, whilst waiting, a young lady arrived and waited for the annoyingly slow thing as well. I nodded and gave her a pursed smile. She did the same in response. It was a long and awkward minute as we both stared at the numbers counting down on the little monitor above the elevator doors.

The doors creaked open but then stopped just to tease me a little. They fortunately gave up on the joke, opened fully, and I leapt in.

"Floor?" I asked.

"Four, thank you."

Silence again. I spent the time staring at the door and drumming my fingers against the side of my leg. I noticed she had pulled her phone out. When we reached my floor, the doors got up to their old tricks just to taunt us both. When there was just about enough room, I stepped out sideways and hurried away from the unwanted moment I had shared with the stranger.

I got back to my flat, quickly unlocked the front door, and barged through with my shoulder. It was home sweet home, so I let out a sigh of relief. I heard the television on and felt a little excitement that Zee was in. I kicked my shoes off, left my bag at my room door, and then strode to the living room. My mouth fell open and my eyes bulged to the point where they tried to leap out of their sockets. I dropped the shopping onto the ground and I sought to find any words that could express my horror of what I saw in front of me.

There was my stoner flatmate in his armchair, lit joint in his mouth, dressed in a black T-shirt and black jeans, looking smarter than usual. He was watching music videos on the television. That part wasn't what shocked me. Sat on the armrest next to him was Ann. What added to the oddity of what I saw was that she wore an exceptionally revealing black cocktail dress, wore make-up that was more suited for a porn star, and a pair of black stilettos. They both turned to look at me and I saw a scowl come up onto my manager's face.

"Ugh, he's here. If this weak human cries too much, I will kill him," she snarled.

"Hey! No! He'll be fine."

I stood there not knowing what to do or say.

"I have come here because your work is awful and you are pathetic. You require punishing, you dog," my manager cackled.

"Oi!"

My flatmate bit into the tip of his finger until a little drop of blood came out. Ann leapt off the armrest and hissed at him, but also looked frightened at the sight of the red liquid.

"Stop killing my buzz. Otherwise, I'll use this on you!"

Zee turned back to face me and took his sunglasses off. I saw his beautiful almond-shaped, hazelnut eyes, completely hypnotic even through the pulsating red roots surrounded the irises.

"Look, Craig, we need to have a brief chat. You probably will need a little of this beforehand. So, come sit down," he ordered.

He passed me the joint, which I more than happily took a few drags from. I edged to the sofa, then ever so slowly sat back into it, still keeping an eye on my social work boss, who rolled her eyes at me.

"We saw Ann, and as you wanted, we have taken care of—" Zee said before I interrupted him.

"What do you mean taken care of? It doesn't seem like you've removed the demons from her."

"What I mean is, she's dead and eaten. In the end, we didn't bother with the demons. Oh, there's a little more to add," Zee explained.

I frowned as I looked at my sneering manager and pointed at her with a quizzical look on my face.

"Yeah, Craig, that isn't Ann as you know her."

My brow creased into deep trenches filled with anxiety as I stared at her.

"You know that demon that looked like she was covered in muscle sinew?" I nodded. "Well, she took your manager's skin before she dined on the rest of her. The greedy cow also ate the husband when I wasn't looking," my flatmate fumed.

"That skinny bitch had no meat on her. I needed something else to fill me up, and he was so plump and ripe," she giggled.

Zee turned to the demon and scowled at her. My mouth fell open and I stared even harder, hoping by focussing I'd see it was all a practical joke that Big Red was playing on me.

"I think I wear it far better than her. Do you think it was better than my last skin, Craig? Perhaps we can christen it with another fuck together?" she mocked in a different voice that somehow sounded familiar.

I tilted my head and looked from left to right as I thought about what she just said and in the voice she had just said it in.

"What do you mean by another fuck together, and what happened to your voice?"

Zee rolled his eyes at Lily, but rather than intervene, he shrugged his shoulders, sat back, and puffed on his joint.

"Have you already forgotten me? I was a lot paler the night we fucked. Don't you remember, we did a little role play. You were you, and I was your mother."

"WHAT THE FUCK?!"

"Lily, you are not making this easy. So, be a star and leave," Zee snapped.

"Lily, I just remembered, that was that woman's name..." I whispered.

"Fine! I don't know why you are so interested in someone so pathetic and weak. You should just let me fuck him into oblivion and then feast on him, then at least he'll have some use," she ranted back in Ann's voice.

Zee flicked his finger, which had the droplet of blood on at the belligerent blondie. She moved in time so that it splattered onto the wall next to her. Ann, Lily, or whatever the hell she was, hissed and snarled at my flatmate before getting up and storming away. The sound of the front door being slammed, slapped my eardrums and echoed throughout the flat.

"Yeah, she's probably going to go party a bit. Hopefully, she'll just sleep with a few people rather than eat them. With her, well, you just don't know," the Devil groaned.

I tried to piece together all the information that had just been fired at me. So, it appeared I had slept with a psychopathic demon, helped this demon kill my manager, she stole her my manager's skin, and then she dined on the husband because she enjoys eating humans. *Bollocks*. My stomach plummeted as if I was on a rollercoaster crashing down as I realised I had been the catalyst to such brutal murders.

I hyperventilated and the reality swirled into a pallet of water colours. My head swayed from left to right, and I just about made out Zee offering me another joint. A part of me wanted to grab it and stomp on it, but such a feeling only lasted for a split-second. The briefest of moments later, I was soon taking deep drags of the drug. I felt my mind slowly solidify, and I could think again. I then looked at the joint and raised a suspicious eyebrow.

"Is this even weed? It smells like it, but no weed I ever smoked does what this does."

"Well, it's stuff I grow, so you know it's going to be different to your bog-standard green. After all, I need something strong enough to work on the likes of me," the stoner chuckled as he reached over to me and, like a tacky magician, he pulled a fresh joint out from behind my ear.

Even though I had calmed down and was able to communicate, the conversation had strung me so tight that I thought I might snap. Instead, I opted to let out a groan and protected my neck with my hands.

"I'm not a murderer, Zee. It's not the type of person I am, and I don't think I can live with myself for helping her die. I didn't actually want Ann killed!"

"Oh, don't take it personally like that, man. Also, no need to lie. She wasn't a nice person and, in different circumstances, you'd be quite happy with her being dead. Here, smoke some more," he comforted before he lit his drug.

I stared at him right into his eyes, but only held his gaze for a second before turning away as I thought I'd see deep down into the Hell he was from if I kept it up any longer. He gave me the new joint, which I inhaled greedily.

"Wanting her to die differs from causing her to die! I had changed my mind about her, but you weren't here for me to tell you," I blurted.

My unholy flatmate closed his eyes and it seemed like he was about to nod off; suddenly, they opened, as if he had just remembered we were still in a conversation.

"Look, Craig, I didn't tell you, but you would've had to use that black crayon at some point. I didn't give it to you to test your resolve against having that power, I gave it to you to see what it would take before you did what it took to right the wrongs in this world. To be honest, I've been that baked twenty-four seven, seven days a week, that it wasn't until recently I realised that myself. At first, I thought I just gave you that black crayon for a bit of fun. But then I had this epiphany about my life."

I puffed myself up with as much courage as I could muster and looked at him to search for more meaning, but the coward in me quickly took over and my gaze was back down to the floor.

"It isn't about collecting demons anymore, Craig. That's just silly shit for children. I want to get back to doing something meaningful again. Like saving humanity." He paused and then puffed. "And to do that, you've got to be forceful."

"What?" I whispered with wide eyes.

"We're going to create a better world, Craig. Except, it's going to be done in the only way that will work. This way," he croaked before he pulled out a black crayon from his pocket and placed it on the coffee table.

The cynic in me could not help but to check my pocket for the crayons, feeling there was only one left. I pulled it out and saw the red.

"But, getting rid of people's demons will make them good, and it'll mean they can rectify the harm they've caused!" I cried without daring to look at his reaction.

"You can't see this world so simplistically as individuals making choices that are right or wrong. It's much too complex for it to work like that. I will have cleansed them of their demons but soon they will become corrupt again. It's like curing someone of a disease in a Victorian hospital, but because the patient remains in absolute filth and everyone around them is diseased as well, they'll simply get infected with

241

the same or an even worse pathogen. The demons will always come back in such circumstances, and the sickness will remain."

I had curled up into a ball on the sofa by the time he finished speaking.

"So, you're saying we have to kill people to save people. That doesn't make any fucking sense," I whined just before taking a couple more drags of his drug.

"Craig, these behaviours that harm humanity are nothing more than a disease. Within such plagues, there are those who are super-spreaders. By focusing on those who transmit so effectively and making sure there is no chance of them contaminating others will ensure that we make meaningful progress. I know you see this, and I know you know who such people are."

I gasped as the image of my mother appeared in my head.

"Then why don't we just look to cure those who spread it?" I whispered.

"Like I said, it's because the disease is too ingrained in their environment. They will simply become sick again and would again spread it to others. So, the only hope we have is to cut it out."

I took in several deep breaths.

"Even if that's the case, we're still killing. It isn't right."

"Craig, who am I?"

"Zee," I croaked

"No, what's my full name?"

"Beelzebub."

"So, why would you ever think I cared about whether we killed anyone? Also, why would I let you say no to what I command?" He guffawed. "But, you know what, I'm feeling kind, so I'll do you the courtesy of further explaining myself. When you can see as much as I can see, you'll realise that individuals do not exist, Craig, only systems do, or super organisms if that helps you to understand. Each person operates like a cell in a human body and each cell needs this greater whole, otherwise, it can't function. Humans are like this. It is what you were designed for, not for this illusion of individual desires but for something far greater and meaningful," Zee explained.

I bit into my forearm, hard, to draw my focus away from what was being said, but it was of no use. I saw another joint dangled in front of me and I again succumbed. Zee did not start speaking again until I had finished it, and by that point, I felt calmer than I was before.

"In a body, when a cell becomes too infected and it is so far gone that it becomes a virus production factory or a cancerous cell, there is only one resort, and that is to destroy it. Your body does this all the time to ensure that it survives. This destruction of cells isn't murder, it's done to ensure the disease is eliminated and does not spread. You cannot see this as you are but a cell."

I turned to him, my eyes half-closed, and nodded. I wasn't sure if the words registered as I was so high, but it felt like I was seeing in my mind what he spoke.

"My father had always believed this. Why do you think he was so wrathful with humans when behaviours he disapproved of developed? I feel he was too clumsy in his approach, but the philosophy behind his methods stays true. It has taken me this long to realise this and what needs to be done," he explained.

"So, why don't you just do all this with your father?"

Zee stretched his arms backwards and he squished further back into the armchair.

"We obviously don't get along. Also, if he found out what I was doing, he'd intervene because...well, he's the type who has to have everything done his way," Zee sighed.

I had uncurled out of my ball and fell onto my side on the sofa. I lay there as we stayed silent and dwelled on what he said. Not only did I start to believe there wasn't an individual, but I'd always known it. I visualised each human as a minor cog that was interconnected with many others and ultimately moved with these others to create the greater being. Each person, each family, each neighbourhood, each job, each company, each local authority and the central government all interlinked to form the whole, all working in unison.

Once that image faded, psychedelic fractals of intensely bright and changing colours replaced it. I do not know how long it was but, eventually, I pushed myself out of the fantasy and back up the sofa.

I saw Zee had his sunglasses back on and was again watching music videos on the television.

"I'll do it, Zee!"

"I know you will," he drawled without turning to look at me.

Chapter 21

""Hi, Sheila. Is Ann still sick? I wonder if it was her who passed this bug onto me...I've got a cracking migraine and a fever at the moment...I don't feel like I can drive, so I'm going to take the day off...cheers, Sheila. Hopefully, I'll feel well enough to come in tomorrow. See you," I groaned.

I lay there on the sofa for a few seconds, wondering whether Sheila had fallen for my acting. She had raised three sons into adulthood, so I imagine she could see right through the bullshit I spewed. Any remorse evaporated quicker than water in the Sahara as soon my thoughts leapt to cover the hours the local authority owed me in TOIL. Of course, they could act like any other decent employer and provide overtime, but no, they felt the guilt of failing vulnerable children would be payment enough for working far more hours than they paid me for. *Wankers*.

My body relaxed and melted into the sofa a little more because it knew for definite that I would not be working. A chill caressed my bare arms, so I moved the throw up to cover me whole. I tried closing my eyes, but as soon as I did, memories of my discussion with Zee and Lily—or Ann, or whatever the fuck its name was—popped up into my mind. I remembered what I had agreed to and what I had done. There weren't any feelings of guilt for my crime, but I thought that might be because I was so very stoned. Even though I needed a lighthouse to guide myself through this amount of haze, my mind could not help itself and further ruminated about what I had done.

"Murderer," I whispered.

Even though I didn't shed the blood with my hand, I knew I played a significant enough role, and I couldn't deny that without my actions, the deaths couldn't have happened.

"Murderer."

I still did not feel any emotional turmoil, even after I spoke the word. Next, I went into deliberations about all the times I had wished for people to die. I didn't realise how long this list was, most of the names being sadists and their enablers that I had worked with. It is difficult to not hope for death upon these people, especially when they cause so much pain and will continue to do so until they draw their last breath.

I remembered it had only been a couple years after I had started in my career that a favourite pastime of mine was fantasising about what death best fitted a parent. On one Friday, I had got work colleagues to join in on such festive imaginations, and we all got quite into it, so much so we had even created a table and voted on the methods of how these people should die. The winner was a ghastly paedophile who had raped his son and daughter until they reached adolescence. We voted to tie him up, place him in a six-foot-deep pit, have his cock and balls smeared with honey, and then pour flesh-eating ants out him. They'd, of course, start on his weapon he so loved to hurt others with and move outwards from there. It was all for fun, but we knew that a part of us would have been ecstatic with joy if these dark fantasies became reality.

My thoughts soon went to Ann being brutally skinned alive and then eaten by Lily. I created quite the vivid image of what her face would have looked like just before the mutilation started, to her imagined gargled screams of pain, and how the demon would have feasted on her like a lion on a zebra. I gave no emotional response. It was something that should have shocked me, but it didn't.

Zee was quite right that I wanted her to die, and it hadn't been just a spur of a moment feeling that lead to me to use the black crayon. I had always thought the obvious reason I never acted on such twisted fantasies was because I was a moral person. Now, I felt it was just because I didn't have the power. As soon as the Devil gave me the ability to kill without impunity, it was only a matter of time before I used it.

I wondered if my regret only came about because I thought it meant I should perceive myself as a bad person, not because I cared one bit that Lily chomped Ann down. Before I could follow this thread and see where such thoughts took me, I heard a loud rumble from my stomach.

"Not the best time to say you're hungry when I'm thinking about people getting eaten, you sick fuck," I said sighing.

I grumbled out an expletive as I decided to get up. I left my dour introspections behind on the sofa. I wrapped myself with the throw and headed to the kitchen. A quick search of what food was available and I found the menu was ice cream, biscuits, or a simple cheese pizza for breakfast.

I went for the pizza as I didn't think I could bring myself to eat the other junk food so early in the morning as that was a step too far. I didn't bother waiting for the oven to pre-heat, I just chucked the food in, picked a temperature, and set a timer on my phone.

I went back to the sofa, and just before I switched the television on, I remembered what Zee had said before he disappeared to do whatever he does—get stoned and play on an Xbox with Lily, perhaps?

"M-aaa-n, I know you won't like this, but I've got to make sure you do your bit and stay motivated. So, I am going to need you to pick someone by Friday. That gives you three days. Oh, it can't just be anyone, it must be someone that is a *disease spreader*, if you get me. Take it easy, Craig," Zee croaked just before he shuffled off to his room.

When he said that to me, my mum immediately popped into my head, but I fought away that desire until I had pushed it back down deep inside me. It wasn't long after that Jacob Smith's father came into my mind's eye. Aside from the evidence of child pornography on his computer that he discredited by blaming such downloads on his other son, there was this visceral instinct which told me that this *prick* was as bad as they came.

There was something about the degenerate that reminded me of all those men I slept with when I was in care. Memories of the way they talked, the way they moved, the way their nostrils flared, their heavy breathing, the beads of sweat on their noses, even the way they smelled, the way they touched me, the way they looked me up and down and the way their skin felt, was what I saw in Jacob's father. I could feel that same slime simmering underneath that mask he wore in public.

I tried to think about potential marks for Zee, but it would only be seconds later that I was back to Jacob's father.

As I ate my breakfast pizza, I had the TV on, but completely ignored it and watched my Jacob's father being mutilated by Lily in my mind. The fantasy made me feel ravenous and I ripped into my food, barely chewing before I swallowed. My breath quickened, my eyes went wide, and my leg shook with excitement. Suddenly, the pizza dropped from my mouth as I realised how much I had readily taken to Zee's philosophy and how much the power excited me. I gave my crotch a quick feel and breathed a sigh of relief as it didn't make me *that* excited.

That shock of realisation brought me fully back into reality and I wrenched my focus to the television as I wanted my mind to switch off. It was a talk show with a vindictive and judgmental host who picked on guests who were from destitute backgrounds. He had a level of belligerence that was usually achieved with a bottle of whiskey and a gram of cocaine. He had this caustic wrath just pumping naturally throughout his veins.

I felt I should've felt sorry for the guests, but I didn't. But I also felt indifferent to the host's faux outrage that turned his head the colour of a beetroot. It was like watching a nature documentary of a predator and its prey. The studio and host being like a Venus flytrap that lured prey with the fetid whiff of fame. I soon wondered about what thoughts must have gone through the guest's head to have led to them thinking it was a good idea to go on the show.

I spent the rest of the day watching terrible TV and filling my face with more junk food. After what happened the day before, I felt I deserved to enjoy such slovenly behaviour and to do so guilt-free before I started Zee's next task. That relaxation all ended when nightfall came. It was not long after I got into an Australian soap when the front door of the flat opened. I had expected Zee to shuffle on in. Instead, Lily came in.

"Oh, you're here," she muttered in Ann's voice.

I raised my eyebrows in surprise and then grunted like a moody teenager. As the haughty demon approached, I felt confidence inflate my chest. I imagine it was because even though Lily could easily kill me, I knew she wouldn't cross our master.

"Of course, I am here, it's my flat. How did you unlock the front door?"

Lily didn't answer. Instead, she went to the armchair and sat herself down. She was still in the same black dress, stilettos, and immaculate make-up. She pulled out a key from a little black clutch bag and tossed it onto me. I looked down and saw it was mine.

"No wonder Zee finds you so difficult to deal with," I said, pushing myself back to sit up.

"I am difficult because I am not a weakling like you," she snapped whilst intently assessing her nails.

Lily then reached into her clutch again and pulled out a file.

"So, did you have fun last night? Eat or fuck anyone, or was it both?"

She filed one of her nails before speaking.

"Yes, I had plenty of fun. Of course, it was both as I can work up quite an appetite from such thorough exercise. I feel I was quite fair and progressive in who I chose as victims. Variety is certainly the spice of life," she chuckled.

I raised an eyebrow. *I probably should be more shocked than I am*, I thought.

"Don't the police ever find out about what you've done?"

"Only if I want them to. I am not as stupid as you humans," she sighed as she went about filing more of her nails.

I waited for a couple of seconds to build up the courage to ask a question I knew would rile her up.

"So, what's it like being Zee's slave?"

Lily stopped, put the file down, and looked at me with a scowl that cracked like a whip.

"I am no one's slave," she growled.

"Well, you do as he says, and you seem more than happy to grovel at his feet."

The seductive monster sat there glaring at me whilst I perused television channels, knowing she wanted to hurt me but couldn't. I heard her breathing quicken before it suddenly quieted.

"If I am his slave, then so are you. You are worse as you do as he commands because you are a coward who is too scared to stand up for himself. I do as commanded because I am bound to him and because I owe him for saving my life."

I felt my ears go hot and my back become prickly as I certainly didn't like the scathing comment. Rather than stay quiet or go into a sulk as I usually would have, I uncharacteristically burst into laughter.

"What is so funny?"

I turned to look at what was left of my manager, sitting with her legs crossed, leant forward, both eyes squinted, and her brow furrowed. I imagined she found it incredibly easy to lure men or women for her pleasures with beauty like that. I then realised I had never really noticed how stunning Ann actually was when she was the owner of the skin in front of me. I thought it must have been the hate I felt that twisted my image of her. I coughed to clear my throat, taking my time to reply.

"It's you I find funny. It's because you have this unique way of dealing with others. You say what you feel and are straight to the point, something I can't knock you for," I confessed with a sincere smile on my face.

Lily raised an eyebrow, uncrossed her legs, and opened them slowly.

"Are you wanting to fuck me again?! Is that why you are acting like this?"

I shivered and forced myself not to retch.

"God no! You did a right number on me last time. You've put me off women for good. Even if you drip-fed me MDMA, Viagra, and GHB, it would still be a no." I laughed nervously, hoping to pacify her.

Lily's frown suddenly broke and a smile beamed through.

"Yes, I certainly did that to you. I must confess it was very fun for me. Such a shame you do not feel the same and don't wish to play again," she chuckled as she looked down at my crotch.

I instinctively responded by crossing my legs.

"Why did you want to sleep with me in the first place? Especially as you have such a low opinion of me," I asked.

Her smile crept from cheek to cheek.

"Zee asked me to, so I did. We needed to rid you of the demon that was created inside you because of your mother. Otherwise, you would have been even weaker than you already are."

"W-w-what?"

"It is as I said. Even a simple human like you should understand that," she snapped.

As repulsed as I was by what she just said, it made sense of why the act was so traumatic.

"I can help you understand more about your mother. Perhaps I can pretend to be her again and—"

"So, how is something like you created or born, Lily?" I quickly interrupted to change the subject.

The skin-stealing femme fatale rolled her eyes and giggled before she sat back in the armchair.

"I am not like those other lowly and weak demons, if that is what you are asking. Zee's father created me because it was deemed so. I am not a product of a lowly human's twisted heart. Who knows why he made me? He is a mischievous one. Why do you ask?"

I raised both eyebrows in surprise.

"Just curious. If we're going to be around each other a lot more, we might as well get to know each other a little. So, how did you and Zee meet?" I asked.

"As you humans say, curiosity ripped the idiot's head off," she replied and went back to filing her nails.

I resisted the urge to correct her and sighed instead. I went back to watching the television.

"He wasn't always like this," she said a couple of minutes later.

I turned my head and tilted it inquisitively.

"Zee. He used to have ideals—none that I agreed with—and he was far less the degenerate he is now. I must admit you seem to have awoken some of that inner fire again, and he appears to have changed a little for the better, so I thank you for that."

"I changed him? Why, what was he like before? What happened?"

"Yes, you did. Do not make me repeat myself. He was boring and believed in stupid things, but at least he believed in something, and he did not hide in his drugs as he does now. He became this way because of you humans being humans. Seven billion people always whining about every little grievance. He has to hear it all. I would not have put up with it. I would have just killed you all for being so loud and annoying." Lily gave me a wink. "But then again, there are some who serve their purposes."

The demon leered at me, so I turned away and stayed quiet. She went back to filing her nails, and I again stared absently at the television.

"I am bored and you are boring. I think I will go and enjoy the night some more," she announced before standing stood up.

As she sauntered by, I felt her hand stroke the side of my face and head. It caused me to shiver.

"Do not disappoint us, Craig. He may be forgiving, but I am not," she called out as she went to leave the flat.

I heard the front door open and then shut. I felt some pity for the poor soul she was going to take a liking to. Such feelings quickly changed as thoughts of pigging out on more junk food again made their appearance. I got up and headed to my cupboard, and just in front of a packet of milk chocolate digestives, I saw a couple of Zee's pre-rolled joints. I raised my eyebrows in surprise, did a little victory boogie, grabbed one, and then lit it on the oven hob.

I walked over to the unholy stoner's room, joint in my mouth, biscuits in hand, and I knocked on his door. No answer. I tried again, but it was the same response. A shrug of my shoulders later, I headed back to the sofa. Moments later, I was back to being horizontal again. I breathed out a sigh of relief and puffed away just as a new episode of the Australian soap started.

Chapter 22

""Feeling better, Craig?" Sheila asked.

We were both standing in the corridor and I had just arrived in the office for the morning.

"Yeah, I feel much better. I had a few painkillers this morning and now I feel as normal as I can be," I said with a polite smile.

"I'm glad to hear it."

Out of nowhere, she opened her arms out and gave me a hug. It caught me off guard, and the warmth of it damn near melted right through my defences. I thought I was about to burst out into tears, but I held it all back.

"So, how's Max?" I blurted to get the focus away from me.

"Oh, that pain in the arse. He found a job as a labourer a couple of weeks ago, but then got sacked from it just yesterday. He telephoned me straight after it happened. I was still in the office and I had to finish early to pick him up and take him home!" she chuckled.

"Why was he fired?"

"Because he was a silly arse. Max said he was at the work site changing rooms with the rest of his colleagues. He said everyone's boots were on the floor and it wasn't just his. The boss came in, had a go about the mess and kicked his boots against the wall. So, Max being Max lost his temper and shouted at him. So, I am back to having him laze around the house and eating all my food. He bloody ate a whole cheesecake yesterday before I could even have a slice!"

She burst out laughing and I soon followed as it was nigh-on impossible not to chuckle along with Sheila.

"Anyhow, I've got to get back to set-up a bloody strategy meeting for this teenager who told her teachers that her brother raped her. Take care, Craig," she said before rushing off.

When I reached the office, I saw only Lisa was in.

"Morning, Lisa, how's it going?"

"Morning, Craig. I'm fine, thanks. Are you feeling better?" she murmured back.

"Feeling a lot better. Thanks for asking," I replied as I set up my laptop on my desk.

"Ann still not in?" I asked with feigned interest.

"No, she's called in sick again. So, if we need anything signed off, we need to ask Sheila."

I nodded in reply, sat down, and waiting for the cogs to turn my decrepit computer on. Finally, it pinged into life. I then tried to access my emails, but the mouse cursor turned into the loading icon and stayed like that with no change. Two minutes went by, and nothing loaded. I wondered if it was actually just IT having a good laugh, typing commands to prevent me logging on, and then spying on my reaction with the laptop's webcam. I shook my head, muttered an expletive, force closed my emails, and re-opened the program again. Again, it would just not load or open. I tried turning my computer off and on again, drummed my fingers on the desk as I waited for it to reload but, again, it was the same result.

"Are your emails fucked?" I asked.

"Yeah, I think something is up with the system. Care Logic seems to work though."

I logged onto our system, but the same issues occurred. The computer simply became stuck on the loading screen.

"Well, Care Logic seems to be fucked for me as well," I groaned.

"Yeah, it seems to have just this second frozen for me as well."

"I wonder how many work hours they lose through this system breaking down?" I pondered.

"I asked one of the IT guys this once. He had a look and calculated it as twenty-one working hours for the past year. Quite a lot of lost hours if you apply that to all staff who use it," Lisa explained with an enthusiasm I didn't know she had.

I sighed but then jolted up as I realised this was the perfect opportunity for me to see if I could use Lisa to get into Jacob Smith's father's home. I imagined if I went to the degenerate's home by myself, and without a good reason, he'd just not open the door. This being quite the hurdle, as I needed to get inside to mark his house with the inverted cross. I yawned and stretched my arms before I got up. I headed over to Lisa, pulled a spare chair next to her, and sat down. The rookie social worker turned her head and gave me a polite smile.

"So, how's this job going for you, Lisa? I remember my first year, it was quite the baptism of fire."

"Yeah, it's definitely a baptism of fire for me as well. I think I am coping but, sometimes, I think I am not," she sighed, still looking at her monitor.

"Are you needing any help with any cases or do you think you've got a hang of them all?"

"Well, I've got a hang of them when Care Logic works!" she exclaimed, still not making eye contact.

I waited a couple of seconds to see if she would get more involved in the conversation.

"So, have you got any other court stuff going on?"

"Yeah, I'll be taking a case to the initial court hearing soon. We've just sent off the paperwork yesterday. I am pretty worried about it. Also, Ann said she will come, but she's off sick so I don't know what will happen."

A flicker of a smile shot up and then went down on one side of my face.

"Yeah, the first time at court can be pretty scary. Especially if the case ends up contested, as they might call you to the stand to give evidence." I waited a couple of seconds to let what I had said to seep in. "You know what, if Ann can't go with you, I'm happy to come and help. My cases have simmered down, so it'll be no bother. At your level of experience, you'll need someone with you as support, otherwise, it really won't be fair to you. Also, aren't you not supposed to have any court cases until you're up to a level two social worker?"

The newbie paused for a couple of seconds, then turned her head to look at me and I saw her brow furrow and panic in her eyes.

"Thank you. I'd really appreciate that. Yeah, I asked them about why I was getting court cases, but Ann told me I'd need to learn how to do them at some point so it might as well be now," she sighed.

"That's really unfair. I know it was like that back when I started, but that was wrong. We should protect you lot until you're ready. It's why they put these policies into place, and it's also to prevent people from getting put off by the profession," I gave her a look of sympathy before saying, "Do you want me to speak to anyone about this?"

I knew full well what her answer would be.

"No, no, no! Please, don't. Thank you, but I don't want to make a fuss!" I nodded, she turned back to her monitor, and silence followed. I quickly thought up another topic to get her talking.

"So, are you finding the job is killing your social life? It did mine, still does, but less so than at the beginning."

Lisa turned back but seemed to look just behind me as she spoke.

"Yeah, my boyfriend has been getting really pissed off at me lately. I keep on cancelling plans and coming home late. Also, we haven't had…" she trailed off and her face turned red.

"Haven't had sex for a while? Oh, God, yeah, in the beginning, this job destroyed my sex life as well!"

"Yeah, I find I am just so tired. At first, it was just the weekdays, but now I am finding it's happening on the weekends as well. I just end up wanting to sleep and mope around. He's getting quite upset about it, and I think he's taking it personally," she lamented.

"Don't worry, it'll come back. Once you get used to this job, you'll become less stressed, and you'll be able to get some normalcy back. Only some, though!"

I put my hand on her hand and squeezed a little. Initially, she appeared uncomfortable and it seemed she was about to pull away but she remained still with eyes moon wide, not quite knowing what to do. I waited for the silence to become a little awkward and then got up.

"Yeah, I better go see if there is any other work I can do," I said, and then just as I walked a couple of steps, I did a Columbo, stopped and turned around. "Oh, just one more thing. About Jacob Smith and that assessment you did on his dad. Have you shown it Jacob's dad yet?" I asked, pretending like I didn't know the answer.

"No, not yet, why?"

"I think it'll be good for me to come with you because I am working the case, and I am worried he might cause you trouble. You know how prone to complaining and lying about me he was, so as the report isn't in his favour, he might do the same to you."

The shy rookie turned her head away from me and I could tell she'd prefer to do it herself.

"Okay, but he might not want to see me if you're with me."

"We won't tell him I am coming. I'll just turn up with you. It'll make it easier like that. Trust me."

"Um, okay…I guess. I am meeting him tomorrow at four o'clock. Do you—" she said before I interrupted.

"Good, good. I'll see you at his house a few minutes before," I announced before turning around and heading to my desk.

I was happy to see my emails back up and running. A part of me questioned why I was doing any work at all as it appeared my main job was now working for Mr Satan himself, but I then realised I still needed to be a social worker as I didn't know many potential marks outside of work that were as prolific in their spreading of suffering as the parents I worked with.

Based on the emails I read, nothing major had occurred during my day off. There were some emails I needed to reply to as soon as possible, some emails I could reply to within the next couple of days, and some emails I could, and would, simply ignore. Instead of starting my work right away, I got up and headed to the break room to make a cup of coffee.

I spent the rest of the day completing reports that were essentially duplicates of other reports and case notes—a big chunk of social work was regurgitating and duplicating information—which I should have done weeks prior. But following Zee meant I wasn't so immersed in the

266

bullshit that they forced us to do, and because of that, I more and more didn't want to let myself become drowned by it all again. Report writing for the sake of managerial theatrics that had no relevance to helping people, *fuck that*. When it was late afternoon, an alert popped up onto my computer and I realised I had a home visit that I needed to do.

The visit was to see Dave—the first person I had marked for Zee—and his family. Since the day we changed the father, he had made significant progress with his family and the work needed to show that he was a benefit to his kids. The troubled dad was doing so well that the council allowed him to have regular and supervised contact with the family again.

I had another cup of coffee before I set off. As soon as I arrived outside the red-brick terraced family-home, the weather turned for the worse, and heavy rain fell from the skies. I sighed just before I opened the door and hurried through the rain as it soaked into the parts of my shirt that my quilted jacket didn't cover. I futilely tried to cover my hair from the rain with my rucksack.

I knocked at the door and it was ten seconds later that it opened. A portly, short lady with her blonde hair scrunched back into a ponytail so tight it pulled her face back like a face-lift answered the door. She wore a plain grey tank top and black sweatpants. I immediately recognised her as Dave's partner, Melissa.

"Come in, Craig," she said gruffly.

I was quick to enter and gave her a polite smile.

"Thank you. It's absolutely awful out there! So, how have you and Dave been?".

"I'll tell you about it in the kitchen," she sighed.

We walked through the hallway and into the living room, where I saw Brandon and Reese on their Xbox together.

"Hi, Brandon. Hi, Reese," I greeted.

The best I got was grunts of acknowledgements back. I thought I'd listen to what Melissa had to say first before I annoyed them by trying to see if I could interrupt their gaming.

We went into the kitchen and sat down at a dining table. I regretted putting my forearms to rest on the table as I immediately felt it was sticky—with what, I did not know.

"Me and Dave are no longer together."

"What?! You guys were doing so well. I thought things had got better since he made all those changes a month ago?!"

"Yeah, we were. I thought the way he changed at first was good, as it was quite sweet. The effort he was putting in with the family, but he soon just became so damn needy. Like he kept on crying loads and wanted me to hug him all the time. It was like dealing with another one of them." She nodded her head in the direction of the children. "I mean, don't get me wrong, there's nothing wrong with being open like that, but it was every fucking... Oops, sorry about the language. It was every day, and it was always about how he used to be such a bad person and how he had hurt us so much. That was nice at first, as he was a proper shit, but it just wouldn't stop. On and on he'd whine," she ranted, barely taking a breath.

"So, what happened next?"

"Well, he then became religious. Nothing wrong with that, but he wanted to push it onto me and the kids. Like constantly trying to push it onto us. He got us to go to church once, and that was a total disaster. Can you imagine those two in a quiet church filled with old people! He then felt the kids' Xbox was the Devil's work and tried to confiscate it. The shit for brains couldn't figure out why them two went loony after that. They became absolutely awful!" She paused, got up, went over to the fridge, and pulled out a supermarket brand can of cola. "Want a drink?"

I shook my head as she opened her drink. Melissa went back to sit down.

"Eventually, I just couldn't take it, so I ended it with him last week. He wouldn't stop crying when I did. He really was not the man I fell in love with. I'll let him see the kids on weekends and whatnot, but that's it. Well, after he comes out of the hospital," she explained.

"The man he was before was one that hit you all the time!" I cried, but then like a dropped potted plant, my face became a jumbled mess. "Hospital? What?"

"Yeah, he's been drinking heavily as well, and the men in white sectioned him. They've shoved him into that unit near Senford police station. I guess he didn't handle the breakup so well, and I think being mental runs in his family. His mother was sectioned and took her own life. Apparently, before they took him, he smashed up his dad's home, punched the old man's lights out, then took an overdose of paracetamol with two litres of vodka. Not only that, he was screaming about demons invading his life the whole time. I suppose it was a good thing I got rid of him," Melissa shared, unable to hold back a chuckle.

I raised my eyebrows in surprise. My thoughts went to *why the hell did the police not update me about this?!* I didn't want my mind to go off on a tangent so I had to drag my focus back to Melissa.

"So, how have the kids taken it?"

"I think they've been all right. They have said nothing, they're just happy to get their Xbox back. They're always playing on the damn thing and haven't said a word about Dave since I broke up with him," I sighed.

So much for saving the family.

"How long are they playing on it a day?"

"Oh, I only let them play on it five hours a day on school nights," she said, and then shifted herself in her seat.

"You know five hours a day is a lot and it isn't healthy for them. They need to be doing exercise, socialising, and using their brain for something more healthy," I groaned.

It went further downhill from that point. She simply couldn't see the downsides of Brandon and Reese being on the Xbox all the time. I imagine she preferred them playing on it as it gave her peace and quiet. When I attempted to interrupt their gaming to speak to them, I got some choice swear words back, and Melissa just shrugged her shoulders when they called me a "four-eyed cunt." I imagine their mum wanted to agree.

I tried to engage them about their father and how they were feeling. This time they degenerated to grunts. Melissa was of no use and barely tried to intervene to get them to stop with their gaming when I asked for her help. All I got was a pathetic "Come on, you two. Craig wants to talk to you both." It became clear I was going to have to do a lot more work with the family.

I left the house feeling somewhat dejected, and it was a confirmation of Zee's philosophy. Simply getting rid of people's inner-demons didn't work as they'd just eventually become corrupted again. I had a little think, but I couldn't come up with any good reason why Dave's family needed him. He was probably back on the path of decline, and it wouldn't be long before he was terrorising his family again.

I looked at my watch and saw it was a quarter to five. There wasn't much point in me heading back to the office as I'd get there after five, so I drove back home, fantasising about what was going to happen with Jacob Smith's dad the following day.

Chapter 23

I had left the office early to get to Mr Smith's home. It was uncharacteristic of me to arrive at such a time where I was the one who waited.

His home was on a generic modern estate filled with new build homes where the builders had tried to squeeze in as many as possible onto the land. There were no front gardens, as the construction company had turned the scant room at the front into driveways. This meant finding somewhere to park that wasn't blocking someone's car was quite difficult. I ended up parked near a corner of a road that led into a nearby cul-de-sac out of view of James' house— I didn't want him to see me until I was at the front door.

Whilst waiting in the car, I tried to smell myself again to see if I still stunk of sex. Last night, I had spent the evening on my mobile phone looking for a bit of fun. I was successful in my online hunt and I found someone who had just finished their night out at a student club.

It was a couple of rounds of fun, and then I went home to smoke one of Zee's joints and sleep. Unfortunately, I forgot to set my alarm clock, so I woke up late and didn't have enough time to clean up and make myself more presentable.

A ping made me look at my phone and I saw I already had a message from my casual fling. I immediately blocked him and went about perusing who might be available later.

After a few messages sent to potential encounters, I noticed the time. I was about to rush out of my car but had to wait a couple of minutes as I realised I had got myself noticeably aroused. I forced myself to think about Margaret Thatcher with her cabinet at a nudist beach playing badminton. It was an imager I'd used many other times before when I needed to rid such feelings from me.

It was half-a-minute later that the Iron Lady and her crew had completely deflated me. I quickly opened the car door and I hurried down the road. I spotted Lisa—in a mint green, tiny toy-looking car—parked near Mr Smith's house.

As soon as I got close to her, she opened the door and got out.

"Sorry, I'm a bit late, Lisa," I blurted before she could say anything.

Lisa gave me a polite smile and nodded.

"Come on," I stated without slowing down and headed straight to the front door.

The house itself was a three-bedroom detached and that degenerate prick lived in it by himself. It used to be where his ex-partner and his other son, Harry, lived. As he never married Harry's mother, and there were no legal agreements, Mr Smith easily booted Harry and his mother out. Lisa hurried after me and was about to say something but stopped herself when I knocked on the door loud and clear.

"Coming," I heard a gruff voice shout from inside.

The door swung open and there stood a tall, middle-aged, square-jawed, and stocky man with a protruding belly in a floral-patterned shirt and jeans. The shirt was too tight and could not stop his belly from trying to peek out through the buttoned seams. His hair was blond, spiked with gel, and was on top of a head that was home to a cherubic face.

"What the hell is he doing here?" James growled to Lisa.

"Um, it's because—"

"Why in the hell would you come here with him? Don't you know how much he has harmed me! It must be all over your case records what this man has done to me!"

"James, if you—" I said before I was quickly interrupted.

"Why is he even talking to me? I refuse, absolutely refuse, to communicate with that man, Lisa," he snapped, still not looking at me at all.

"James, please, let—" again, he interrupted me.

"This person has had it in for me since the very beginning. He is corrupt and doesn't believe in the rule of law. This so-called social worker believes people are guilty until proven innocent. He does not realise this is not communist China, this is England, a nation of free people ruled by law!"

"I'm so sorry, James," Lisa stammered.

"Good, that's a start. You can come in, but he cannot!"

"Um. Sorry, Craig, but I don't think he's going to let you in," she whispered to me.

My neck went hot and my skin went prickly as I felt sweat wriggle out of my pores.

"James—" I tried to say more but, again, he would not let me finish.

"Lisa, you can come in now without that man or you can go!"

Lisa nodded, moved past me, mouthed, "*I'm sorry,*" and went inside. The door slammed shut behind her.

"I need to use the toilet!" I cried at the shut door.

There was no response. They left me feeling frustrated and humiliated. Suddenly, the thought of disappointing Zee helped me push down my feelings of professional embarrassment. In my desperation, I thought of going around to the back of the house to see if there was an open window so I could draw the inverted cross on the inside window ledge. However, I stumbled at the first hurdle as I came across a locked back gate that was just about taller than me.

Initially, I tried to see if I could unlock the tall gate from behind, but there were no sizeable gaps for me to squeeze my hand through, and the lock wasn't high enough for me to reach over and use. So, I took a deep breath and tried to climb it. At first, I tried pulling myself up, but I found I was far too weak to manage more than a few centimetres off the ground. I tried a couple more times, none of which were an improvement over my initial attempt.

I then tried using my feet on the gate or wall to vault myself over but found them both too slippery and one such attempt at doing this caused me to slip and bang into the gate face-first.

"For fuck's sake!"

I had to take a minute break after that as the pain really smarted and caused my eyes to tear up. After a couple more swear words, I gave jumping and pushing myself up a try, but found I wasn't even close to getting high enough for this to work. By the time I had given up, I was gasping for air.

Frustrated and angry, I stomped back to the front door and banged on it with a clenched fist. No reply came, so I banged on it again.

"It better not be that prick," I heard Mr Smith growl from behind the door.

The door swung open and he stood there red-faced.

"I told you to bugger off. This is my property and you are trespassing on it," he snapped before slamming the door in my face.

I banged on it again and kept doing it until he eventually came back.

"If you do not go away, I am calling the police, and I will make another complaint against you!"

"I need to make sure Lisa is okay," I blurted, not knowing what else I could say.

James took a couple of deep breaths before shouting for Lisa. He moved to the side and I saw her standing in the hallway.

"I'm fine, Craig. Seriously, don't worry about me. I'll see you in a bit," she yelled.

"Okay," I shouted back before I turned to speak to James. "Um…can I use your toilet before I go?"

James shook his head and slammed the door shut.

"Bell end," I muttered.

I realised I needed to think up a plan and if I waited any longer outside his home, he might actually call the police on me. The degenerate prick would look for any excuse to cause me grief as he felt I was to blame for his family being broken up, not him. I headed back to my car and when I reached it, I took my keys out of my pocket and dropped them onto the floor.

"FUCK!" I roared into the sky.

I picked them up, opened the passenger side, reached over, unlocked the driver's side, got out, and then got in through the driver's side. I slammed the door shut and closed my eyes. There had to be some way to manipulate James into letting me in, but nothing believable came to mind. I thought about offering sex, but I was probably much too old for someone like him and possibly the wrong gender.

I let out a cry of frustration and banged my head back into the headrest many times until I started feeling dizzy. I tried a different tactic for my deliberation and thought about what Zee would do in this situation. The obvious answer to that was to get stoned, and that really wouldn't accomplish much at all. Rather than give up, I thought, *what would Lily do?* That was thankfully obvious, and after a minute of thinking about it, I realised that was probably the only possible way I could get inside. I sighed and decided to try the new strategy after Lisa had left and when it was dark so there was less chance of a nosey neighbour being a witness.

Lisa took quite some time but, eventually, I saw in my rear-view mirror that she drove off just as daylight dimmed. I took the black crayon with me as I leapt out of the car, slammed my car door shut, and stomped to enemy's house. Moments later, I was knocking lightly on the door. I heard footsteps and the door swung open. Before the human-shaped-slime could say a single word, I pushed him aside and barged my way in.

"OI!" he shouted.

I was just about able to shut the door behind me just as he regained his balance. I took the crayon out of my pocket but was only just about able to scribble one line before he slammed me so hard onto the laminate floor it squeezed the air out of me.

"WHAT FUCK ARE YOU DOING?!" James roared.

I gulped a couple of breaths and scrambled down the hallway to buy me some time to draw a cross on the wall, but felt my leg being grabbed, and James wrenched me down to him. As I twisted to get away, I felt his heavy frame move down onto me. It was only a couple of seconds later that he pinned me the ground as his heavy mass sat on me.

"Now, you're breaking into my home!" he bellowed just before a giant club of a fist headed straight into my nose.

My head rocketed back into the flooring. Just when my head stopped swirling from the first blow, I felt another punch on the left-hand side of my jaw. I let out a groan and then choked as my mouth filled with what I soon realised to be blood. I coughed and spluttered, causing the red liquid to go all over my face. As more punches rained down onto my head, I could somehow process the thought through the haze of what I needed to do. I spat out blood again and this time felt a tooth go with the liquid.

"Please, stop. Please," I moaned.

"Why would I do that when I'm having so much fun?!" he hissed in my ear.

"I'll do anything you want, and I mean anything," I cried, hoping he would stay near my ear and not notice my outstretched arm with a black crayon in it.

"You have nothing I want. You're *much* too old for me," he mocked just as I finished drawing what I hoped was an inverted crucifix on his hallway skirting board.

I felt James get up off me, but I was much too dazed to recognise him in all the swirling water-colours my vision provided. Suddenly, I felt a sharp hit in the side of my ribs, then the air rushed right out of my lungs and I couldn't breathe. Straight after, I gasped for oxygen but, instead, choked on my blood.

"Yes, officer, he broke into my home, attacked me, so I had to defend myself...does that sound believable enough?" he taunted.

As I retched and gasped, I felt another hit go into my abdomen. By this point, I was convinced I was going to pass out and could barely process what was happening. I wanted to scramble away, but my body simply didn't have the strength to. I thought the next blow was going to send me into unconsciousness or kill me but, instead, I heard the noise of what sounded like a tree branch snapping, and then a scream of pain.

"My fucking arm! You cunt! Look what you—" another snapping sound interrupted James.

More screams erupted, and that was when my brain realised I was no longer getting the shit kicked out of me. I crawled to the side of the hallway and propped myself up. Although it was dark, I could make out a couple of blurry figures standing in the living room.

One was short and feminine and the other seemed to have the outline of a large and overweight man. The shorter one had the middle of the taller one's forearm in its grip. It was peculiar because the top of the forearm and hand appeared to be dangling as if only a piece of cloth held it together.

"I dislike those that are so pathetic and weak that they prey on children!" I heard a familiar voice growl.

I saw a swift movement come from the smaller figure's leg and I heard another tree branch *snapping* sound. Again, I heard the cry of pain, and I saw the larger figure fall to the floor.

I still could not quite understand what was going on, and I couldn't connect what I was seeing and hearing together.

"Your other leg is feeling left out! We can't have that, can we?" the familiar voice chuckled before I heard another crack.

Wails and blubbering followed. It was not long after this that my brain and mind soon returned to their battered homes and I recognised that the smaller figure was Lily.

I was just about able to push myself up off the floor with shaking arms. Just as I got up, I almost fell back down as standing brought vertigo that caused me to lose my balance. I propped myself against the wall to stabilise.

Suddenly, I retched and coughed out blood all onto the front of my shirt. . I groaned and wiped my mouth with my forearm and hobbled to the entryway of the living room and leaned against the door frame. I saw snapped bones protruding out of James' forearms and shins, blood seeping out the wounds. Jacob's father wept and begged for his life.

I turned my head as I saw a little spark of orange in the dark room's corner and immediately recognised Zee lighting up a joint.

"Well done, Craig, my man. Again, a damn excellent choice. Happy to see you were so willing to put yourself on the line for the cause as well," my master enthused, and then softly applauded me.

I gave him a polite smile and, straight after, felt blood trickling out the corner of my mouth. I turned to the side and spat on the floor.

"You!" Lily barked after she swung to face me. "Do you want to have some fun before I eat him?"

I shook my head and watched James' distorted face flinch at the words.

"Please, Craig, please, save me. I'll do anything! I'll pay you all the money I have!" he begged when he saw me.

I turned away from his pitiful gaze. A part of me still felt guilty about what was about to happen. Zee must have sensed this as he intervened.

"Craig, you only know about the child pornography on his computer. Why don't you ask him what else he has done with children? Ask him what he did to his son, Harry," he drawled before he took a couple of drags.

I swung my head back to the injured man and hobbled to the father.

"What the fuck did you do to Harry?" I snapped, grabbing his shirt collar and shaking him.

"NO! NO! I did nothing. I'd never touch any kid. I'm not a sick pervert like that. I'll do anything, Craig, anything!" he cried.

At that moment I remembered what he said to me when he was pummelling my head. I got down as close as I could to the wretched vermin.

"Sorry, mate. You're *much* too old for me," I hissed at him before I stood back up. "Those were your words to me when you were smashing my face in. You're an absolute fucking scumbag, James. Harry and Jacob are going to be a lot better off with you gone and out of their lives."

I then turned to a sneering Lily.

"I hope he tastes nice," I said.

The demon then turned to Zee and he nodded to her. She grabbed the insides of her cheeks and somehow stretched the skin of her mouth enough so she could pull it back over her head like a hood until she revealed her true self. James screamed in absolute terror as soon as he saw what she was.

"I'm going to start from your feet and move up from there. The more pain there is and the more terrified you are, the more adrenaline it produces, and this will help give you quite the nice flavour," a bass-heavy voice giggled.

Her opened, revealing the myriad of writhing, tentacle-like tongues. As disgusting as the sight should have been for me, I only felt a stillness within. James screamed and screamed until Lily had reached just past his crotch. Straight after that point, he fainted or perhaps died, I could not tell.

It was a messy feast for the demon and she did indeed go at it like a lion feasting on a zebra, but she somehow consumed every single drop of blood and every little part of the pervert. When she was finished, she put Ann's skin back in place and was back to the stunner in a little black dress.

"NO! NO! NO!" she yelped.

"What's up, Lily?" Zee asked.

"I've ripped my dress!" she whined as she felt the split near her back.

I raised my eyebrows and rather than try to further process the horror that had just happened before me, I hobbled over to the unholy stoner, grabbed the joint out of his hand, and took a few deep drags.

"Zee, I'm a bit fucked. I don't know how I am going to drive back home," I sighed just after I let out a puff of smoke.

"Don't worry about it, man. Lily, you take Zee's car. We're going to head back through the shadows."

"I have to use that junk! Fine!" Lily snapped as she went to me and yanked my keys out of my pocket.

"Come on, Craig. She'll clean up any evidence. Follow me."

My master pushed himself up off the sofa and then headed to the large wide-screen television. I was perplexed as I didn't know why he wanted me to follow. As he reached the TV, I saw he wasn't walking to the device but the shadow behind it. The stoned Devil ducked his head so his entire body was in the darkness and disappeared into it. It did not flabbergast me as I had become inured to such oddity. However, I needed prodding to follow, and Lily did so by shoving me into the shadow.

"Hurry, so you don't lose him," she ordered.

I went with the momentum of the push and bent down into the darkness. As soon as I was in, I felt the oxygen ripped out of my lungs. I immediately panicked as I couldn't breathe. Also, the feeling of floating and it being pitch-black all around me didn't help with my nerves. I was about to turn back around when I felt a hand grab onto my arm and tug me in its direction.

"It's a weird one but you don't need to breathe to survive here. The only issue is your body panicking when it realises there is no air, so try not to breathe, and you'll be fine. Just ignore the fear and it will naturally die down as your body realises you are not coming to harm."

It was difficult to follow his advice. I tried and soon found I was perfectly fine, even though I was not breathing. But then moments later my mind would wander, I'd forget I didn't need to breathe, and then my body would panic as it would try to gasp for air again.

This process of me panicking and then my attempts to calm down took place many times before I saw a faint light ahead in the shape of a crooked parallelogram. It was bright enough to illuminate some of my unholy chief as he pulled me along. As we got closer, something about what I saw through the hole seemed familiar. I saw Zee clearly now as we arrived right next to the opening.

"You first. It's a bit disorientating but once you put your arms through, you have to pull yourself up. I'll push you from behind so you're able to get out," he said.

I obeyed, stuck my hands through the hole, gripped onto what felt like hard flooring, and pulled. With Zee helping, it was easy work. I came out and rolled onto the floor. Straight after, I gasped for the oxygen that was surrounded me, and it felt like a wonderful feeling being able to breathe again. It took a fair few joyful breaths before I realised I was in my living room and next to the shadow my sofa made. I laid there and closed my eyes momentarily.

"Come on, it won't be good to fall asleep on the floor."

He grabbed my hand and pulled me up onto my feet. My master then sauntered to the armchair, fell onto it, and switched the television on. I hobbled to the sofa, collapsed, and laid on my back. When I turned to look at him, he was already rolling a joint.

"Fancy a smoke?" he asked.

"Yeah, sure," I croaked.

I closed my eyes just to rest them.

"Zee, I think I love you. I know you don't feel the same, so don't worry...I'm going to do whatever it takes to make your dream true, whatever that might be. I'll follow you, I'll follow you all the way until you bring about a better world," I whispered whilst I waited for him to finish the joint.

Before he could respond, and before I could feel any regret, I fell asleep.

Chapter 24

My eyes cracked open as daylight obnoxiously shone onto my face. I groaned and moved my head as I felt a wetness on my pillow where my face lay. As I turned around to lie on my back, the cold air brushed against my bare arms and caused goose pimples to pop up like thousands of little mole hills. I shivered and grabbed at my duvet to pull it over myself. Just as I did, I remembered what happened the day before.

The feeling of wanting to return to sleep shattered and my eyes shot open. I scrambled up my bed and sat pressed against the headboard. I looked around me and recollected that I had not fallen asleep in my bed. Zee or Lily must have carried me here, and I then felt a smile creep onto my face as I thought it was quite a lovely gesture.

A yawn trundled out and I stretched my arms as high as they would go. I turned to look at the wall mirror and inspected myself. I appeared as I always did, dressed in only my bright, multi-coloured briefs. A moment later, I noticed I shouldn't have appeared this normal as my face was supposed to be littered with bruises and swelling. There wasn't any sign of injury. I moved my tongue around my teeth and felt they were all there. The ones I lost had somehow come back.

After all that had happened, and with it all being so fantastic, I guessed my master had somehow healed me. Next, the memories of what happened to James flooded into my mind like a torrent of water through a broken dam. Zee and Lily had etched every gruesome detail of his demise into my mind but I didn't feel a single bit of remorse.

It was quite unexpected, more so because I felt quite the opposite, as I was chest-puffed-out-proud and giddy. The good guys—that being the Devil, his demon, and his plucky acolyte—had won. He deserved it and the world was a better place. I knew it was only a marginal change, and the world would not hold hands to sing kumbaya any time soon, but it was a start. I put my feet on my bedroom floor and stood up. As soon as I did, it felt as if my gut plummeted, like I was on a roller coaster, and terror gripped my chest hard.

This wasn't all a crazy delusion, right?!

I quickly scrambled around my room, picking up my dirty clothes to find the shirt and jeans I had on the day before in the hope of finding them blood-covered and torn. They weren't anywhere to be found. I was going to run straight out of the room to bang on Zee's door, but my aversion to the cold made me put on a dirty T-shirt and sweatpants first. I swung my door open and hurried to Zee's room but, to my horror, saw that there wasn't even a door there anymore.

"No! No! No! No!" I whined.

I searched around the wall where his door should have been, and there wasn't a single sign that one had ever been there.

"Oh, God! Oh, God! Oh, God!" I cried as I rushed into the living room with my hands gripping my hair, convincing myself that all that had happened was actually a delusion.

"He certainly won't help you," I heard a posh, baritone voice say.

I swung my head in the sound's direction and breathed a sigh of relief as I saw a bored-looking Lily, dressed in a black skater dress, sat on the armchair's armrest and looking at her fingernails. Before I could greet the prettiest carnivorous monster that I've ever known, I noticed that in Zee's place was a man I did not recognise, who sat back into the chair with his legs crossed with the type of feigned politeness that interviewers of job applicants would exude.

A blond-haired man who wore an immaculate three-piece burgundy suit and a black skinny tie sat there. His hair was shaved on the sides and completely slicked back on the top. His chiselled face was gaunt and a well-trimmed goatee rested on it. When I saw his eyes, I knew I should be concerned as they were without pupils; the entirety of them was completely black. I stood there with my mouth agape, not knowing what to do or what to say as I felt a suffocating menace from this man.

"So, this is the man my little brother has taken such a liking to?" he asked.

Lily stayed quiet and continued to assess her nails.

"I just can't think what colour to have them," she pondered out loud.

"Lilith, you will answer me when I speak to you!"

"HA! If your father does not scare me, why do you think you would?! I only will come with you because your little brother has abandoned me and because I am bored," she snapped without taking her gaze from her fingernails.

The stunning man-eater rolled her eyes and stood up.

"I will wait for you outside," she yawned.

"Take care, my pathetic little human, he is not as forgiving as your old master," she warned as she stomped by.

Zee has abandoned Lily?! Does that mean he has abandoned me?! I gulped and stood frozen, not daring to say a word or move. As soon as she left, I felt the air heat around me to the point where my lungs struggled to breathe, and then, suddenly, the room cooled back down.

"Perhaps taking her is not the best of ideas," the stranger said.

He then raised an eyebrow at me.

"Why are you still standing? Come and sit," he ordered and pointed at the sofa.

My body suddenly switched back on and I immediately complied. I sat perched on the edge of the sofa, facing him, wanting to not look into his terrifying eyes but being unable to look away.

"What do you require of me, my lord?" I stammered.

Why the hell did I call him my lord?

"Manners maketh man," he chuckled.

The intruder looked me up and down with obvious disdain, then back to my eyes.

"I don't imagine you have gathered yet, but I am Satan," he drawled.

I blinked and felt my eyes moisten as though on the verge of tears.

"I know my brother has been claiming to be me, but I can assure you that I am the one and only. I had naively hoped that such identity theft was out of idolisation. Instead, it seems it was for manipulation and perhaps to be a nuisance to me. Unfortunately, he has become quite the coward, not just in his behaviour but in his willingness to accept who and what he is," Satan sighed.

I opened my mouth to speak but immediately closed it for fear of what the repercussions might be.

""I must admit that it's not the healthiest sign of familial love when my brother flees as soon as I arrive at his new home. If the silly thing wished to have stayed hidden, he shouldn't have let you into the shadows. Honestly, did he not think I would not notice a living human in such realms?" He snorted and grumbled. "He fled as he knew I would try to put a stop to his self-destruction and send him back to where he belongs."

I stayed silent and stared at his feet as I dared not look up at his eyes.

"Speak and say what is on your mind, so I may understand his new toy and himself somewhat better."

"Thank you, my lord," I whispered.

My mind raced to find what to ask and to make sure it wasn't something that would offend. I would have preferred to have run away and hide, but as that wasn't an option, I knew I'd have to keep him interested in conversation as otherwise, I knew I would not like the consequences.

"Who actually is your little brother then, my lord?"

I could feel Satan staring at me for long, uncomfortable seconds. My skin handed its notice in and tried to crawl off me.

"Have you not figured it out? I forget humans are so primitive."

He waited again, appearing as if he was deep in thought, and then his eyebrows furrowed with sadness.

"I remember when I first met him. He had so much belief in this world and you humans back then. This was when he actually thought your species was redeemable. Allegedly, I tried to tempt him away from such silly notions of righteousness at our first introduction. I simply tried to help rid him of his naivety and help him see what you humans really are and can only ever be. I did this out of love as I knew his naïve belief in humanity would only ever cause him to suffer."

I nodded along as I did not know what else to do.

"Yet, he still went forward with pointlessly sacrificing his life for your species on that dreadful cross in the hope it would bring about a lasting change."

I tried to process what he had just said and I found it all too difficult to believe. What felt like an eternity of silence filled my head and brought me to a state of near catatonia, but then suddenly, my mind was electrified back into life by one raised eyebrow from my guest.

Such an alleged identity made sense when I thought about Zee's kinder side and his desire to want to create a better world, as it never felt right that Beelzebub would act in such a way. But then, he had endorsed and taken part in murder, took copious amounts of drugs, and hung around with demons. Also, as fantastical as all that had happened before was, adding this new discovery on top just seemed almost too much to believe. My head suddenly spun and I thought I was going to faint, but I fought against it as I needed to know more. I gulped.

"My apologies, my lord. Your brother, he seems to have changed a lot compared to what I have read about him. What happened?"

Satan frowned, uncrossed his legs, and leant forward as he looked into my eyes. Suddenly, I became covered in flames. All over, a searing pain erupted, and my blood boiled, causing me to want to scream and flail, but I could not move at all. I felt my skin crisp, my flesh cook, and my eyes melt as the heat tore in and out of me. Even becoming so disfigured, I somehow still had my vision, and saw thousands of little flame-like worms sprout out of me. They threaded back into my flesh to scorch what little remained. Even with my body so decrepit, I still felt the pain of these fire beasts ripping me apart, until, finally, I crumbled into ash.

A second later, the pain had completely disappeared. I felt whole as I did before. My hand shot up to my face and I could see that my flesh had not been burnt, and I looked down at my body to see fire hadn't actually scorched it to dust. I then turned back to look at the monster, far more terrified than before.

"It was you humans being humans, that is what happened," he drawled, and then let out a deep sigh. "My dear little brother, he was such a sweet and sensitive one. He did all that he could to help humanity. Little did he know his undying love and sacrifice would help you apes create a monstrous religion, one that would kill millions, rape millions, torture millions, and mutilate millions, all in his name. It was all this pain and suffering, all of which he felt, all of which you humans said you committed for him, that changed him for the worse."

One tear of blood came out of the unwanted guest's eye and trickled down his still face, which he dabbed with a handkerchief from his front jacket pocket.

"The guilt and betrayal broke him. So, he tried to hide from such hurt with his drugs and became a degenerate in doing so, and now I find out that, in his despair, he wishes to act like his father and I by resorting to murder."

I wanted to look away from the face filled with anger but simply could not. I realised I had to say something to calm his feelings, otherwise, I would become victim to his wrath.

"My lord, your brother's aims are still noble. They are more brutal than they once were, but the aim is still to create a better world, which he believes to be possible. It is the creation of demons and humans infected by them that spread like a disease—"

"Ah, yes, the demons. A scapegoat for why mankind act the way they act. That notion is quite incorrect, as demons are simply a by-product of humans being humans. Homo Sapiens acts the way they act because that is their innate nature. You are designed to cause pain and suffering. Although I must add that such brutality is not unique to your kind, it is commonplace in many other lowly animals." He yawned and stared at me with a raised eyebrow that told me my species did not impress him one bit. "Arguably, since the improvements in technology and increased self-awareness, you apes have managed to direct less violence against each other. However, it is easy to see that such savagery has simply changed direction and is now aimed at the world and its other inhabitants. I tried to help him understand that there is no hope for your kind all those years ago, but he refused to think any less of you."

"But, my lord. I honestly believe we can save—"

"Well, you can't even save yourself and you haven't even attempted to save the one you love the most. So, why would I ever think you to be competent to complete such a grandiose act?!"

My mouth opened but no words came out, and I then winced as I realised who he meant. Satan pushed himself back into his chair and crossed his legs.

"If you believe in what my little brother preaches so much then why did you not pick your mother to be *saved*?"

"I-I-I don't know," was all I could stammer.

"I believe it is because you need her to be the way she is to maintain this pathetic identity you have created. You need her to always be your rapist and for her to always continue to cause you pain. Otherwise, you will have nothing to rally against, no purpose or reason for your sad little life, as ultimately you only help others because you think you are rescuing yourself when you were so powerless. Without her like that, you would become just another beast with an empty existence that degrades itself to its baser instincts." Satan sighed. "Perhaps my brother is like you, perhaps he needs human savagery to create purpose and to march for a better world. But this belief will only bring bitter disappointment and it will only cause him to fall further than he already has."

"Yes, my lord," I said because I did not know what else to say.

Satan drummed his fingers on the armrest.

"I grow weary with such talk. Now, we must move on to the subject of what I do with you. On one hand, you have somehow given him hope in a futile cause that will eventually lead him to despair, so to me, death seems most appropriate."

I gulped, terror gripped my stomach like a stress-ball, and tears filled my eyes.

"Then again, if I dispose of you, I am sure my little brother will find out and become most upset and far more headstrong in following his silly plans."

I implored Satan to go with the second option by giving him a teary smile. He let out a heavy laughter.

"It is decided," he declared and disappeared.

I stayed frozen and held my breath for half-a-minute, expecting I would become engulfed in flames again, but nothing came, so I breathed out a sigh of relief. I looked around my flat and saw that it was empty and I was alone.

"Zee! Zee! He's gone, you can come out," I shouted.

I realised I still called him Zee and then decided I would continue to do so unless he said otherwise. There was far more trust in him than whatever that thing was who had just been in my living room. I hurried over to where his door had once been but there was still no sign of it.

"Zee!" I cried out as I knocked on wall.

I spent the next five minutes calling out for him and knocking, but the silence was my only reply. Eventually, I went back to the sofa and noticed as I went to grab the television remote that my hand shook. I realised I had tears rolling down my face, and I was hyperventilating.

I knew what would cure me of such distress and immediately set about a search for one of his joints. I felt confident he would have left me at least one. Just the thought of smoking the joint calmed me down and I could slowly and precisely search the living room, but no drug was to be found.

I moved into the kitchen and noticed that I was shaking uncontrollably. When I looked in Zee's cupboard, I found it was completely empty. I moved into my bedroom and by this time tears were trickling down my face.

I tore up my room and went through every crevice and every nook but, once more, I did not find any of his joints. It wasn't a completely fruitless search as I rediscovered an old packet of cigarettes that had two sticks still left inside. I quickly tried to light one with hands that would not stop trembling.

Before I was able, I fell to the floor, curled up into a ball on my side, and wailed as a pain deep within cracked open. There was no reasoning or thought about what this was, just a visceral feeling that exploded out to cover every part of my being. At that moment, I thought this hurt was what there only ever was and would be.

I held myself tight as I wept and wept as that was the only thing I could do.

Chapter 25

I sucked in the hot smoke from a joint that looked like a decomposing witch's finger. It was on the verge of breaking apart and spilling its guts but it somehow had the determination to hold itself together. I kept the cannabis fumes in my lungs for as long as I could and then blew out. Rather than relish in the effect it had, I quickly smoked the rest out of desperation.

It certainly wasn't as smooth as Zee's joints, and this sorry attempt at a spliff caused me to cough and splutter to no end, even after I had smoked the entire thing. I sat up on my sofa and, with naïve optimism, went to find an open cider can that wasn't empty on my coffee table. I found no booze, not even dregs.

It had only been a couple of days since Zee had disappeared and my once clean living room had become littered with empty cans of cider, used cigarette butts, odd socks, and an army of empty ice-cream cartons.

Since he left, I'd spent the days following in a drunken state, caught between weeping despair and manic laughter, all of which were instigated by memories of that stoner devil. I didn't realise how infatuated I was with him until it was too late. Out of desperation, I even went back to Ann's house, hoping Lily would be there with him, but I found it a cold, empty, and silent as a mausoleum.

Without him here, my body fluctuated from feeling alone, empty, and scared of all the problems the world would send at me. I descended into a manic hyperactivity that involved a lot of dancing and chanting, begging for his return. I wanted him back, his stoner mannerisms, his grimy hair, the fusty smell he brought, his perfect joints, the purpose he built up inside me, the alluring terror he instilled into me, and most importantly, just his company.

Me being more smashed than a rugby team holidaying in Magaluf, meant time had gone quickly and, suddenly, I was back in the working week. It was natural that I called in sick. Straight after that, I had the bright idea that if I scored some weed then after smoking it all would be right with the world again.

As I no longer knew any dealers, I went on a search at lunchtime and I decided unwisely to approach some tough-looking teenagers who I found hanging around a park bench. Before I even had finished my sentence, I saw one was about to swing for me as I must have looked like such an easy target, but for once social work came to the rescue.

"Hey, nah, man!" a kid with his hood up ordered and put his hand on his friend's clenched fist. "I know him. It's Craig, innit?"

I was much too drunk to recognise the talking blur. All I did in response was frown and sway.

"Anyway, this guy, he helped my sister get away from that rat fuck Billy Burgin. Remember him?" A couple nodded. "He helped sort out a house for her and all that. Swear down, she was close to topping herself, but this man proper helped her out," he exclaimed and put his hand on my shoulder.

Even with him being so close to me, I still hadn't a clue who he was and who he was talking about. The teenager turned to me and he grabbed my hand. I felt a little plastic bag placed in my palm.

"I know you helped my sis and all that, but business is business, so twenty quid that," he said with his face turned away.

"Thank you," I slurred before paying him.

It wasn't long after I finished that first joint that I realised the drug would not help with my woes. Instead, it made me feel a hell of a lot worse. It bashed me across the head with an intense dizziness and my limbs became filled with lead. I fell onto my side on the sofa and felt a nausea that gripped and yanked at my stomach. It wasn't long later that I puked—all down the side of the sofa and onto the floor.

Only the cider I had just consumed came out, as there was nothing else inside me. Some of the vomit seeped back onto me and into my hair, but I was much too disorientated to care. I groaned and focused on the noise in hope it would distract me from this rollercoaster ride for my stomach. Eventually, after however long it was, I passed out.

I awoke to loud knocks at my front door. My eyes opened to a room darkened by dusk. I peeled my face off the wet leather on the sofa and the smell of bile mixed with regurgitated cider immediately hit me. I pushed myself up to get away from the fumes, and then instinctively reached over for a can but found it was empty. Moments later, I had checked all the cans on the coffee table and became dismayed as there was no booze left.

"For fuck's sake," I grumbled.

More heavy knocks came from the front door, each bang causing my head to pulsate and my ears ring.

"Come on, Craig. Open the door!" I heard Emma shout.

It took me a couple of seconds to figure out what was happening. I suddenly remembered that last week we had agreed I'd cook her a meal today. I leapt to my feet and almost fell over when I realised how jelly-like my legs were. Then my brain tried to defy gravity and attempted to carry on floating upwards. I felt a heave coming but I forced it back down.

"Coming," I slurred.

The dried, sticky cider on the floor tried to glue my feet down like cinema-flooring as I stumbled across to the kitchen. I tried to put my face under the tap but ended up banging the top of my head against it instead. A couple of choice expletives later, I tried again, was successful, and then switched on the cold water. It helped jolt a bit of life into me and I scrubbed the vomit from my hair and face.

I stumbled over to the front door, forgetting I was still just in my underwear, and swung the door open. There was Emma with a beaming smile so warm it would easily melt butter. When she saw me, her face quickly changed and became furrowed with worry and concern.

"I'd give you a hug but I'm a bit wet and I think covered in sick," I chuckled.

"What the hell happened? You look awful, Craig!"

I moved to the side so she could come in.

"It bloody stinks in here!" she exclaimed as she stormed in.

I groaned as I knew the criticism would not stop there. I let go of the door and it swung shut.

"Your shoes, Emma," I mumbled.

"HA! Not with your flat being this grim," she baulked as her shoes made Velcro noises on the sticky floor.

She hurried into the living room.

"Craig! It's as bad as Tommy's!" she teased.

That last comment stung a little as Tommy's flat was the drug-den we frequented when we were teenagers. I stumbled along the corridor and into the living room to see she had already started to tidy the flat up. She hadn't yet taken her dark green quilted jacket off or her scarf.

"We can talk after. Come and help," she ordered.

I stared at Emma for a few seconds. She had so much energy, none of which I wished to have. However, I knew there was no way to avoid her, and the path of least resistance was to comply. I let out a heavy sigh and went to the kitchen to find bin bags. With her enthusiasm, we had the living room, kitchen, and bathroom spotless within the hour. She dared not go into my bedroom and that was probably a good thing.

"Um, want a brew and...pizza? It's all I have," I asked with a sheepish gaze averted from hers.

"Better than nothing. Aren't you going to go get changed?"

I turned red as I realised I was still in my briefs. I quickly scurried off and slipped into a pair of jeans and the cleanest T-shirt I could find. By the time I came back, I saw Emma was in the kitchen and she had already put the pizza in the oven. She also had the kettle switched on.

"Sit, sit, sit!" I scolded as I slapped her hand, which was on the cupboard handle as she looked for the tea and coffee.

Emma raised an eyebrow but a second later did as she was told. I made her a cup of tea, strong with no sugar, and a coffee with three sugars for me. As I was doing so, I noticed my friend's visit had completely switched my focus and I had briefly forgotten about Zee, his weed, and the brutality that came with him. Annoyingly, this realisation brought all that pain back. I forced myself to focus on my guest and I got the drink across to her with minimal spillage. She was sitting in the armchair, so I sat on the sofa.

"So, Craig, are you going to tell me what's wrong?" she asked with her gaze fixed on me as she sipped her tea.

I let out a deep sigh and tried to decide on how much I'd reveal to her.

"It's a guy," I groaned.

"I thought as much. You could never handle rejection, which was why you were never with someone for long."

Cunt. I gave her a scowl, so she knew where the line was and not to cross it.

"He was different. I thought we were just starting to gel, and then he disappears. I think it's because of his fucking family. They're so controlling and seem to be more fucked-up than mine!" I sulked.

"Your family would be hard to top. Was it this Zee guy?"

I turned away and tried to remember what I had told her about him.

"I thought as much. As when you told me he was your flatmate, I swore you only had a one bed flat and became a bit confused. So, you guys were sleeping and living together but not quite at the level where you were boyfriends?" Emma said and took another sip of tea.

I nodded.

"You know how it is with me. Regular sex first before I can decide if they're boyfriend material," I chuckled nervously and averted my gaze from hers.

"Well, it sounds like he had you hooked. I am guessing he didn't feel the same about you?"

I put both my hands up to my neck and grabbed it before speaking.

"Yeah, I supposed that's a good way to describe it." I took a deep breath in and exhaled. "I thought I was going crazy when I was with him and we did a lot of weird things together." My friend gave me a look that said she didn't want to know what kind of weird these things were. "You know, being around him gave me this feeling of having a purpose in life again, like

I was heading somewhere good and…and he had the best fucking weed!"

I paused and felt my eyes moisten. I swallowed and tried to force the sadness and longing down.

"But now, without him, I don't feel like I can cope with what the world throws at me, and it sounds so pathetic, but I feel like I am lost again. Everything in my life just seems so irrelevant and…and I miss him so much," I croaked.

Emma immediately got up, sat next to me, and gave me a cuddle.

"I even miss his stupid fucking friends. One of them is this mega bitch who can destroy anyone that pisses her off, but she's quite the character," I laughed through my tears.

I put my head on my friend's lap. It had been there many a time when I was upset. I remembered the one time my head had been right in that lap, a time when we had taken way too many drugs, an experience which we had never talked about due to complete embarrassment. Once that memory came into view, I pushed myself back up, gave her a cuddle, and sat back.

"Why do you think it went so differently for you and me?" I asked.

Emma's eyes went wide in surprise.

"What do you mean?" she stammered without her usual confidence.

"I know this will sound like I am jealous. Well, it will, because I actually am," I explained with a polite smile.

"Go on."

"Well, your life is so fucking perfect! You have Miguel, you have an amazingly cute kid, and a job where you're going somewhere! Whilst I am a fucking shambles, alone, still getting smashed all the time, and when I feel like I am picking myself up something comes along and kicks me back down," I ranted.

"Honey, raising a child isn't easy and I've had to work hard to get to where I am. Also, I've had to work hard with Miguel to make sure we stay in each other's good books. It isn't easy and I definitely wouldn't say it's perfect," she explained in a manner that felt patronising.

"I'm not saying it's easy for you, Emma, but your life is still pretty damn fucking good! Look at the car you drive compared to mine! I know I worked just as hard, or maybe even harder than you." *Definitely harder,* I thought. "But we've got such incredibly different lives. We both went through fucked-up upbringings, we both had the same fucking social worker, and we both went to the same university! We both fucked God knows how many people and we both took God knows how many drugs. Yet, our lives seem so different now. It has become so different that we rarely even see or even talk to each other anymore."

I felt my eyes moisten and realised I wasn't actually jealous of her having all she had, but I was jealous of the time she spent with others over me.

"What's happened to me, Emma?! Why am I so fucking alone? Everyone keeps leaving me. My parents, my friends, you, and now Zee. What the fuck is wrong with me? Why don't people want to be around me?!" I cried out.

Emma quickly reached over, hugged me, and kissed me on the top of my head.

"I'm always alone, Emma. I feel like if I died in here, no one would know and no one would care. Everyone's left me behind," I blubbered, with tears rolling down my cheeks.

I felt her hug tighter.

"Come on, Craig. I'm here, so you're not alone," she comforted me.

I fell back down onto her lap and wept into it. I do not know how long for, but where my face lay on her jeans became sodden with my tears and mucus. As soon as I turned my head, I saw a tissue being offered. I grabbed it and blew the gunk out of my nose. She gave me another and I did the same again.

"You know, I used to work hard in my job because I cared about helping people, but then it all changed. I don't know when or how, but I worked all those extra hours,   so I didn't have to come back to this empty fucking flat and so I didn't have to realise I had no one. When I would come back, I'd get so fucking drunk by myself to hide from that fact. I don't know how many years it has been like this for me, Emma, I just know it has been for way too long."

I felt the soft, deep, long breaths from her on the back of my head. She stayed silent for a minute as she stroked my head. During that moment, I was with the Emma I had grown up with and she was looking out for me.

"You've been through a lot, Craig. But I didn't know about all this until now. You really need to tell me," she sighed.

"I have told you before," I snapped.

"When?!" Her frown went down so hard it could have crushed rocks, but then her face went back to its warm self. "Never mind. I am sorry if I didn't listen, I really am. You know I really do care for you and always will. I know I have been prioritising Hayley and Miguel. I am sorry, but I really need to. But!" she said and then shook me a bit before giving me a kiss on my head. "It breaks my heart to see you like this, so I will make more time for you and it will be different now, okay?"

She bent over and was just about able to kiss me on my forehead again.

"Okay," I whispered.

"Come on, sit up," she said.

I sat back up again. I saw that her mascara had run a little and I leaned forward and gave her a tight hug.

"Craig, there'll still only be so much time I can spend with you because of my job and Hayley. So, you're going to have to make changes to your life as well. You can't just keep doing what you're doing, as it'll only get worse for you. You're going to have to meet new people and make new friends," she stated with her eyes looking right into mine.

"I do meet people on—"

"Casual flings you find online do not count! You don't even meet them twice!"

"Yeah, you're right. I guess," I grumbled.

"Also, I think some therapy would help. A lot of traumatic stuff has happened to you and finding out the reasons for it will help. Those five years of therapy I had did me a world of wonder, you know that because I told you about it twenty fucking times! You've got to confront your past..." I completely zoned out at that point but nodded to pretend I was still listening.

Confront your past. The thought resonated throughout me and I focused on the notion as Emma carried on talking.

"THE PIZZA!" Emma cried suddenly.

She rushed to the oven, opened it, and giggled hysterically.

"I didn't even switch the bloody thing on!"

I let out a chuckle and went over. I switched on the oven and we both went back to sit down to talk more. As we did, I thought she would have made a good social worker as she wasn't content with just talking; she made me plan out what I needed to do and even set deadlines.

She assured me she would make sure I stuck to what we agreed. Even with all that we revealed, and after I had bared so much to her, I kept my reaction to the message of hers that hit me the hardest hidden as I knew she wouldn't like what I had in mind for it. But I knew it was what I needed to do to move on.

Confront the past. That I will.

Chapter 26

I sat in my car, staring at the house. It was an end-of-terrace three bed home that was in possibly the roughest part of Senford, Grimsmoor. All around the house and down the estate, litter and dog shit covered the pavements. It was as if the council had long since given up on trying to clean the streets up and had decided to just let it fester as the slum it was.

Many of my cases came from this area, and many had to be escalated to the point where we removed the children from the care of their parents. It was also the area I was raised in as a kid.

My mother's house almost looked exactly the same as it always had. The house was red-brick with a red door. The graffiti of a gigantic buxom, bikini-clad babe on the open-wall side of the home was something new. I doubt she'd condoned or provided the design. There weren't any signs of life from within other than the living room light shining through the drawn curtains.

I imagined she was sitting in the living room, watching television, which she probably did all day and all night when she wasn't praying for God to fight off Satan. The imagination of her became so real that it felt as if I was right there next to her as a cheesy game show, she would shout along with, came on.

I tried to remember how long ago it had been since I had stayed there. To my shock, I realised it was around eleven years ago I last visited the house. It was in my last year of university when I had moved back to live with my mother and it didn't take long before she thought I was in cahoots with the Devil again due to my male one male fornication.

This subsequently led to me being kicked out onto the streets. I suddenly burst out into a fit of laughter, as she very well may have been right about Satan and me. She was just wrong about the timing of such influence. I immediately stopped chuckling when the blond-haired man who claimed to be the supreme terror suddenly came into my mind's view. I had to wait for an uncomfortable five minutes for him to disappear from my thoughts as I was much too frightened to move until that happened.

As soon as I felt capable, I quickly opened the car door and stepped into the cold Senford night. Shivers immediately slithered from my spine to my arms and legs. I took three deep breaths before I shut my car door. It took me a couple of seconds before I could make myself walk towards *her* door.

As I approached, I realised I didn't have a clue about what I was going to say or do. I shrugged and told myself planning what to do didn't matter as I couldn't rehearse or practice such an important confrontation. I carefully avoided the dog excrement and rubbish like they were landmines as I moved on. Fortunately, by the time I reached the house, the road had become empty of pedestrians and locals. I thought it a good thing, just in case she chased me out and threw a load of Bibles at my head. When I reached the door, I stood outside, frozen, and without a thought going through my head. Then, suddenly, without wanting it to happen, I moved my arm up and knocked on the chipped, tatty red door. The noise reverberated right through me and I felt it echo within.

My anxiety gripped my chest so hard I thought my heart would stop. I fought through the fear and knocked again. I hit the door harder and for longer this time. Just as I was about to try one more time, I heard the door unlock and it swung open, causing my stomach to plummet.

When the door opened fully, I saw a blonde, middle-aged woman with electric blue eyes standing there. Wrinkled trenches covered her gaunt and long face. Her eyes were sunken with dark circles beneath that were so deep they appeared chiselled in. She was petite, ghostly pale, and she wore a haggard pink dressing gown that was stained and mottled with dirt. Her furry slippers and pyjama bottoms were of a similar colour and stained with dirt.

There stood my mother, Sylvia Jane Mors.

"It's you," she said without a hint of emotion.

"Yes, it is. It has been a while, hasn't it?" I replied in the same flat manner.

"Yes, it has. I suppose." She took a deep breath. "You want to come in?"

"Please."

I noticed all my panic had fled at the sight of her, and my breathing had become slow and calm. Without saying a word, she walked back into the house. I followed, shut the door behind me, and breathed in the smell of damp and fried chips. The former came about as she refused to open windows, and the latter was because she always deep-fat-fried damn near every food she'd eat. I kept my shoes on as I knew she didn't like people wearing them inside the house.

None of the steps I took into the hallway registered and it almost felt as if I floated. The walls of the hallway were still a bright white. I always imagined she chose such a colour as she thought it somehow helped counter the continual Satanic corruption she always saw. Even with me going deeper and deeper into her lair I so despised, the expected flood of emotions still wasn't there, there was simply silence. I followed her to the living room and there on the television was a game show. The room itself was, of course, painted a bright white.

In the mostly empty room, there was only one large reclinable armchair close to the television, a large rug underneath it, and a little table next to it. On the table was an assortment of pill bottles, a bowl of half-eaten soggy chips, and the remote. My mother went to sit down on the armchair and I stood near the television, so I was in her field of vision. She didn't look up at me and remained focused on the game show. I waited and waited, propped against the wall, glaring at her, and it wasn't until the program finished that she spoke.

"You can't stay here, you know," she grumbled.

"I didn't come here for that and I wouldn't want to as I have my own flat. Bought and paid for with money I earned!"

"Earned through the Devil's work you're so good at?" she asked, still without looking at me.

"No, I am a social worker now. What do you mean, anyway?" I asked, even though I knew full well what she meant.

My innards heated and cooked. There was the briefest flash of me throttling the life out of her in my mind, but instead of the aversion and worry that used to come after, I felt such intrusive imagery actually calmed my nerves with feelings of pleasure.

"Well, your cavorting with men for money and drugs," she mocked and laughed.

I let insult run through me.

"Of course, I'm not doing that anymore!" I gulped in breaths of air and then sighed. "You know there are reasons behind why I did such things."

"Yes, there are reasons. One is that Satan corrupted and perverted you long ago," she muttered, but then swung her head to look me in my eyes. "Come to church with me, Craig, and repent! Let the minister cure you of your sin and let him rid you of the dark one's grasp!" she pleaded.

My chin went in, and my eyes went moon-wide with surprise. A second later I guffawed and burst out laughing.

"Yes, laugh. You won't be doing that when you're in Hell and the demons are torturing your soul!" she hissed before turning back to watch the adverts on the television.

"I'm not an agent of Satan." A wry smile crept up onto my face as Zee's image flashed into my head. "I do social work, for Christ's sake!"

"Don't you dare use his name in vain!" she snapped after she swung her head back to face me.

My mother continued her scowl; a look she that hadn't changed since I was a child, and it was a look I felt belonged more on a Halloween witch mask. She turned away when she saw I would not back down from such a glare. I took a couple of deep breaths to help push down the acid in me.

"I'm not here to convince you that there is nothing wrong with being gay. I'm here to talk about what you did to me."

"What?!" she shouted.

"I said, I'm here to talk about what you did to me!"

"I KNOW! I am asking what did I do to you?"

I opened my mouth but no words came out.

"I said, WHAT did I do to you?" she demanded.

"You fucking raped me!"

She quickly averted her gaze from mine and went back to watching the television. I saw her eyes moisten and then her face buckled down with a heavy frown. I noticed my breath quicken and my skin tingled all over. My head felt lighter and lighter as I held my stare on her.

"NO, I DIDN'T! Don't let the Devil make you lie and say such horrible things!" she screamed as she swung her head back and glowered at me.

"WHY THE FUCK DO YOU THINK SOCIAL SERVICES TOOK ME INTO CARE?!" I roared in exasperation whilst flinging my arms outwards. Even though I was hyperventilating, I forced myself to unclench my fists and pry open my gritted teeth. "It's on their records that you admitted to it!"

She had turned back to face the television again. I went behind it and yanked the plug out, so she turned to me again and snarled.

"They took you because you lied to your teachers, and you did this because Satan made you do it! That social worker was a liar, a slut, and a cheat! I'd never do such a thing like that to you. NEVER!" she screamed with tears streaming down her face.

I was dumbfounded and shocked as I did not expect she would completely deny it ever happened. I had never confronted her about that night, even when I momentarily went to live back with her after being in care.

"Don't you dare spread such lies! If my minster heard them, he'd, he'd…Oh, no, he wouldn't believe it. He'd know that it's the Devil's work and not true. He'd know," she ranted to herself as she stared at the blank television. "You must repent, Craig, you must! Save your soul and be a good boy again. Just be a good boy and you will find that God will reward you!"

At that moment, I felt as if I had taken ten steps back so I wasn't me but watching a distant projection. I could see on this screen that my mother was wide-eyed, gripping the armrests tightly with her nails, imploring and begging me to change. I watched me walk away from my raving mother and go into the kitchen.

I saw my hand search through a couple of drawers, eventually find a large kitchen knife, and pull it out. This distant me then turned around and walked casually back to the living room. Then, without even letting my mother turn around to see what was happening, that person stabbed the knife right down into her throat just after she screamed. Blood gushed from the wound and gurgles followed. Her eyes emptied of all the pain that clung to her like a shadow, and for the first time on her face there was peace.

"No, Craig, no," I heard a whisper in my ear.

Suddenly, I blinked, I was no longer watching a projection, and returned to my body. My mother was back in front of me and still ranting at me to repent. I turned my head to look at my hands and saw there was no blood on them. I lifted my head back up and realised she had stopped speaking and looked at me with an intense glare.

"Do you remember all those times I had to patch you up after whoever you were fucking battered you?" I whispered with tears trickling down my face.

Her mouth went to open but she said nothing.

"Each time you would hold me and cry, you did so tight and like I was the most important thing in the world. You'd then fall asleep on me. As much as I hated seeing you so hurt, as much as I blamed myself for not being able to protect you, I weirdly became so grateful for those moments as they were the only time you seemed to want me," I stammered.

Tears rolled down the sides of my mother's face. Her mouth opened again but words still did not come. I felt the heat within me creep up to my throat.

"Do you know what it's like to watch this? Watching your own mother, the one you love the most, beaten to a fucking pulp and then having to mend her every fucking time?! Do you?!" I screamed.

I I glowered at her but she held my gaze and I saw her face crack like dried clay as she winced.

"I do, Craig. I know what that is like," she gasped.

I felt the breath rush out of my lungs and my mind went blank. I turned away from her look and waited until I could think again. She remained silent. I then saw what I saw damn near every day in my job; the transference of hate and suffering that moved down and infected entire bloodlines. The old corrupted the young with this disease and they then passed it on further when they themselves had children.

It was a story repeated through generations of some of the families I worked with; they were too far gone and too far damned. *She will not change,* I said to myself and repeated it in my head over and over again. Just as I finally accepted this, I saw her face distort into a wide-eyed manic grin.

"It was the Devil who sent all those men who were nasty to me. He sent them to test my faith, sent them to harm me because I am a child of God. But when he couldn't get me, he got you instead, Craig. He got you! Please, come to my church with me. God will save you! You can find a nice woman after and then have a child with her, one that Satan can't touch, can't defile!" she ranted.

I tilted my head at the madness spewing from her mouth. It took me a minute but I finally breathed a sigh of relief.

"I'm sorry, I'm so sorry, Mum, but I need to go. I can't stay...I can't ever stay," I sighed.

I went to leave and had to walk by her to do so. As I did, she went to grab my arm, but I moved it out of the way.

"Craig, I need to save you! Please, let me save you!" she cried without getting out of her chair.

I ignored her pleas, left the house, and shut the door behind me. When I got onto the street, I noticed my body felt so light that it was as if I floated. I forgot to look down to avoid the dog shit and rubbish as I made my way back to my car without a perceptible thought in my head. At my car, I realised I wasn't careful in my steps, so I had a quick look at the soles of my shoes and saw I hadn't trod in any.

I went to the passenger side, unlocked it, went in, and opened the driver's side. I went back out and got in the car from the other side. As soon as I did, I let out a heavy sigh and my head fell back against the headrest. I felt a smile creep up my face and, suddenly, I laughed. It started off slow, a chuckle that came deep from my belly, but it quickly sped up, becoming high-pitched as it did until it hurt my ribs.

I stopped and came to my senses when I saw an anxious-looking teenage girl walk by my car. I tried to think of what I had found so funny, but I couldn't figure it out. My thoughts next went onto what I was going to do tomorrow, and that was to write out my notice to quit that council as soon as possible. I stopped at that as I didn't think I was quite ready to think of what I was going to do after, but I felt confident that whatever came, I could handle it.

I put my key in, turned the ignition, and headed back home. I stuck to the speed limit and kept it slow and precise, even though there was minimal traffic. For once, I actually enjoyed the drive as I purposefully felt the shift of the gears, the slow acceleration, and how my body moved as I went around a corner.

When I came to a roundabout with traffic lights, I saw the lights turn yellow, so I put my foot down on the accelerator. I timed it wrong and reached it after it turned red. As I didn't have time to stop, I drove through, but as soon as I entered the roundabout a couple of metres, I heard a loud horn. I thought nothing of it, but then saw a bright light blind my right eye and the noise of crunching metal stabbed into my ears. I then blacked out.

Complete darkness greeted me when I came to. Next, I heard panicked shouts from outside. I tried to figure out what was wrong, but I wasn't able to as I couldn't see anything. I felt a warm liquid pour all over my stomach and legs.

Fuck's sake. What is that and where the hell am I?!

I then thought if I moved, then maybe I could get out of the darkness so I could see what was going on, but my legs and arms stayed still.

Why can't I move? Why the fuck can't I see? I tried to say, but no words came out of my mouth. A second later all within and around me became swallowed by absolute silence.

Chapter 27

The game show volume blared at ear-deafening volume. Craig's mother cared not one bit that day in and day out, her neighbours had to put up with such auditory annoyances. A sneer remained on her face from her son's visit, and any semblance of sorrow had migrated away to somewhere far more hospitable. Expletives about her child and the Devil fled her lips whenever her television distracted mind brought up such recent memories. The brightness of the game show that had started caused an even larger and deeper shadow to form behind Sylvia's chair. Suddenly, two male hands plunged up and out of the thick darkness.

Zee's dishevelled hair popped up first, and then, like a scene out of Apocalypse Now, the rest of him came out of the abyss. He, of course, had his sunglasses on. The messiah opted for a more sensible fashion than usual and wore a black fitted suit, white shirt, and black-tie ensemble. He stood up and stretched his arms up to the ceiling when he got out. His lungs pushed out a sudden cough.

"Who's that?! Is that you, Craig?!" Sylvia cried, swinging her head around, trying to identify the intruder.

Zee walked around, stood in front of the television, and stared down at the frightened woman.

"If you don't go right now, I'll telephone the police!" she shrilled.

The supernatural being lowered his sunglasses so she could look into his eyes, and suddenly she quietened. However, it was not out of reverence but absolute terror.

"Your son, he was a friend of mine," he sighed, "there is an unfortunate emphasis on the *was*. I must confess that I abandoned him out of cowardice, worried that history would repeat a pattern for me. The one where I keep becoming a catalyst for an infinite pain." He choked up but then took several deep breaths to regain his composure. "I never wanted people like you to think it is so easy to be granted redemption. To think that all you need to do is support the right team, say the right words, and my father would forgive you."

"W-w-who are you?" she whispered, staying planted in her seat.

"I'm just someone who is like many others on this blue world, just trying to get through the suffering, hoping it'll eventually end." He coughed to clear his throat. "One thing I must tell you before my gift to you. Sins will not be forgiven because you spout a prayer or because you ask for such absolution. Forgiveness must always be earned. Pain and suffering must always be repaid through the sinner's blood, sweat, and tears." He drawled and then chuckled.

"Basically, words are cheap, and actions are so much louder."

"P-p-please don't hurt me."

"Do not worry, my child. I will not hurt you. I am here to free you," he soothed, bending over and caressing both sides of her face.

Craig's mother closed her eyes and felt a peace she had never felt before, as the words reverberated a sensation of kindness right down into her core. The bliss led to tears of happiness tumbling down the sides of her face. Such a feeling was short-lived as Zee, ignoring the laws of physics, penetrated her skull, reached into her brain with both hands, and grabbed hold of the thick tar that had suffocated her spirit. Screams of agony and pain charged out of Sylvia's mouth, and her eyes exploded to beg for the supernatural being to stop. Minutes of the torturous pain went by, and the elderly woman's cries became whimpers when suddenly the cause of her pain pulled his black slime-covered hands out of her uninjured head.

The terrified woman's eyes became full moons, and she began to spasm as the sludge squeezed out of her eyes, ears, and mouth. It trailed downwards, fell onto the ground, and kept trickling out as if there was no limit to its supply. Zee raised his eyebrows with surprise as he hadn't met someone with so much in them before.

Eventually, the last droplet left its vessel, and Sylvia awakened to her living room being half-filled with the black slime, reaching her knees. Tears flooded out of her eyes as she had never in her life felt so light. The fear, hate, and sadness that encased her heart and lungs in lead had melted away. The intruder no longer appeared to be the bringer of doom but one she had always sought salvation from.

"I knew you would come and save me! I knew that if I prayed long and hard enough, you would bring me redemption, as for I am a child of yours, and I am here to fulfil your every need! Do not worry, for I will bring forth your word and make sure all will hear it!" she exclaimed, still tears of happiness flowing down her face.

"What of your son?" the messiah asked.

"What of him? Oh, yes, my Lord. I seek your forgiveness for his crimes. I will repent for his sins and do what I can to save his soul for you!" she ranted.

He let out a sigh and felt his shoulders become heavy before saying, "that is unnecessary, my child. Now, wait and watch with me."

Confusion etched across her face, but she then nodded obediently. The black slime all around them swirled in together as if a drain existed in front of the television. Sylvia initially looked on in terror but then saw her saviour maintain a face with no anxiety, so she puffed up her chest and prepared herself for whatever would happen next. The nightmarish liquid condensed and compacted into a blob that stood a little over five feet tall. As if invisible hands used the material to sculpt, a human figure eventually formed. The fragile woman's eyes shot wide in fright when the horror completed its shape. Standing in front was her child, younger than he should be but also disfigured to the point he looked like a nightmare.

"Well, I suppose I shouldn't be surprised that is what it has taken shape as. Do you recognise him?" Zee asked.

A naked twelve-year-old Craig with a malevolent face-ripping grin, dripping black slime out of his mouth, stood in front of the television. His eyes were also the same colour as the sinister liquid and leaked the same substance. There were also two other obvious differences between it and the child she once abused. One being his right hand and forearm appeared to be made of an obsidian blade. The other was a large and open gash being in the place of the genitals. The nightmarish sludge leaked from the grim injury and flowed down the sides of his legs, pooling onto the floor.

Craig's mother went to grab at her saviour's arm for comfort, but he stepped out of the way, so she pushed herself back into her chair and hugged her sides.

"It is a demonic vision of my son," she gasped, "when he was twelve."

"Well, do you remember what happened when he was that age?"

At first, she shook her head and then sheepishly looked up at Zee to see his reaction. He had his sunglasses down, and his accusatory gaze connected with hers, communicating across that lying was of no use. She closed her eyes for several long seconds before re-opening them and turning her vision back to the horror in front of her.

"I remember," she stammered and then gasped, "it is my greatest sin."

"There have been a lot for you, but, yeah, I'd say it's up there," Zee replied.

The abuser's eyes then filled with tears of sadness rather than happiness and her face became distorted as she slowly realised the pain she had caused. Zee let out a chuckle whilst shaking his head. His face creased in pain as if wounded but quickly became serene again.

"Listen here, Sylvia. I've done what I needed to do, and after speaking to the likes of you, well, I now need to go sort my head out. I'm probably going to have a spliff or two to help, and I'd prefer not to spark up here as your home isn't my cup of tea. So, before I bounce, what I can say is that you're free from your prison, free to do whatever you wish and choose to do." He snorted. "However, your creation over there, well he's also free to do whatever he chooses to do. So, whatever happens between you two, well, it's just the laws of nature," he ranted quickly and slapped her on her back.

Her contorted face of pain turned into one of confusion.

"Wait, you're leaving me here? What about—" she blurted but saw he had disappeared.

Sylvia pushed herself up to look behind but saw that her saviour had disappeared. The frightened woman turned back around and saw that the twelve-year-old horror remained, his head tilting in curiosity. The demon then opened its mouth to laugh, but no sound came out, only splatters of black slime did in its place. It then took slow and purposeful steps towards its creator, moving like a zombie from a horror film. Craig's mother gasped and whimpered, but she remained glued to her chair because she was too frightened to flee. She did the only thing she could do, pull her legs up and curl up into a ball.

Zee stood outside the house with a joint in his mouth, waiting and listening. The screams of terror soon erupted and cut through the silence of the night. It didn't take long before Sylvia's wails quickly became disfigured and gargled. A part of him wanted the suffering to go on for as long as it could, but another side of him hoped it would end soon. The latter won as the noises of the slaughter soon stopped.

The messiah grabbed a lighter out of his pocket, lit the spliff in his mouth, and took a couple of deep drags.

"Well, now what?" he asked after blowing out smoke.

He shrugged his shoulders, let out a deep stoner laugh, and then sauntered down the road into the Senford night.

Chapter 28

I woke up to the noise of clicking fingers next to my left ear.

"Come on, Craig. That's it, big m-aaa-n, you can wake up now," I heard Zee's voice croak before he coughed and spluttered.

I let out a groan and went to reach down for a duvet, but found there was nothing there. Confusion slowly wriggled its way through my groggy brain. This only got worse as I noticed that although I was lying down, it didn't feel like I was lying down on top of anything at all. There was no feeling of material or pressure from below.

Suddenly, the memory of the crash exploded into view and I shot up. My eyes sprung open and in that instant I tried to gulp in air but found there wasn't any. I panicked and saw that all around me was pitch-black.

"There's no air here for you to breathe, so don't try. Just take your time and let yourself get used to it. You can take however long you want until it's second nature. Remember all that time ago when we went into the shadows?" Zee said.

I do not how long it was and how many times I tried and ended up gasping for air in panic, but it eventually got to where I stopped trying to breathe and my body accepted this.

"Where am I, Zee? Or do I call you Je—" I blurted before he interrupted me.

"No, stick with Zee, I've grown accustomed to the disguise. Also, I know me using this name really pisses my brother and father off," the stoner chuckled.

"Okay. So, what's happening?" I asked, facing the darkness where I thought the Messiah was.

"Yeah, about that, Craig. I hate to break it to you, but you're dead. Well, you died in a car crash. A van hit you right on the driver's side of your tin can car."

"What?! I don't feel dead!"

I heard his deep and rhythmic stoner laugh. It somehow helped pry away the panic that had been digging its claws into my chest.

"Yeah, just so you don't get it twisted and so you understand, this isn't an afterlife. This isn't your soul, as it doesn't exist in the way you humans think it does. Death is just transformation, and since your first transformation…well, I've transformed you back. Momentarily," he drawled.

"What do you mean *momentarily*?" I whimpered.

He cleared his throat.

"You see, the universe wants you to be dead, so it will eventually get its way. Let me explain. Every part of the universe interconnects and it is like this swirling mass of energy and matter that moves together and exists together. Suddenly, this one minor part that is you has changed its direction in this sea and doesn't flow how it should flow. You're like a little current going the wrong way, so you will naturally get corrected. But I've intervened to stop this, but I'm only half-God, so I can only do so much. So, I'm sorry to say, it'll only be a matter of time before I can no longer shield you, and you will be dead once again."

"Oh…"

"We also have to hide in the not so obvious places, so it takes longer for this process to happen," he said and then I felt a hard slap on my back.

"So, what about Emma? My mother?"

"I'm afraid that's all irrelevant, and hate to say it, it has been so long since you first died that they've all moved on. Your mother," he cleared his throat, "well, I've not kept track of her, but last I checked, she was still struggling with her demons. Emma took your death pretty hard at first, but she's now doing pretty well. She's a partner in her firm and her kid Hayley is doing pretty well; she's now studying law in Cambridge. Also, she's had another kid, and it's Craig. Yeah, he's challenging to say the least. He's into the ole' sex, drugs, and rock-n-roll."

I felt tears come to my eyes at the thought that Emma had to feel such pain because of me, but then I pushed my feelings down as I didn't want to spend what little time I had left feeling guilt. I told myself she had moved on and I just knew she was happy with her life. Then the name of her youngest child registered and an ear-to-ear smile leapt onto my face.

"Yeah, m-aaa-n, he eerily looks like you as well. Anyway, I didn't bring you back to talk about them," the holiest of stoners said.

"So, why did you resurrect me then?"

Carnal thoughts suddenly appeared in my mind.

"It definitely isn't because of that," Zee snorted and chuckled. "I guess I just wanted to apologise to you and also to thank you. First off, sorry for leaving you alone like that at your flat. My brother is quite the dick and I am pretty sure with me being there, he would have lost his temper and destroyed you in some horrific way. Also, I'm really not a fighter so I wouldn't have been able to stop him anyway."

"Well, it doesn't seem to have mattered if he did or didn't kill me, as I still died not long after," I laughed, and then stopped as it shocked me that I could after such a morbid comment.

"HUR, HUR, HUR! That is very true, man!" He paused for a couple of seconds. "It wasn't just that. When you told me you loved me and wanted to follow me, it just brought back too much pain from those old days. You know, the hands nailed into wood days. It also reminded me of all those who've said similar things and they only ended up dying or harming others because of me."

A couple of mumbled expletives followed.

"I never wanted people to be hurt, I just wanted people to chill out and be cool with each other. Instead, I got the total opposite. So, yeah, I didn't want that to happen to you."

I raised my eyebrows in surprise, and I felt the urge to tell him that made him climb even higher in my estimations, well not that he could get any higher, with being the son of God and all.

"So, what have you been doing all these years then?" I asked.

"Did a lot of soul searching, *a lot*. I looked you up and found out what happened. After that, I felt pretty guilty, but knowing what you did, and all those old feelings you brought up, well it changed me somehow and since then I've come to accept that what happened has happened, there is nothing I can do about it, and I am now letting myself move on. So, I brought you back alive because I wanted to thank you for that."

He chuckled softly at first but then his stoner laugh got louder and louder until it boomed throughout the entirety of the darkness and almost sounded as if it came from all directions.

"So, yeah, I'm back on the mend because of you. I smoke fewer joints as well. No more wake and bakes, m-aaa-n!"

I felt another hard slap on my back. Suddenly, I burst out into another fit of laughter. This time it felt as if it came from deep within, and it wasn't just about what Zee had said. It was about every grievance I had ever felt, big or small, and how I had wasted so much time pointlessly reacting to these. It was about trying to create a different me with all the drugs I took. It was about the loneliness that had clung on and tried to drag me down ever since I was old enough to feel it.

It was about all the pointless fucks that I chased, all because I was too scared to grasp onto something more. It was about the twisted love I had for my mother and would always have for her. And, most of all, it was about the simple absurdity that being alive actually brought.

Zee's stoner laughter joined in with my chest-wrenching mirth. Somehow, and at some point, we both calmed down and there was silence again.

"It won't be long before you're going to have to die again," my old flatmate sighed.

I shrugged at the darkness, confident he could see me. I knew I couldn't hide from dying, and with divinity chilling next to me, I thought there were worse ways to go.

"Better than dying like this than in that car crash, I suppose."

There was a silence from him and just when I thought that meant my time was up, I heard his stoner laugh.

"You know what, fuck it. There's still time. Do you want to see how much Lily is pissing off my brother? He really doesn't have an idea of what she's capable off and what she's like! Yeah, I've been helping her a bit as well. It's really funny, m-aaa-n!"

I guffawed.

"Yeah, fuck it. Let's do it."

I felt an arm grab mine and pull me up.

"Come on, then. Hold on tight, as if I lose you, it'll be difficult to find you again!" the stoner ordered as he pulled me along by the hand.

I held on, looking forward to seeing Lily raze Hell, and hoped the universe would give me just enough time for me to do so.

Author's Note

I hope you enjoyed this one. I know it was a different pace and level of emotion in comparison to my last series. If you were hoping for something more balls-to-the-wall action and farcical humour, then you'll see more of a return to that style in my next series. However, it'll have more depth to it than the first series. The plan is to rapid release three books of this series late next year. The series and first book will be called *Primal Payne*.

Back to the story you just read. *Shock horror,* I am a social worker, so this book is a bit personal. The main character is based on a kid I once worked with. Of course, I imagined him older, and I did utilise some creative licence when it came to his past. All I can say is that the care system is shite, and in social work, you work with some of the worst kinds of people, so it messes you up a bit. Not only that, you have a management structure that is so risk-averse that they force all the shit to roll downhill to those workers at the bottom, care only about looking good on paper, and base any structural changes on whims rather than evidence. It's a job that I should thrive in, but the bureaucracy and the corporatization have turned it into a means to pay my bills. Anyway, apologies for that rant, but I hope that gives a bit more understanding!

Please, leave a review as it helps people decide on whether to get the book. Also, you can find updates and my mailing list on https://louis-park.com/. Cheers, for reading.

Printed in Great Britain
by Amazon